Praise for the novels of Seraphina Nova Glass

"*Too Close to Home* is an exciting and wild ride depicting how lives can spin out of control when someone is hell bent on revenge. . . . A definite standout in the cul-de-sac thriller genre."

—Jaime Lynn Hendricks, bestselling author of *Their Double Lives*

"Explosive, addictive, and impossible to put down—Glass just raised the bar for domestic thrillers."

—Noelle Ihli, bestselling author of *Such Quiet Girls*, on *Too Close to Home*

"*Too Close to Home* has one of the best twists I've ever read. Nobody does 'suburban thriller' like Seraphina Nova Glass. A masterclass in tension building."

—Nicola Sanders, author of *Don't Let Her Stay*

"A story so startling that it will make you question everything. A magnificent read."

—Samantha M. Bailey, *USA TODAY* bestselling author of *Hello, Juliet*, on *Nothing Ever Happens Here*

"*Nothing Ever Happens Here* is a twisty, propulsive read. At once decidedly heartwarming and darkly disturbing."

—Kaira Rouda, *USA TODAY* bestselling author

"A riveting page-turner with a sly sense of humor."

—Robyn Harding, internationally bestselling author of *The Haters*, on *Nothing Ever Happens Here*

"[An] entertaining thriller [that] maintain[s] tension and intrigue through to the satisfying end. The author's fans will devour this."

—*Publishers Weekly* on *The Vacancy in Room 10*

"Seraphina has once again proven she's a master of domestic suspense. No one weaves a twisty, dark tale quite like her."

—Amber Garza, author of *In a Quiet Town*, on *The Vanishing Hour*

"In [Seraphina's] heart-racing new thriller, she hangs you off a cliff, hits you with red herrings and suspects at every turn, and takes your breath away with her final startling twist."

—Katie Tallo, internationally bestselling author of *Buried Road*, on *The Vanishing Hour*

"A fast-paced, highly enjoyable and compulsive read that may well make you look at your entire neighborhood a little differently . . ."

—Hannah Mary McKinnon, internationally bestselling author of *Killer Motive*, on *On a Quiet Street*

"A twisty thriller in the vein of *The Girl on the Train*."

—*Bustle* on *On a Quiet Street*

"Bold, racy and masterfully plotted, *Such a Good Wife* kept me guessing from the very first page to the scorching, jaw-dropping conclusion."

—Rose Carlyle, #1 internationally bestselling author of *The Girl in the Mirror*

"A taut and intriguing suspense that held my attention from the very first page. . . . A stunning and impressive debut."

—Alessandra Torre, *New York Times* bestselling author, on *Someone's Listening*

Also by Seraphina Nova Glass

Nothing Ever Happens Here

The Vacancy in Room 10

The Vanishing Hour

On a Quiet Street

Such a Good Wife

Someone's Listening

TOO CLOSE TO HOME

SERAPHINA NOVA GLASS

PARK ROW BOOKS

ISBN-13: 978-1-525-80007-8

Too Close to Home

Park Row Books
22 Adelaide St. West, 41st Floor
Toronto, Ontario M5H 4E3, Canada
ParkRowBooks.com

HarperCollins Publishers
Macken House, 39/40 Mayor Street Upper,
Dublin 1, D01 C9W8, Ireland
www.HarperCollins.com

Printed in U.S.A.
$PrintCode

For Dr. Yonit Arthur, whose brilliant work changed my life and allowed me to continue writing.

PROLOGUE

Regan

The last days of summer have felt endless, bringing with them an insufferable, dripping heat and something bleak hanging in the air. An unease I haven't been able to explain—something intangible in the background like a distant, electric buzzing.

Almost everyone in the Cloverhill Lakes community attends the Labor Day party. It's always held on the little beach between the Millers' docks and the country club, and it's usually something I look forward to, but tonight I'm just ready to go home. Something is off.

"Sasha, hi, sweetheart," I say, waving as she arrives, a potato salad in one hand and a bottle of prosecco in the other. She's trying not to get her stiletto heels stuck in the sand while remaining graceful at the same time. I see someone gave her—the newcomer to the neighborhood—the memo: that even though we call it a barbecue, we still wear sundresses and carry our good handbags. She waves back and looks for a place to set her things, but it seems someone has *not*, in fact, given her the memo that around here, barbecues are catered. I pretend not to see her toss her offering into the trash can when she registers this.

I sit at a picnic table in the gazebo and stir my martini. The strings of fairy lights twinkle in the trees and the crickets take their turn playing the night's soundtrack between the deejay's sets of pop music. There are round tables and folding chairs set up across the grassy bank of the lake, small plates of cake in people's hands and lots of champagne bottles poking out of buckets of ice. It almost looks like a Seurat painting minus the parasols. I even fan myself with a paper plate and very much feel like I'm having "a fit of the vapors"—a joke I want to share with Andi as she plops down next to me with something fruity and frozen in her hand, except I'm certain she wouldn't get it.

"God, she's an absolute twat," Andi mutters.

"Who are we talking about?" Sasha asks, walking into the gazebo and pouring herself a margarita from the sweating pitcher on one of the tables.

"When Andi is using the word *twat* or *cow* or *slutbag*, it's only ever in reference to . . ."

"Tia Hainsley," Sasha interrupts. "Right. I do know that. Sorry."

We all look in Tia's direction and watch her hanging on her new husband's shoulder, showing a small group of women her blingy ring. I was certain everyone had already seen the thing, but I guess I was mistaken. There are a couple people left on the planet who hadn't. It is a notable size—something you could probably see from space. I see Andi's eye twitch as the circle of women's squealy shrieks waft over the soundwaves of Beyoncé coming from the deejay's speakers and echo off the vaulted gazebo ceiling, but she ignores the giggling admirers and swears she doesn't care about Tia and Ray. Perhaps she is actually over her ex-husband's marrying Tia freaking Hainsley. I mean, she *has* remarried herself, so she really shouldn't care, but . . . methinks the lady doth protest too much.

"It's not a good color on her," Sasha says. "I mean, in case that's helpful." We all look back to Tia again, flinging her hair over her shoulder and tossing her head back to laugh. I fight the urge to laugh myself when I see she's wearing—not *a color* but a rainbow-striped dress. Sasha was clearly just reaching for anything to say to be supportive.

"Yeah, she looks like a packet of Smarties," I add in solidarity. Andi sighs.

"Thanks, guys."

We sit in a row, sipping our drinks and watching the crowd. An occasional bark of laughter pierces the air, glasses clink and our kids dance in bare feet on the makeshift dance floor on the sandy patch by the water. Hallie sees me watching her and waves at me. I blow her a kiss. It's these times when I miss Jack the most, like *really* miss him, where the wave of it hits me unexpectedly and it's like realizing for the first time . . . that he's gone. It steals my breath. I hold my chest and stand, walking away from the others.

"You okay?" Andi asks.

"Fine," I say, futzing with a jar of olives, keeping my back to them until I can collect myself. I drop a couple stuffed olives into my drink, pop an Ativan under my tongue and breathe. It's not the place for an anxiety attack. Breathe in for four, out for eight.

"We have an emergency," I hear a panicked voice say behind me, and I turn to see Ally Whitlock speed-walking around the tables in the gazebo, plucking at a couple bags full of paper plates and napkins and opening the coolers along the wall.

"Oh no." Sasha stands. "What happened?"

"We're out of ice. Seriously? I mean, how does that even happen? This is a disaster," Ally says. She's the unofficial coordinator of the Labor Day party because she inserts herself into the committee's business, and they let her do whatever she wants and micromanage all she pleases because she's willing to do all the work—delighted to, even.

"Should I call the fire department?" I ask.

"Regan. I don't appreciate that. I did a lot of work making sure everything was . . ." She trails off, opening one last cooler and then standing, hands on hips.

"People expect a certain experience each year. The bar can't run out of ice. It's not a good look."

"I would offer to go get ice, but this is my second . . ." Andi shakes her glass.

"Same," I say.

"I'll go," Sasha offers, because of course she does.

"No, this is your first year, darling. You stay, but please order the signature drink from the bar. I have fifty pineapple coolers melting into oblivion. I took a poll. People voted 'pineapple cooler.' Why no one is drinking the damn pineapple cooler is beyond me."

"Of course," Sasha says.

"I'd go myself, but I came with Connie and I can't find her anywhere. She has the keys."

"Here." I take my keys out and toss them to her. "My car is in the first lot."

"Oh, wonderful. If you see Connie, tell her I didn't leave. I'll be back in a few . . . and oh, God, the wind took the paper plates right off the . . . Ugh. Good Lord! What next?" She holds her head in her hand a moment and then shakes it off. A warm breeze nudged one paper plate off a table and somehow it's Hurricane Sandy about to destroy the party and then the whole town.

"We got it, Al. Don't worry," I say.

She nods with exasperation and rushes off to my car to go get her emergency ice. We watch her hold her skirt down so it doesn't blow over her head as she makes her way down the grassy embankment to the lot.

"Do you think her and Connie are . . ."

"Are what?" Sasha asks.

"Like, you know?" Andi says.

"What?" I say.

"Doin' it?"

I actually spit out my drink.

"Oh, like you don't already think that!" Andi says.

"Well, you're not supposed to say it out loud, for Christ's sake. They're gal pals."

"Lady friends," Sasha agrees and holds up her drink. We clink glasses, chuckling at this.

"And that's okay," I say.

"Good for them," Andi adds.

And that's when we hear it. A noise so loud it hardly seems real.

At first, I think it's fireworks because I see sparks in my peripheral vision. Sometimes folks light a few fireworks at the Labor Day party, although it's more likely for people to do sparklers on the beach. But this sound is not fireworks.

It's an explosion.

I don't clock that right away. I'm paralyzed with shock as everyone around me starts to scream. To run. A few people run toward the blast to help, and some hold others back from running toward the danger. It's sudden chaos and screaming. I just stand, motionless.

"Oh, God!" I hear Andi say, and then after what seems like minutes but was probably only a few seconds, I move—I run, calling out for Hallie, and I hear Sasha and Andi crying, panicked, running for their kids, too, and everything blurs and moves in slow motion as I see Hallie, sobbing, running toward me with her arms outstretched and fear flashing in her eyes. I hold her in my arms and the terrified crowd moves around us, and people don't know what to do with what they're seeing—they can't make sense of it.

At the stop sign at the end of the parking lot, a car has blown up. My car. *My car* has exploded into the night air like a firework sending shrapnel and . . . flesh scattered across the pavement.

Within minutes, the area is swarming with police, paramedics and the fire department. Families and friends huddle in small groups, terrified but seeking answers—me, most of all. After some time, the fire is out and officers are surrounding the car, taking a closer look. Suddenly, several officers rush toward the crowd, shouting, "Clear the area! Clear the area!" They've found an explosive device on the car. This wasn't an accident.

Ally Whitlock is dead. And it was meant to be me.

CHAPTER ONE

Andi

One month later

It's funny how time makes us forget. Like a school shooting on the news—you're shocked, outraged. How can this still be happening? But you're also helpless, and letting yourself feel the horror of it for too long will start to change you and jab sharp fingers into your sense of safety. It will eat at your mental health and destroy any illusion of security you might have carved out in your small pocket of the world, and that's why we forget. Or try to, at least. It's only been a handful of weeks since the explosion, but we're all moving on with our lives.

Except Regan. If I knew someone connected an explosive under my car, set to detonate within minutes of the car's starting, I'd have trouble moving on, too. Surely it was meant for someone else—that's what everyone says anyway. Maybe some teenagers in science class were playing a joke. One of the police officers used an example of four high school kids who threw a jar of acid off a freeway overpass—it crashed through the windshield of an innocent woman just driving along on her way to a hair appointment, and there she was, over 80 percent of her body burned so severely that she was left disfigured even after seventy-four surgeries. They think it's just some unhinged delinquents who don't really understand the consequences of their actions. Because what other explanation would there be for targeting a widowed mom in an affluent lake community?

Everyone is on edge, even if they believe that explanation. Nobody talks about it much since Ally's funeral, not out loud, not in public, but the wondering sits heavy on everyone's chests and people exchange pensive looks of solidarity in the streets, speaking more quietly to one another than they used to—an us-against-them sentiment—even though we don't know who "they" are.

"Just because I'm a newlywed doesn't mean I want to have sex in the hot tub," I say to Carson when I walk onto the back deck and see him jabbing at the buttons on the side of the Jacuzzi to heat it up.

"It's unsanitary," I add. He's peering at the football game on the TV in the outdoor living room over my shoulder and only half paying attention. I see the gas fireplace is lit and a couple of wineglasses are resting on the coffee table.

"That's very presumptuous of you." He smiles, still distracted. "I didn't even ask you to join me."

"Mmm-hmm." I grab my sweater off the outdoor sofa and

he grabs my ass as I pass him. "I'm taking the kids to what's-his-face's."

"Their dad's?" he says.

"Yeah, that guy," I say, going inside and hollering up to Roxie and Dez to get a move on. Dez will want to bring the cat, and Roxie will want to drive because she just got her license, and I'm not really in any mood for it tonight because I have to spend the drive over thinking about my strategy to deal with Tia, who will inevitably be the one to answer the door and push my buttons. How will she do it today? Who knows? It's always new and inventive and I have to remember the meditation I did last night and how I promised myself I would rise above the drama and be the better person and not react. I have to get into my Zen place no matter what shit that bitch tries to pull.

Ray will pretend he didn't hear the door so he doesn't have to get involved, and Tia will find a way to say something insufferable, like the casual way she says "our kids," like they have anything to do with her, and then she'll try to backpedal and say when they're with her and Ray they're her family, too . . . and don't I want them to feel loved and accepted? She'll turn it around on me like I can't see she's trying to help Ray steal them from me—she actually thinks the custody battle will go his way and that they're somehow "her/our kids" and not my fucking kids.

I let out a growl of frustration thinking about this as Rox and Dez come outside with their overnight bags. I know they can sense my mood because there is no talk of bringing the cat or Rox driving. They pile in and I white-knuckle it on the two-lane road around the lake, thinking how if Tia twists her giant ring around on her finger, pretending she's not doing it to irk me, or if she brings up some personal thing about Ray just to demonstrate their intimacy—the fact that she knows him better than I ever did or ever will even though I was married to him for fifteen years and she barely fucking knows him—it will take all I have not to . . .

"Mom!" Roxie yells and I slam on the brakes and swerve, just barely missing a blur of something running across the road.

"Shit!" I scream, trying to gain control of the car. When I screech to a halt, the car jerks and I see all of our lives flashing in front of me for just a moment. Then I breathe. I turn and make sure everyone's okay.

"It was just a deer. It's okay," I say, but I see the silent tears on Roxie's cheeks and the fear in Dez's eyes. Everyone has been so shaken, so traumatized from what happened to poor Ally, that it's far from okay. Every loud sound is a shock—any raised voice is a reminder of people screaming in terror, a reminder of the fragility of it all, which they shouldn't have to feel at ten and sixteen years old. They've been forever changed and I'm helpless to comfort them.

"Look, it ran into the woods. Nobody's hurt," I say, and Roxie nods and wipes her tears bravely, not saying a word. Dez turns and looks out the window.

"Nobody's hurt," I repeat under my breath, then restart the car and slowly pull back out onto the road.

At Ray's new, stupid house—the one he bought across the lake from ours in order to be close to the kids—I pull into the driveway and pop the hatch so the kids can grab their things. I get out to hug them goodbye, and before I can just drive away in peace, I see Tia leaning against the door frame, twisting her giant diamond ring as the kids bolt past her into the house, where I know there's Friday-night pizza waiting for them.

Be the better person; don't react, I tell myself. She waves. Would the better person wave back or see through the condescending nature of the purposefully taunting wave and just get in the car and go? I can't decide which is the high road. Before I have a chance to, she saunters up to my car.

"Oh hey, I just wanted to tell you that you really need to fix the lock on the gate to your backyard. You have a pool so it's actually illegal not to have a working lock."

"Uh. What?" I snap.

"Just a warning," she says.

"Um . . . *You* are the one who broke the lock," I say, wondering where exactly this is going. She literally smashed the padlock with a hammer a couple of months ago, stating she heard a dog barking in the backyard and that we left our corgi outside in extreme heat and she was going to call animal services on us. We weren't even home and Toots wasn't outside. She was with us, safe, in air-conditioning, eating an abundance of Beggin' Strips at the cabin. Stupid twat. She didn't even manage to get into the yard before the alarm scared her away, but she still made an official report of animal abuse.

"Oh, let's not get into that again," she says.

"Yes, let's not get into that again. I have a couple estimates to fix the lock and the places where you dented the gate," I say. "Would you like them? Then maybe we can drop it." I really was taking the high road when I decided not to send the estimates and make things even more volatile.

"Listen, it's a violation. It's not safe to have a gate unlocked when you have a pool. Anyone could wander in and drown."

I meet her eyes, and I can tell she'd probably like to reword that—she knows I'm thinking I would welcome her over to the pool anytime in that case.

She hands me some photos. I take them and flip through the half a dozen printouts.

"What the hell?" I say, looking at the images of my broken gate lock.

"I had to report it to code compliance. You left me no choice. You've had weeks to fix it." I feel my mouth go slack and hear a sharp bark of laughter escape my body.

"Are you on crack?" I ask.

"I'm on the right side of the law is what I'm on," she says self-righteously.

This woman has been snooping around my house for months. She calls herself a stay-at-home mom now that she's married to Ray, even though the kids are at school all day and she's not their mom. She literally has nothing else to do. I've caught her three times snapping photos, trying desperately to catch me in the act of being an unfit or abusive or neglectful mother so she can bring her evidence back to Ray for the custody case and win the day—she's his own little Barbie doll minion. She's made it her full-time job to dig into my past and catch me doing anything slightly distasteful.

When I met Sasha and Regan for margaritas just last Saturday, she was leaving Finnigan's across the street, and she waited in the fucking parking lot, making sure I didn't drink and drive, ready to follow me and call the cops. I had a virgin and went home early.

Somehow, the woman I walked in on while she was fucking my husband in a utility room at the Lakeview Inn during the town's holiday banquet is the morally superior one now.

"You reported it?"

"Also to your HOA. You should be getting a warning from them. I'm just looking out for the children," she says, tucking her glossy blond bob behind her ear and smiling with her flashy veneers. She twists her ring again and gives me a wink before turning to walk back to the front door.

Don't react, don't respond, I tell myself. Everyone in town has seen us go at it. Everyone has seen me react to this taunting, and I always look like the psycho. I used to be the one who looked like the victim, until enough time went by where people thought I should be over it, I guess . . . but they don't see what she's doing. She's a master at making it appear like she's just looking out for the greater good, and I'm some sort of menace to society. And that would be fine if it were just about me, but what if she's sinking her finely manicured little hooks into my kids? Could there really be a scenario where Ray would win custody? She literally has a file folder full of allegations and accusations. I get out of the car and take out my phone and stab at the camera icon.

Before Tia gets inside, she sees me practically speedwalking toward her back gate. I snap a photo of the grass in the side yard.

"Overgrown grass. HOA violation," I say, then swing open the gate to the backyard, where Ray sits on a deck chair, drinking a craft beer and listening to Journey. I take a video.

"Noise violation! The music is too loud," I yell over the Bluetooth speaker on the table, and it is pretty loud so I feel good about that one. The kids are inside, no doubt eating pizza in front of a video game, so I keep going. Ray has been startled to his feet and Tia is marching over to me, holding up the ends of her weird linen dress with fire in her eyes, but I duck past her and march to the opposite side yard with both

Tia and Ray following behind, and I hear some mumbles from Ray about "taking it easy" and "going on home," but I ignore him. I knock over the recycling bin and start snapping photos.

"Look at all this shit that shouldn't be in the recycling. Jesus. Bubble Wrap? An aerosol can? Are you some kind of Neanderthal?" Just as I notice she's hovering over me in a rage, Tia swats the phone out of my hand and it hits the grass with a thud. Then she pushes my shoulder.

"Get off my property! You're trespassing!"

"Oh, is it yours? Is it your property? I guess I thought Ray bought the house. Am I mistaken? Can a part-time Pilates instructor afford a three-point-two-million-dollar house these days? Well, pardon me, I guess." With this, she slaps me across the face.

I'm a little shocked she had the balls to do that, so it stuns me into silence for just a moment. Then I pick up my phone from the ground. Soft landing, thank God, so it's not broken. I press Record on the camera.

"This woman just assaulted me. For the record," I say, camera in Tia's face. I'm not trying to be one of those women who ends up on the Dr. Phil show. I'm really not trying to be petty, but goddammit. This is about my children and someone actively plotting to get them taken from me. It's time I get a little angrier and stop taking the high road, because nobody can see me way up here on this freaking road. My voice can't be heard way up here. I keep thinking surely people will eventually see who Tia is, that her true colors will come through, but nobody can see through her. This can't go on.

I turn off the camera, satisfied I have something to show now, too. Even though I didn't get the slap on video, it's something.

"All right, Andi, get the hell outta here, come on," Ray says weakly, and he tries to put his hand on Tia's shoulder and walk away with her back into the house, but she loses it. She absolutely loses it and lunges at me with a shriek, and before I know it, I'm on the ground with grass-burned knees, breathlessly trying to push her off me.

"Give me that fucking phone," she growls. She's trying to wrench the phone out of my hand as she straddles me on a bed of Russian sage.

"Are you out of your mind?" I scream. I can see a couple neighbors watching now. Tia is small but wiry, it turns out, and she manages to get the phone out of my hand, just as Ray finally pulls her off me. She takes the phone and flings it into the driveway, shattering the screen.

I really cannot believe what I'm witnessing. I push myself to stand. I brush wet grass off my jeans and pull a leaf out of my hair and just stare at both of them.

"Go inside, Ti," Ray says. She pushes his hand away.

"I can sue you for this, you know. Assault. Destruction of property!" I yell, infuriated now.

"Just try it. You'll see what I can really do to you," she hisses under her breath.

"Is that a threat? Everyone hear that?" I say, looking to the neighbors who pretend not to see now, all of a sudden, and go about their business. "You're the one who better watch your back! You think breaking my screen erased that video, psycho? You want a fight? You have one. I'm done. That's it!" I peer into the living room window and get a glance of the kids. Thank God for loud PlayStation games and a well-built house—it looks like they didn't hear anything. So I pick up my phone and walk to my car, resisting holding up my middle finger because this doesn't really need to sink any lower than it already has.

"Don't threaten us," Ray says pathetically, probably feeling like he has to do something.

"Oh, fuck off, Ray," I say. Then I drive away.

I drive around the lake blinking back tears, partly because I'm just so pissed off, but also because of how everyone has witnessed my war with Tia and I'm embarrassed, honestly. It's not the person I want to be. It's not the person I am.

Do I need to wear a sign that says Ray begged for me to stay and forgive him after I caught him with her? I was the one strong enough to walk out—she got him by default, and I'm not some victim here. I'm not the jealous scorned ex causing drama, but that's what it looks like to everyone. And how am I even thinking about this after what happened to Ally? It makes me feel even more pathetic that this is what my energy is focused on. I know this is similar to the way people see Regan. She pops pills and flies off the handle and snaps at everyone, but because of what happened to her, there's a sense of quiet pity, and people rally around to support her. My husband's not dead, so I don't get to act like this. There was a certain window of time allotted for me to lose it, and now I'm expected to shut up and move on.

I try to shake it all off as I walk into the kitchen and put my shattered phone on the counter, grabbing a kitchen towel to wipe the wet leaves from my hair. I see Carson standing in front of the sliding glass doors leading out to the back deck. He's on the phone and I can tell something is wrong by the tension in his posture and the way he hasn't turned around to give me a silent greeting. Shit. What now?

He hangs up the call and turns to see me.

"What the hell happened to you?" he asks, and I'm just too humiliated to tell him about what was essentially a catfight.

"I had a tumble. The grass was slippery. I'm fine. What's wrong? I can tell something's going on."

He sighs. "Let's sit." He nods to the door and I follow him to the deck, where he's already poured a couple glasses of wine. We sit on the sofa next to the fireplace.

"What?" I ask.

"There was . . . a sort of bomb threat at the elementary school." I put my wineglass down and leap to my feet.

"Oh, my God. Dez!"

"Babe, you just dropped the kids off at what's-his-face's house. He's fine."

"I know that, but it could have been . . . What if it was . . . God, what happened?"

"Everyone is fine. It was a prank—like a false threat. Someone left a box—a wrapped package with a kitchen timer inside—in the middle of the hallway."

"Why? Who?" I sit back down, my mind trying to wrap around what the hell is happening. Bombs? *Another* bomb, for Christ's sake. It's too much.

"I don't know any more than that, really. They say there was a note taped on it that said, *Bang. You're dead.*"

"Jesus!"

"Yeah."

"There are cameras in the halls, though."

"Well, a few, but they only pick up some main traffic areas. There was nothing caught on security cam from what I'm told."

"And who *did* tell you all this?"

"The school. They're calling all the parents. Said they left a message for you. They're trying to get ahead of it before it ends up on the news and they're raked through the coals for not having a clue."

"Right," I say. "God, what's the world coming to?"

We sit for a little while and he pretends not to be distracted by the game on the TV, but I don't care. Our date night at home is no longer on my mind. I drain my glass of wine, pour a second, and kiss him on the cheek before announcing I'm headed to take a hot bath and change.

The sun begins to sink and paints purple and crimson watercolor strokes across the horizon as I lie in the hot water and gaze out the picture window. I think about my kids in the slimy grips of Tia fucking Hainsley—how she micro-manipulates them, puts bugs in their ears attacking my character in a carefully crafted way so they won't know that's what she's doing. I blow out a hard breath and pick up my wineglass from the side of the tub and tell myself to let it go for the rest of the night. Just let it go.

When I finish and exit the master bath, drying my wet hair with a towel and slipping my feet into UGG slippers, I notice something odd. The locked bedroom safe is open, and the gun case we keep inside is lying on the bed—and the gun is missing. I feel my heart skip a beat. I rush out to the deck, whipping open the door and staring at Carson.

"Uhhh. Anything you wanna tell me?" I say. He clicks off the game, saying something about it being a blowout anyway, whatever that means. I see the gun on the coffee table in front of him.

"Was there an intruder when I was in the bath or something?" I say, sarcastically gesturing around. "What the hell?"

"Well, with everything going on, I think it's time you at least learn to protect yourself. What would you do if there *was* an intruder?"

I sit in the armchair across from him and set my empty glass on the table. He fills it. Two is usually my limit but I'm riddled with anxiety and so I take it to calm my nerves.

"Bomb threats. You want me to learn to use the stupid gun against a bomb? Solid plan," I say.

"Andi. We don't really know what's going on, do we?"

"Do you know something I don't?"

"No," he says, but I can see a little flash in his eye that tells me differently. One thing I fell in love with, after the whole Ray disaster, was Carson's honesty and seeming inability to effectively lie about anything without giving it away. I appreciate this quality, but not right now.

"What is it?" I ask.

"It's nothing. I don't know."

"What?"

"The other day, I . . . I don't know. I thought I saw someone. Like a figure. I didn't want to worry you for no reason. Probably nothing."

"What do you mean? Where?" I ask, because we live on the lakefront but behind us is fifty acres of wooded land, so a figure usually means a rustle in the trees from an animal or something innocuous.

"I don't know—just out in the woods. It looked like a guy standing there, staring. I don't know if it was, but I think that's what I saw. I . . ."

"You know it was Tia, right? She's always skulking around the property taking photos."

"No. It was . . . different. Eerie."

"Maybe a hunter wandered over. It happens—they don't know it's private property if they're out in the thick of it."

"Yeah, maybe. But seriously. I think about you out here. I have to go to Albany for work tomorrow. You'll be here alone for a couple days. Don't you want to feel like you have some hope to protect yourself if something ever happened?" he asks, leaning back in the sofa with a resigned sigh.

We've talked about this before, and of course I've thought about it, but there are a lot of mixed feelings. Touching that thing scares the hell out of me.

"It's just . . . ugh. I don't know if I can. I've gone this long, right?"

"But shit's getting weird. You let Dez shoot cans with me, learn responsible gun owning and all that."

"Because he has an interest in it, and I want him to be educated—"

"Right," he interrupts. "So all you need to know is the very basics. You don't need to go to the range and have it be this whole intimidating thing. We have a billion acres to practice on. Just let me show you how and make sure it's accessible when you're home alone, and then I'll never bother you about it again," he says. He waits, blinking at me.

"Now?" I say, curled up in the chair, wearing comfy yoga pants and holding my glass of wine.

"I leave for two days in the morning, so yeah. It will be fun. Date night can-shooting." He reaches out to take my hand and pull me up. I hate the idea of it. Hate it. But he has a point. Something is happening around here and some figure lurking in our woods doesn't exactly make me want to stay here alone. Would I feel better if I had any hope of protecting myself against danger? I mean, I'd never have to touch the thing again, but knowing it's there and that I know how to load it, hold it . . . I don't even know what cocking a gun really means, but I've heard the term on TV and it's probably something I should know how to do.

I let him pull me to my feet. I put my glass down and grab his hoodie from the back of a chair and pull it on.

"One and only time," I say. And I follow him out past the clearing of the yard, into the trees where the fence sits about fifteen yards in the distance, already set up with Dez's Dr Pepper cans for shooting practice.

It's dusk and I'm happy for the sun to set in the next thirty minutes because that will mean this is short and sweet. Carson shows me bullets and explains things like caliber and releasing the cylinder and whatever the hell a magazine is, and when we finally get down to the "me shooting" stage, my hands shake. I'm standing under a canopy of towering pines in my UGG slippers and stretchy pants and I'm about to shoot a gun. I feel detached from myself—everyone would say I'm making too big a deal of it, but it feels wrong. There are only a few cans left on the fence, but I don't plan on actually hitting them anyway, so that's fine. I take a deep breath . . . Then I shoot.

I miss by a long shot, and he smirks.

"That was good," he says. And in my defense, it's getting dark and hard to see that far in the shadowy light.

"Shut up." I try again. I don't hit a can, but I'm closer. I find myself laughing at this.

"Holy crap. I was close that time," I say.

He smiles and nods at me proudly. Okay, this isn't terrible.

"You're doing great," he says. He comes over and helps me line up the shot perfectly and then backs away. I shoot one more time, and to my shock, I hit the can. Well, Carson's alignment hit the can, not so much me, but still.

"Oh, my God! Yes!" I cheer. "I did it."

"You're a pro," he says.

"We need more cans up," I say, and he laughs.

"Well, all right," he says. "I'll grab the empty Michelob Ultras, and I have to get some more ammo. I didn't think you'd last this long."

"Ammo," I mimic. What a dumb word. He shakes his head and starts toward the house. Then his phone rings and he takes it from his pocket and answers. He holds up a finger as if to tell me he needs a minute and goes toward the house. I know with his job, a minute means an hour, and so I almost decide to give up on the whole thing, but then I notice one more can left on the fence, so I take another shot. I miss, but I have to admit it's kind of fun. I decide to jog out to the fence to gather the fallen Dr Pepper cans even though they're mostly bent and obliterated. More cans lined up across the fence means better odds I'll actually hit a target. Carson will be over the moon I'm making an effort . . . but when I reach the fence, I see something.

Something that steals my breath. Something horrific and life shattering that I can't believe I'm looking at.

I cup my mouth with both hands and stifle a scream. I drop to my knees and try to breathe, but I begin to hyperventilate.

"Oh, my God, oh, my God!" I hold my chest and tears prick my eyes. My hands shake violently and I'm paralyzed in terror. What have I done? What have I done?

In front of me on the ground, just behind the fence I was shooting at is . . . a body. God help me. It's Tia Hainsley. Shot. Dead.

CHAPTER TWO

Sasha

The leaves are turning so early, Sasha notices as she sits on her front porch, wrapped in a long cardigan on a drizzly Saturday morning. She sips her coffee and watches the wind bend the tree branches of the old oak, shaking loose yellow and orange leaves that dance their way down to the wet sidewalk. A typical New England autumn, but she'll never feel accustomed to the damp and cold even though she's spent her whole life in it. Sasha was meant for a beach . . . or even better, the desert. Anywhere warm and less depressing.

The drizzle turns into a steady rainfall just as Drew runs out the front door, passing her without a word. He hoists his backpack over his shoulder and jogs down the drive to meet a car pulling up. A car she doesn't recognize.

"Where are *you* going?" she hollers over the rain thundering on the roof of the porch.

"Out," he says, pausing slightly but not stopping.

"With who?"

"A friend. Tom said it was okay." As if that means Sasha has no say in the whereabouts of her sixteen-year-old. They've talked about this. Tom is not his father and all he's supposed to say is "ask your mother." That's his only line. How hard can it be to remember? It's not that Tom can't parent him. Tom is literally the kindest person on earth, and he does a good job as a stepdad, but Drew is in a weird teenage phase and Tom deferring to her is just what they agreed would be best to do whenever possible. Better for everyone. She knows she could let it go this time, but she also knows it's important to keep some semblance of control over her increasingly unknowable child, so she's about to put her coffee down and go barefoot into the rain to make sure he's aware of who's boss—but then she sees a girl in the driver's seat. She shields her eyes with her hand to squint and see who it is. To her surprise, it's Andi's daughter, Roxie, and Sasha is suddenly sort of thrilled he's not only made a friend, but a friend who's a girl. And one she sort of knows . . . one she would maybe go so far as to say she trusts.

She remembers them chatting by the lake at the Labor Day party. Roxie calls herself a "theater nerd," so it makes sense that Drew would be drawn to her. The band and theater nerd worlds collide, so she could see it. And even though, of course, he wouldn't tell her they'd become friends, because he doesn't tell her anything these days, this is a good thing, Sasha decides, so she does not follow him and list the house rules and tell him to get his happy ass back inside. Instead, she brings her coffee into the house and puts the mug in the sink. Then she returns a missed call from Regan.

"A bomb threat? Jesus. No, I didn't hear anything. You gotta be kidding. When?" Sasha asks as she sits at the kitchen table, feeling the blood drain from her face. She listens as Regan goes over what little detail she has about what happened, peering across the kitchen island and into the living room, where Chloe is watching *Junior Bake Off* on the Food Network and mindlessly twirling the hair of a Malibu Barbie around her fingers. A bomb threat. My God. Sasha feels nauseated.

Regan explains that there's a meeting at the school this morning—a few of the parents are demanding the school take it seriously and make a safety plan, so they're all meeting there in a couple hours. Sasha says she'll get ready and meet her there, and even though everyone is safe and they're calling it a prank, she feels something stirring—an unease, a weight on her chest like a thumb pressing into her solar plexus.

When they hang up the call, she stands at the kitchen island and stares, taking in the back of Chloe's head poking out above the couch. If she's honest, she's scared—scared something terrible is coming. Tom sits next to Chloe, eating Raisin Bran out of the box, and his father, Al, who is an absolute dear, sits on the recliner with a cup of coffee. He comes almost every Saturday with something for Chloe—today it was blueberry pancakes—and he always watches some kids' show with her, and sometimes they go to the park or aquarium in the afternoon, especially when Tom has to be in New York for work on the weekend.

It's a lovely routine, but right now Sasha wishes they were well on their way to the zoo, which is the plan today, because she wants Chloe shielded from all of it—from the school and safety concerns, even from the look on Sasha's own face that she is very much trying to arrange into a smile. She's never been good at hiding her emotions.

"The buttercream is grainy," Al says, pointing at the kid on the TV who's mixing up something pink in a metal bowl.

"She didn't sift her flour," Chloe says.

"Rookie move," Al says.

"Yeah," Chloe giggles.

Then Tom turns around to look at Sasha. "Jesus. What's wrong?" he asks, coming into the kitchen.

"Nothing." Sasha stands, smiling at Chloe and Al as they turn to look. "I was just zoned out. Coffee?" she asks, then makes a gesture to Tom, telling him to drop it after Al and Chloe return their attention to the TV.

"Dad said 'Jesus.' He's not allowed to say that, I thought," Chloe sings, partly teasing him but too engaged in her show to pay any more attention to what's going on as the cupcake judging begins.

Sasha pours Tom a mug and takes creamer from the fridge door.

"Thanks," he says, rubbing her back with his hand and giving her a concerned look. "You okay?"

"There was a bomb threat. At her school," she whispers, pointing past him at Chloe.

"Jesus," he says again. "You're kidding. An elementary school? What is the world coming to?"

"I know," she says, and he puts his arms around her.

"It was bound to happen," he says.

"What does that mean?" she asks, but she knows what it means because the fact that the school has little security is a bone of contention in town. Sure, they could afford all the bells and whistles—face recognition, vape sensors, access control—but that would make people feel like they no longer live in the safe bubble they pay so much money to exist in. The school has the basics: a lock and checkpoint at the front doors, a sign-in system. But bars, clear backpacks, metal detectors? Those things aren't necessary in a peaceful little community. Nobody wants them to be necessary. Folks want to drop their kids at the steps of the school and wave as their children happily run over to their friends like in a movie scene. They want to see hopscotch chalk on the sidewalk and backpacks in a pile on the grass and kids hanging on monkey bars. Nobody wants to watch their kid frisked as their bag goes through an X-ray machine like the place is a prison. Nobody wants the world to change like this. But it already has, and Cloverhill Elementary is behind the times.

"I just mean, the fact they've gone this long with no issue is surprising, but this will change things," he says, pouring Chloe's Count Chocula cereal into a bowl and plucking at the dry pieces.

"There's a meeting for parents this morning. I'll go if Al is still taking her to the zoo."

"Yeah, of course, hun," he says, looking for the milk in the fridge. "I have to interview a couple folks at the restaurant today for the hostess position, or I'd go with you."

"It's fine," she says, then changes the subject as she sees Chloe get up and start to come their way.

"Hey, by the way, Drew says you told him he could take off for the day. Why didn't you ask me first?" Sasha asks, trying to keep the annoyance out of her voice.

"I haven't even seen him today. He didn't ask me about it," he says, pouring his coffee into a to-go mug and pulling on a coat.

She sighs. Drew is now just outright lying even though he knows she'll find out, because of course she'd talk to Tom and figure it out. Super. She can't think about his odd behavior and how it's escalating. Not right now, even though the embers of anxiety are beginning to smolder inside her and she knows something is very off with her son.

By late morning, she's worked herself into a state over Drew and the school meeting and the gloom that seems to follow her around since they moved here. She wonders if it was a mistake. Still, she goes through the motions and heads to the school to join the other worried parents so they can all fan the flames of the panic together.

The rain taps at the windshield on her drive down the curvy, tree-lined streets to the school. Soggy red leaves drop from the stunning, towering maples and get caught in her wipers, and the gloom settles into her bones. When she pulls up, she takes her Starbucks from the cupholder and joins the other moms, standing in a circle at the base of the school stairs. It's a familiar sight—all messy buns, yoga pants and puffer coats. Everyone is attempting to look like they aren't trying, but the full makeup and immaculately covered roots give them away.

Rebecca Elsher has set up a table with apple cider donuts and hot chocolate for the kids, calling them "sweetheart" and "poor thing" as they come up for the goodies, as if they've been the victims of some enormous offense, even though none of them knows about the threat. As far as the kids know, it's just a school meeting and they get to play outside with their friends and eat donuts for an hour.

Some of the parents brought their kids because of the last-minute nature of the meeting, and Rebecca seems to be enjoying her Mother Goose role a bit too much for the type of occasion, but the moms only side-eye her instead of saying anything—they are here for more important reasons and to call her out would appear petty. They have nothing if not a healthy sense of decorum, after all.

"They need to shut the school down until they get to the bottom of it," Melissa Winterman says, and others nod in agreement. Sasha goes and stands next to Regan, who's looking over at her daughter, Hallie, eating donuts with a couple of girls by the side fence.

"Morning," Sasha says, startling Regan into noticing her.

"Shit, is that a pumpkin spice latte?" Regan asks, looking sideways at Sasha's Starbucks cup to read the barista's scrawl.

"With whipped cream," Sasha adds.

"I was too busy calling all the moms this morning to ingest caffeine. Hot chocolate isn't doing it. Rebecca burned the chocolate, to boot. Tastes like a campfire."

"Here." Sasha hands her the cup and Regan takes a couple swigs.

"Bless you."

"Where's Andi?" Sasha asks, looking around.

"Left her a voice mail, I don't know." Regan glances over at Morgan Dyer, who's clapping her hands in the air and yelling, "Okay, inside, everyone. We're starting." Sasha sees Regan roll her eyes.

"I guess Morgan's in charge now," she quips, giving a little mock salute.

Sasha smirks. She became fast friends with Andi and Regan when she moved in at the beginning of the summer and Sasha brought cupcakes when it was her turn to be "snack mom" at Little League practice. The newsletter clearly stated it was healthy snack week and she was to bring only approved items from a list that was provided. When she did not show up with Cuties oranges or Fruit Roll-Ups, some of the moms lost their minds, but Regan and Andi stepped in. They understood what it was like to be outsiders in this town, too, it turned out—since Regan's husband's death and Andi's very public divorce. Now the three women are inseparable.

As folks start moving up the school stairs, Regan calls to Hallie to mind Miss Elsher until they're back, but before Sasha can hoist her tote over her shoulder and go in, a Range Rover pulls into the lot and the screeching brakes make her and Regan turn.

It's Ray Davila, Andi's ex-husband, and she can see that Dez is sitting in the back seat. Ray leaves the car running and gestures to Dez that he'll be right back. He walks swiftly over to where Sasha and Regan stand, staring at him.

"Oh, hey," Regan starts. "Hallie was just asking about Dez. She has his baseball glove from—"

Ray cuts her off. "We're not staying. I . . . Listen. Have either of you seen Tia?"

"Uh, Tia? No," Sasha says, wondering why she'd be here since she doesn't have kids in elementary school. "Is something wrong?" Sasha asks, noticing the swelling and redness around Ray's eyes and the panic in his voice, which he's deliberately trying to keep calm.

"I'm . . ." He glances at the car and then back to Sasha. "I haven't told the kids. Roxie's out and Dez thinks we're running errands, so I can't alarm them just yet, but she's just . . . gone. I mean, she's . . . I guess, missing."

"Oh, Ray. Oh, my God, what do you mean?" Regan says, touching him on his arm.

"Last night she said she was going for a run after dinner,

so me and the kids went to see an eight o'clock movie. She said . . ." His voice breaks. "She said to go without her. When we got home at eleven, she wasn't there. I spent an hour calling everyone she knows, but nothing. God, I . . ."

"Jesus," Regan says. "Did you call the police?"

"Yes. I made a report around midnight, but I can't just—I'm just trying to drive around and look. I need Andi to take the kids, but I can't reach her."

"I'm so sorry," Sasha says. "I'm sure there's an explanation," she adds, because it's the sort of thing you're supposed to say and she's at a complete loss.

"Drop Dez with me if you need to," Regan says. "Hallie wants to toss the ball around with him anyway. It's all she's talked about. If you can't get in touch with Andi, I should be home in an hour or two. It's no problem," she says.

"Thanks, okay. Yeah. Please, if you hear anything. Please . . ." he starts to say.

"Of course," Sasha says. "Of course." She puts him out of his misery so he doesn't have to finish his sentence—so he can go and keep looking.

"Or you can leave him with me now if you need," Regan says.

"I'm going over to Andi's now. But I'll let you know. Thanks."

They watch Ray do a half jog to his car. He disappears inside before pulling out of the gravel parking lot quickly. Sasha has heard the stories over margarita nights with Regan and Andi and a few of the other girls, and she knows that a couple years ago Ray spent a few months on the most-hated-guy-in-town list after word of him having an affair went public. Now, though, he looks so small and broken that it's hard not to have empathy for the guy, even if she only really knows him as "what's-his-face who's engaged to slutbag."

"God," Regan says. "I'm sure it's nothing, right?"

"I'm sure," Sasha agrees.

"Maybe she already spent all his money and is leaving him for some even older guy with even more money. God, I'm a dick. That was inappropriate," Regan says. Sasha represses a smirk. Regan takes a small pill from her pocket and slips it covertly under her tongue, then inhales deeply. Sasha pretends not to notice.

"I hope Andi's okay," Sasha says as they begin to move toward the school doors.

"Maybe she went out of town with Carson or something," Regan says. "He goes away for work sometimes. They're newlyweds. Maybe they made it a weekend away. Not like her to ignore my calls, though . . . or Ray's . . . at least not when he has the kids, I mean. Things are very strange around here."

Inside the school building, a couple dozen anxious parents pile into one of the classrooms and begin demanding answers, solutions, explanations from the principal and board members. Sasha thinks about that horrific day only weeks ago when they all watched someone from their own community murdered in front of them—ripped into pieces of flesh and bits of bone and brain matter that fell from the sky like a bizarre scene in the most graphic horror movie you've ever seen. Even for the folks who didn't witness it, the ripples of fear and unease spread across the surface of the community, putting everyone on edge.

Sasha sees one of the moms silently weeping into the hood of her Burberry sweatshirt and another whispering about homeschooling and taking all their kids out of this school. When one of the senior board members, Atkinson, finally gets everyone to quiet down, he speaks in a consoling tone that could be interpreted as condescending, but it's hard to discern his true intent. He definitely looks in over his head, though.

"I understand everyone's concern, so let's first just outline the facts so we can all get on the same page as we discuss what next steps are."

"Oh, for God's sake, Roger," Libby something-or-other says. She's Samantha's mom. "Just tell us what measures you're going to take to make sure the place is secure. Drop the formal bullcrap."

"Yeah," a few other parents murmur in agreement.

"Look, Lib," Atkinson says. "We are taking it very seriously, of course, but the reason we firmly believe that it's just a prank—that it's most likely one of the students—is because the box the kitchen timer was inside of has a batch number and tracks back to one of the teacher's supply cupboards. It was a box mailed directly to the school—to Ms. Brown's classroom—and it was full of washable markers. The sign that read *Bang. You're dead* was written on red construction paper."

"So what?" one of the dads shouts. "The freak who did this could want you to think it's just an innocent thing, right? Remember someone actually got blown up in this town not long ago."

The mention of that has everyone stirring, nodding, shaking their heads. I see a few moms in full sobs now.

"I get it," Atkinson says. "I'm not saying this is nothing, that it shouldn't be of great concern. I'm only saying, to hopefully belay some of your fears, that the police believe a student is responsible. Also, a lot of older siblings from the high school have clearance to pick up younger siblings, so it could be a teen prank, and . . ."

"Just like Sandy Hook was, huh?" a voice from somewhere in the back says.

"Oh, Lord, here we go," Regan says under her breath. Sasha bristles at this. Her eyes widen as she looks around the room to see who shouted that.

Atkinson tries to settle everyone down. "All I can tell you," he continues, "is that there are cameras at the front and back doors—the only two entrances to the school besides the emergency doors, which have not been engaged—and no unknown person came in or out yesterday. The note taped to the box was a circle cut out of construction paper with a spark drawn in, like a cartoon version of a bomb. Very childish and made from supplies inside the building . . ."

Atkinson attempts to go on, but someone starts up about how he's insinuating one of our kids is a psychopath, and others start demanding security checks, cameras in the halls, armed guards, and then a few parents start to yell at each other, and all in all, not much gets accomplished besides a promise to install more cameras next week and a committee vote on metal detectors being installed. Still, the whole thing is exhausting and unsettling.

When Sasha returns home, she feels like she ran a marathon. The drizzle has stopped, but it's overcast and dreary. When she pulls into the drive, she sees Tom raking leaves in the backyard, which apparently he finds therapeutic, the reason he doesn't hire a service like everyone else. Chloe is in her pink raincoat swinging on her rope swing, then jumping into piles of leaves and squealing. Sasha waves on her way into the house, and Tom blows her a kiss.

Inside, Sasha relishes the rattle of the heat coming on as she turns up the thermostat higher than anyone else in the house cares for, but she's chilled to the bone and upset, if she's honest. She puts the teapot on and sits at the kitchen counter to text Drew and remind him that he said he'd spend the weekend writing a term paper he's put off. She sees the read receipt but no immediate reply.

Soon enough, the bubbles appear and disappear a few times as he forms a response, but in the end, all that comes through is a thumbs-up emoji, which is good enough for Sasha right now.

She pulls off her boots and takes her mug of chamomile tea upstairs while she considers a hot bath, but as she passes Drew's room, she pauses and peers in. There's crap everywhere. Dirty clothes on the floor, a bowl of mac and cheese that's formed a patch of blue mold sitting on his desk, empty soda cans. She sighs, places her mug on the hall table and goes inside to pick up.

Once she stuffs his clothes into a laundry basket and starts for the congealed mac and cheese bowl, she sees something that catches her eye. Something that before today would not have warranted a second glance. She stands still for a moment and she can feel her heart thump against her rib cage. She tilts her head and examines what exactly she's looking at.

There is a wisp of red sticking out from a pile of school folders on top of Drew's desk. Sasha's heart speeds up even though it's nothing, of course it's nothing, but still, she drops the soda cans into his waste container and hesitantly walks over to the desk. She removes the science book and folders on top and carefully arrives at the folder with the red scrap. It has a Cloverhill Wildcats sticker on its front cover, along with some doodles. She flips it open and her heart leaps into her throat.

Inside are three sheets of red construction paper. One has a circle cut out from the middle with a notch on one side, eerily in the shape of a cartoon bomb.

CHAPTER THREE

Andi

For a few brief moments when I wake up, I have a flicker of relief truly believing it was all a bad dream. I was up most of the night, but exhaustion finally took over after Carson left at 4 a.m. and I drifted off for just a short while, and now I sit here, excruciatingly aware that it was not a dream. It all comes back in fractured, wine-blurred images as I stare numbly at the bedroom wall.

I ran. I saw her lying on the ground with blood down the side of her head and I almost threw up, but I swallowed it down, and as I felt my own blood rushing in my ears and the adrenaline and fear coursing through me, panic took hold and I ran. As fast as I could back to the deck—the hot tub still bubbling away, wineglasses half full on the table, ESPN playing on the outdoor TV—all of it still existing like nothing at all had happened. My head was spinning and I dropped to my knees, trying to hold in the vomit creeping up my esophagus when Carson came back out the sliding glass doors and stopped cold upon seeing me.

I started to say the words. I started to tell him what had happened. I shouted for him to call the police, I thought. But no. I didn't do that. No words came out. I was paralyzed in fear. Carson rushed to my side, asking what was wrong, and then he saw my colorless face and assumed I was sick.

"God, I hope it's not food poisoning," he said and started to help me into the house, into bed, in such a foggy haze, I scarcely remember it at all—I don't know if he carried me, if I walked, because everything was spinning. Then he brought me saltine crackers and made tea and placed it on the bedside table, and I looked at the ceiling and I said nothing. He kept asking if I was okay and I just nodded, and he said he'd let me rest awhile and went back to the porch, where I heard the cheers of patrons in a football stadium between the TV announcers' commentary and I just . . . I couldn't move. It must be what absolute shock feels like.

I stared at the peppermint tea and the sleeve of crackers on the nightstand, and I heard the rain that the forecast had promised start to tap at the windowpanes, and I thought of Tia's body on the cold ground and then . . . what I had just done started to sink in.

Then sometime in the middle of the night, I realized this was all a drunken haze of a memory—a dream. This could not have happened in real life. It wasn't possible. So I quietly forced myself off the bed and made careful, silent steps out of the bedroom and downstairs. I pulled on a parka from the front hall closet and pushed my feet into old sneakers and then I used my phone flashlight to walk all the way back out to the fence and prove to myself that this was all just one drink too many and not real life.

There was a moment I almost laughed at myself—my stupidity. I probably had one of Carson's edibles and forgot and that's why I was so delusional, but when I reached the spot where it happened, I had to suppress a bloodcurdling scream as I saw Tia lying there. Very real. Not a sick nightmare as I was praying she would turn out to be. Her skin was ghostly white, her pale hair rain soaked. My heart ached. "I'm so, so sorry. I'm so sorry," is all I could mutter over and over.

I stood, paralyzed, a few moments. Then I numbly moved to the utility shed a few yards away. I pulled an old paint drop cloth from a shelf and went to cover her with it.

I stood over her in the black night air and I could barely breathe. The shock of it was still sending ripples through me, my thoughts reeling. I knew I needed to confess, to tell Carson, to call for help, but I didn't move. I moved back to sit on the floor inside the shed and stared out into the darkness, the dim moonlight reflecting off the cloth covering her body, and it felt almost like my life was slowly playing out before my eyes. Every ruined life that would fall like dominoes in the wake of this when the news hit, my motherless children, a lifetime in prison, the hatred and accusation and press and threats . . . my kids, my kids, my fucking kids.

I stayed up all night playing the scenarios over and over again in my mind. It was an accident. How could I have known Tia was snooping around the house again? But nobody, not one person, including Carson, would believe this was an accident. He heard the shot I took after he left. He said I should have waited for him and thought I was afraid of guns. I thought he'd be thrilled I was taking an interest, but he made a big deal about it being unsafe. He seemed almost suspicious, or maybe I was reading into it. But he knew I fought with her. He knows she snoops around. He would say he believed me, probably. But would he, deep down? The palpable hatred we had for one another displayed for everyone to witness at each public event and social occasion. There's no way I would ever, in ten thousand lifetimes, be believed. The fight on her front lawn just hours before with all the neighbors watching. Slutbag, home-wrecker, twat, fuckface, whore. Her name actually pops up on my phone screen as "cow" the rare times she has to call about something to do with the kids.

I can't change what's happened. The words repeated over and over in my head. What would become of me if I told? More importantly, what would happen to my kids? Their lives would be torn apart.

Not just because they'll have a murderer for a mother, whom they will spend their weekends visiting in prison, but their shattered futures, the way they'll be treated by everyone for the rest of their lives, the irreversible damage it will cause to the two precious babies that it's my job to protect—my only job.

My husband and my own mother—would they ever really believe me? Would even *they* think, somewhere in the back of their minds, that this might not have been an accident, no matter how much I implore them to understand that it was? As my mother struggles with a third resurgence of breast cancer, she'll have to wonder if her daughter is a killer—she'll have to go to her grave with this question in her consciousness, even if she says she believes me. And after beating cancer twice, would learning about this, going through a trial and police questioning, all the inevitable press coverage—would it put her over the edge with no chance of recovery? Goddammit. What have I done to my family?

These thoughts looped through my head as I sat still in the darkness all night, the rise and fall of Carson's breathing next to me. The whipping wind picked up, howling through the trees, and as the thoughts and all the scenarios played through, I came to my senses. I resolved to tell Carson and call the police. Yes. Of course I had to. But then the flashes started over again: my kids losing their childhood and being the children of a murderer; my mother in hospice; Ray hating me even more than he does now and poisoning the kids against me—the whole world forever thinking that I'm a killer. All of it crumbling, one destroyed life, then another, then another. No.

It's private property. We have a legal right to shoot cans within our acreage. I wasn't doing anything wrong. I can tell them that, right? Maybe they would believe it. These conflicting thoughts just keep fighting one another—keep looping and looping, and tugging back and forth, until hours have gone by and now it's dawn and the sun is barely visible above the tree line as the rain falls in torrents.

And now it's too late, isn't it? Even if I wanted to tell, I have waited so long that now I am guilty no matter what. They'll know when she died. I watch TV; I get what forensics is capable of. They'll know how long it took me to call and since they already would certainly not have believed my story, now . . . waiting has hammered the last nail in my coffin.

I can't change what has happened. But I can change what happens next, so that's it. What other choice am I left with? No one can ever know.

There's a knock on the front door that jolts me out of my thoughts so hard, I leap to my feet and suppress a scream. I hold my racing heart as I quickly take inventory of how I must look. Guilty. Of something, I'm sure. What if it's the police? What if they know? My eyes are swollen and my face is ghostly pale. I'm hungover on top of it all . . . and just then, before I can do anything at all, I hear the front door dead bolt click open.

I race to the front door just in time for Dez to fly past me with a bag of McDonald's in his hand.

"Hi, Mom!" he says, and then I hear him take the stairs two at a time up to his room. The door slams. I look at Ray standing in the door frame.

"I've been calling you all goddamn morning," he says. His eyes are bloodshot and his face is crumpled and distorted. He looks me up and down.

"Well, you look like shit. I guess that explains it. You must have tied one on last night. Great. Of course you did. Right when you're needed, you're useless," he says, and in all the years and arguments and extremely one-sided and tumultuous divorce, he's never talked to me like that.

"What?" is all I manage.

"I need you to keep the kids this week. Tia is . . . I don't know. She didn't come home last night. She's missing. Like actually fucking missing," he says, and his voice breaks. He runs his hands through his hair and takes a deep breath.

"I texted you a dozen times," he said.

"I . . ." I stumble over my words. I have to be careful, because I am very aware of how I look right now and that what I say in this moment matters.

"My phone was on 'do not disturb.' I forgot to switch it back," I say, and Ray glances past me to the glass doors leading out to the deck, where the wine bottles still sit and the cover is off the hot tub. He blushes. Even in a moment like this and even though he's the one who cheated, any slight suggestion of me and Carson being intimate still somehow gives him a reaction after all this time. His chest gets red and blotchy and he changes the subject.

"Yeah, well, don't tell the kids what's going on yet. I hope it's nothing. Maybe there's still a chance there's an explanation."

"Of course. Of course there is," I say. Jesus, God, what am I saying? I'm a monster. I place my hand on his shoulder and to my surprise, he grips it tight and hangs his head. I think it's the first time I have even come close to touching him in a couple of years. My instinct is to pull away, but I see he's crying.

"Tell me if there's anything I can do to help. I'm so sorry, Ray. I'm sure it will turn out to be nothing. I'm sure . . ." Before I finish my barbaric, heartless sentence, he lets go and flicks away a tear.

"Yeah, thanks," he says, putting his macho mask back on and walking to his car. I close the front door and try to breathe. I rest my forehead on the door a moment, my mind reeling. Then I slide down the wall and sit on the floor . . . and weep.

CHAPTER FOUR

Regan

By Saturday evening, the whole town has heard about Tia. I drive over wet roads on my way to the community center. Hallie has been rehearsing *Beauty and the Beast* for weeks, and although she is playing Mrs. Potts and not Belle, she's no less enthusiastic about her theatrical debut. She sings the familiar lyrics, warming up her voice in the back seat. I think about the Belle snow globe Jack bought her for Christmas a few years ago and how he'd have given anything to be here for her special night. Then I shake the thoughts away quickly because when the darkness starts to push in, I lose myself in despair, and I can't let that happen tonight.

I sit at a red light and when it turns green, there is still a man in the crosswalk, walking as slowly as humanly possible. He has his hands in his pockets and then he looks over and I feel like he's looking right at me—like he might pull out a gun and shoot. I panic and lay on my horn. The man startles and leaps back with a gasp.

Then he bangs on the hood of my car with his fist as he passes.

"What's your problem, psycho?" he yells, and I remember Jack always telling me never to honk at anyone. You can't get away with it anymore, he used to say. Everybody in the country has a gun and they'll shoot you for a lesser offense than honking these days. I instantly regret it. I didn't think. Hallie is in the back and she looks scared, and that was stupid of me. He yells something else and then hurries across the street, away from me. As it turns out, I'm the scary one—the threat. Because I see it's someone I know. It's Dave Wilfers, and I know his wife. She said he's still recovering from back surgery, which is probably why he's walking so slowly, and now I watch him disappear through the door of a used bookstore with a copy of a Dickens novel under his arm for God's sake. Jesus. I almost put him back into a spinal fusion procedure and he was just trying to go to the Victorian Era Literature lecture at the Reading Nook . . . not, in fact, trying to shoot me in my car. Shit.

"Sorry, sweetie," I say. Hallie just blinks at me from the back seat. "Let's hear your opening lines again," I say and watch her mood reluctantly shift as she refocuses on rehearsing her role.

I've been careful and meticulous with how I manage whatever is happening to me. Grief. The doctor prescribed a slew of meds after Jack's funeral. I didn't want to take any of it. I thought I could cope. I'd been working as an English Lit professor at a small college west of town for a long time, but since his death, I couldn't focus, I canceled classes all the time, I snapped at annoying students; it was clear I wasn't capable of keeping a job. And then I had a moment that went very public when a student recorded it on his phone. A sophomore was giving a presentation on French playwright Alexandre Dumas and pronounced his last name "Dumbass" the whole time. I don't know what came over me. I threw my coffee mug at the presentation screen, where it made a gash and sprayed brown liquid all over the front row of students. I screamed, "Who's the fucking dumbass?" and I tore up the notes in his hand and threw the pieces at the class. Something came over me and I just saw red. Maybe before Jack's death, I would have simply laughed at something like that, but I am different now.

I'm not proud of it, of course, but after someone put it up as an Instagram reel within five minutes, my career was over, and now I live off Jack's life insurance and try very hard not to have violent episodes like that. It takes a careful balance of medication, but I do it for Hallie. I work full-time on not losing my mind solely for her. I don't always succeed.

I read all the time about how to get off benzos. Sometimes I think I can do it, but most days, stopping them seems more horrifying than I ever imagined. A doctor was interviewed in some online thing I was reading, and he talked about how he used to visit patients in the hospital who had been on benzos long-term and were being medically supervised as they were weaned off them. He said the thing he remembers most from that time is the wailing down the corridors—patients would stay in the fetal position howling and sobbing all day. "It's the grief," he said.

Every day it's the grief. Right now, driving Jack's Suburban out of necessity, since the tragedy with Ally and my car, only makes it worse. I sigh, try to shake it off for a moment. All

I get are moments free of it. The grief. I adjust the rearview mirror and smile at Hallie encouragingly as she sings and gesticulates each lyric. Driving Jack's car feels somehow strange and wrong even after all this time, and I found the most peculiar thing—a small key taped inside the back of his glove compartment. I was looking for the registration so I could get it updated in order to drive, and there it was. Now it's on my key chain and I have racked my brain trying to think what it opens, what it means. I honestly feel like I could go crazy with all the unanswered questions.

In general, I don't let myself think too long about the what-ifs in life: What if he didn't make that business trip that ended up being his last? What if on the night of the explosion, I had volunteered to go to the store instead of Ally? What if Hallie wanted to come with me? The kids were complaining about wanting sparklers and she might have asked to tag along. Stop. I have to stop. There is no earthly reason for someone to want me dead. I don't have any enemies I can conceive of. There have to be a billion white BMWs in a ten-mile radius of the party. It must have been meant for someone else. That's all that makes sense. The police have no other explanation, so this is all I can repeat to myself when I need to find a calm headspace.

I drop Hallie at the door so she can get into costume, and after I finally find a parking space in the crowded theater lot, I join the other parents in the lobby. Everyone is standing around in small circles, chatting to one another and drinking wine out of plastic cups from the refreshment stand. I see Sasha and Chloe come through the front door and shake the rain out of their coats. I wave them over and pick up two paper cups of red wine from the concession table, then hand one to her.

"Thank you." She smiles. "You wanna go in and pick out our seats?" she asks Chloe, who clasps her hands together excitedly and nods before disappearing into the theater.

"She's over the moon to see this," Sasha says.

"Oh, good. Hallie is excited you guys could come." Chloe is a few years younger than Hal and adores her, so I know she really is thrilled, and Hallie likes to show off for her and soak in the admiration.

"I guess Roxie and Dez aren't coming. God, did they tell the kids yet, about Tia? Or I guess maybe they're waiting to see if she turns up before worrying them?" Sasha asks.

"God, no. The kids don't know. Shit, it's all so weird. Like, where could she vanish to? They say her phone is off—not traceable or pinging off any towers. I think that's the most alarming thing I've heard so far. Doesn't sound good."

"All of it's so odd. Scary," Sasha says, and then the lobby lights blink, indicating that folks should take their seats. Once inside, we sit in the dark as the stage comes to life, with the narrator standing under a spotlight. He starts the show with "Once upon a time." What's that kid's name? Jamie, I think. Hallie can't stand him—says he cheats off her math tests from the desk behind her and steals her Fruit Roll-Ups from her bag. I should talk to his mother about that.

The music booms suddenly and my hand instinctively flies to my mouth. Sasha squeezes my knee and smiles to console me. Everything makes me startle now. It's embarrassing. I imagine every building blowing up into thin air, the bomber lurking somewhere in plain sight everywhere I go. I take a deep breath and try to focus on the show. I told Andi I'd record some of it for Dez to watch since he wanted to come, so I push Record on my phone camera and capture Hallie's opening song. She stumbles on a couple lyrics early on and looks offstage at the pianist, who nods at her to keep going, but other than that she delivers all those lines she practiced in the living room for weeks perfectly, and I feel pride swell in my chest followed by a tight fist of pain—a longing for Jack.

At intermission, I look over the video I took; it's dark and muffled as one would expect, but Dez will still like to see it. He's in Drama with Hallie and they love making up little plays together, so it's a shame he couldn't come.

"I told Andi I'd document the occasion. Should we take a photo for Andi and Dez?" I ask Chloe. She nods vigorously and the three of us squeeze into a selfie, Sasha and I holding up our plastic wine cups and smiling at the camera, and Chloe giving a peace sign. I send it off to Andi, telling her we wished she could make it. I can imagine she's trying to help Ray keep it together for the kids, or maybe the police are questioning them about Tia. It's always the spouse, isn't it? God, that's awful of me. We don't even know if this is anything to really worry about yet.

Sasha gets up and takes Chloe out to use the restroom, and I'm about to stand to see what the refreshment stand has when I get a text back from Andi.

WTF, Regan?

I reply back with three question marks and an exclamation point because what the hell does she mean?

Jack behind you. WTF? Andi's next text reads. I shake my

head and scoff instinctively at the nonsense I just read, but then I feel suddenly breathless. What does she mean? So I look at the photo I sent her and my heart stops cold. I gasp and hold my throat and stare at my phone screen. A man with sandy hair, a black jacket and a dark wooly hat, looking very inconspicuous with his eyes cast to the ground, is sitting a few rows behind me. The photo is dark, but there is no doubt that it's him. It's Jack.

I whip around in my seat and look to the back row of the theater. The seat he was in is empty, but the back of a figure in the same jacket and beanie is standing, walking up the stairs, moving past a few people coming back to their seats with wine and small pieces of cake on cocktail napkins from concessions. He rushes, almost knocking the cups out of their hands as he takes the stairs two at a time and disappears into the lobby.

I leap to my feet and run up the stairs after him.

"Jack!" I yell over the heads of the people in my way. "Jack!" I practically scream, and a handful of people are looking at me now—people I only vaguely know, but they know everything about me, of course, because that's what happens when you're the victim of a tragedy. Everyone knows Jack is long gone, dead. And the looks of pity I receive are not lost on me even though I'm focused on stopping him before he vanishes.

I burst through the door into the lobby and shout after him again. All of the parents standing around drinking wine are stunned into silence. I see Sasha cover her mouth with her hand, wide-eyed, as I stumble desperately through the theater doors and out onto the wet street. "Jack!"

But I see him, already a distance away down the sidewalk, his jacket pulled up on one side to shield his face from the rain. He's jogging. I watch him hail a cab; they're usually nonexistent in this neighborhood, but they hover around these sorts of events to drive the tipsy moms home, so he gets one straightaway. I pause a moment too long, thinking about whether I can leave Hallie's big night to chase him, but I have to! Of course I have to. I don't say anything to Sasha or turn back around. I'll be back before the second act of the show is over, but I have to go now. I run to my car in the lot and pull out to the street, where I see the cab pull away from the curb and start east down Sixth Street. I'm a few cars behind them, so I try to swerve and pass to get closer, but I'm also trying not to be reckless, especially since the streets are slick.

Jack? How can that be? It wasn't just me. I'm not delusional. Andi saw it, too. He was there. I feel my eyes blur from the tears welling up, and I blink them away and try to focus—to catch him. I see the stoplight ahead turn yellow and I have a moment of hope that the car will stop and I'll be able to pull alongside and see him—stop him. But the driver just barely makes the light and I'm stuck on red. But I don't stop. I race through the red light and hear a symphony of honks as I pass.

After a couple of miles, I have maintained a few car lengths of the cab and then I see him signal; they're turning into the Amtrak station. Who takes a train anymore? Like a regular train, not a subway or the L. I can't make sense of any of this. It feels so surreal and otherworldly that I am watching my dead husband . . . do what, exactly? Run away from me? What the fuck is actually happening here?

The cab pulls up at the front entrance of the station, and I'm about to step my foot on the gas when I hear the bell of a train crossing ring out and the arms over the tracks begin to lower in front of my car, stopping me cold before I can reach him. I'm stuck watching a train pass between me and Jack on the other side. I watch him, in the gap between train cars. It's like a flip-book from childhood—I can only view him in bursts of movement that seem to fast-forward, disjointed with every short glimpse I get.

I register him getting out of the back seat and walking in through the front doors, which are a wall of glass, so I can see him approach the ticket counter. He exchanges brief words with the attendant, and then I watch him walk to a platform and sit on a bench and wait. Shit. I can still reach him. My heart pounds so hard I can hear the blood rushing between my ears. I pound the palms of my hands on the steering wheel, screaming, "Come on! Come the fuck on!" but it's another few minutes before the train finally passes and the arms lift.

I squeal into the parking lot and jump out of my car without even turning it off or closing the door, and I run, breathless, to the platform. I clock the bench Jack was sitting on, but he's not there. I run down the length of the platform, calling for him. I rush into the small snack bar, where a couple men sit drinking cans of beer and eating fries from a paper plate between them. The woman behind the counter starts to look up from her phone and ask me what she can get for me, but she must register my wild eyes and panic, because she just takes a step back and stares a moment. Before she can say anything else, I'm out the door and charging into the men's restroom, calling out for him.

I hear a couple of men mutter "Hey!" and "What the hell?" from inside the stalls, but I don't care. I run back to the ticket counter and ask about the schedule. A train bound for Windsor Locks, Connecticut, just left, and the next one isn't until tomorrow. The man behind the Plexiglas window hands me a paper schedule.

"Did a man named Jack Hoffman get on the train? Please? Can you tell me that?" I beg.

"Ma'am, I can't give out information like that. Come on," he says, more condescendingly than necessary.

I'm so utterly shocked that I look around the station one more time—a few people who arrived on the train from Newark stand with luggage, presumably waiting for a ride. One woman pulls her kid closer to her like I'm some wild animal about to attack, and my heart drops. Jack's gone. I've lost him.

I walk numbly to my car and drive the five miles back to the theater. I've been gone less than an hour, but I don't have time to process any of this or drive to follow each of the train's stops like I thought about doing for a split second. I have to get back to Hallie before she knows I was gone.

The drive back is a blur. My head spins, creating far-fetched scenarios and reaching for explanations—anything that could make this logical. There has to be a reason. Losing my mind and hallucinating is top of my list, but I know what I fucking saw.

When I get back to the theater, I rush in and stand in the back and watch the last song of the show and the curtain call, and I clap and clap and try not to fall apart in front of my daughter and her peers and the parents who are already forming texts in their minds if they haven't already sent them to friends and spouses about Regan Hoffman going mental at the school play. They pity me too much to let me get wind of this, but I know.

The house lights come up and the kids are milking their standing ovation, and I think about what could have possibly just happened and why? Is Jack really alive and well? Did he show up here because he's been keeping tabs on our life and couldn't miss Hallie's milestone event? How can any of this possibly be? I was at his funeral. If this is some elaborate hoax or scam, then why? The man I was best friends with since college and knew better than anyone in the world is a fraud? That's not possible.

If he's capable of disappearing for two years and having the world think him dead . . . then he is completely unknowable and a stranger to me. If that's true, he has to be involved in some very serious shit. And now so am I, because someone is trying to have me killed. Right before he shows back up. It has to be connected. What the hell is he running from?

CHAPTER FIVE

Sasha

When they get home from the play, Sasha can't stop thinking about Regan. She didn't say anything to her afterward, but she saw Regan standing in the back and then waiting for Hallie outside the dressing room, going out of her way to avoid the judgmental gazes from the other parents after her outburst. Sasha's heart aches for Regan's loss. She's in such desperate despair that she thought she saw her dead husband at her daughter's play. Maybe the event triggered something. It's unimaginable.

Tom's on the sofa in sweats and a T-shirt when they come in wet and starving, and Sasha's envious and can't wait to be in a bathrobe drinking something hot out of a mug. Every time she looks at him, though, she feels a twinge of guilt for not yet telling him about what she found in Drew's room. She doesn't know if she should involve Tom. Drew's not his son, and he loves to remind Tom of that any chance he gets. She's sure it can't be easy for Drew that Chloe is Tom's biological daughter—he must feel somehow second fiddle, even though he swears up and down he never thinks of it that way. Of course he'd say that, though.

They get along, Tom and Drew, but there's a small chance Tom would want to go to the police, and Sasha can't let that happen. She needs to find out if it's a cause of concern first. Chloe has a stack of orange and red construction paper she cut autumn leaves and pumpkin shapes from, to decorate her bedroom door with for Halloween. What if that's all it is? She needs more information before she overreacts.

"Hey, any leftovers? We're starved," she says to Tom, shaking the rain out of her coat as Chloe pops into the kitchen and opens a juice box.

"Hey, guys." He gets up and comes to kiss her on the head and take her coat. Still such a gentleman. "Sorry, thought you ate," he says.

"We were running late, and then . . . things got weird," she says, peering into the fridge at a couple raw chicken breasts.

"Where's Drew?"

"Hanging out at Blanc's, he said."

"I'll just go pick something up," Sasha says.

"No, I'll order in," he insists, but she's already in rain boots and out the door before he can protest, because the real reason she's rushing out has nothing to do with dinner. If Drew says he's hanging out at Blanc's, she wants to see if he's lying. If he is actually there, she wants to see his demeanor. Is he subdued, acting off with his friends? Will she even be able to tell? She hasn't seen him since she found the stuff in his room. Ever since they got him a car for his sixteenth birthday a few months ago, she lives on more of a hope and a prayer that he's doing the right thing, trusting him without any reason not to. Until now. Now it's time she starts finding out for herself.

As she drives the short distance to Blanc's Barbecue, she feels like she'll never get used to actually being a "Blanc." It was different in New York. Tom and his father and brother have a restaurant in Manhattan and had another in Baton Rouge where it all started, so Tom was the one who ran the New York location alongside his father, and his brother ran the Baton Rouge store until it closed some years ago due to family drama they don't talk about. Even though Sasha and Tom have been married for seven years, she never gets used to the semi-famous last name. Tom's family grew a multimillion-dollar business off their first endeavor, "Blanc's Brisket," which made a killing in the frozen-food space. After selling the company for a stupid amount of money, his dad started the first two restaurants, and now they've opened a Cloverhill location. Guy Fieri from the Food Network even came to film an episode there and called it some of the best barbecue north of the Mason-Dixon.

Maybe it feels weird since it's not Sasha's success, but it makes her immediately defensive when people comment on it—like she didn't have her own successes and a whole life before she met Tom—but she supposes that's her own baggage to sort out. In New York it was different because nobody knew who the hell she was outside of her close circles. Here, however, she can't hide the association with the name. When Tom's dad wanted a slower pace of life in his golden years, he thought it would be nice to have a Blanc's Barbecue location in Cloverhill Lakes—one of the Northeast's safest and most sought-after communities.

She thinks he mostly wanted to give Tom permission to move his family out of the city, and Sasha sort of leaped at the chance when Tom proposed the idea. She would have preferred Baton Rouge or somewhere warmer, of course, but it was still a good move since they thought it would be better for Drew—not that they were trying to manufacture his popularity at school or anything, but they figured the restaurant could be the place all the teens hung out—they'd create a back room with pinball machines and a soda fountain, and *bam*. And it worked. All the teens do hang out there, but Drew still skulks around mostly by himself. He'll be angry at Sasha about his father the rest of his life, but there's really not much she can do to change that at this point.

And he does have friends, of course. He has a couple boys from band he hangs out with—a tuba player and a bass player—and that's great. They're good kids. It's all fine, she tells herself. Everything is going to be okay. He's a good kid, too, at heart. She knows he is.

She decides to enter the restaurant through the side door by the kitchen to pick up the order she called in on her way over—that way she can canvass the dining room quickly and look for Drew before he spots her. Wally smiles from the kitchen and brings out two large bags of barbecue chicken with all the sides as soon as she steps inside, so she's standing in the back hall hugging the giant bag while trying to look nonchalant at the same time. She spots Drew right away in a corner booth and breathes a sigh of relief. He's there like he said. Not somewhere planning bomb threats. Of course not. She does not see tuba guy, Brian, or bass player, Elija, with him as expected, though. Instead, he sits looking across the checkered tablecloth and drippy candles at Roxie, Andi's daughter, whom she figured would be on a short leash at home while all the Tia stuff is being sorted out, but there they are.

She's sitting at the edge of the booth with her coat still on, holding a take-out bag of food. Drew pulls apart a bread roll mindlessly, and she grabs a piece of it and shoves it into her mouth. They laugh. Oh, my God, they're flirting. Sasha's not sure how to feel about this. She edges around to the hall where the restrooms are and gets as close to their booth as she can to see if she can catch just a sliver of their conversation.

"I should probably go," Roxie says. "My mom already texted twice. She's totally freaking out over all this."

"I thought you said she hated Tia. Why is she freaking so much?"

"Right? Tia is fine and everyone knows it. She's trying to get attention. Her and my dad had some big fight after my mom dropped us off and she's just making my dad pay for it. That's what I think. That's what happens with gold diggers."

"What do you mean?" Drew asks her.

"She's half his age and looks like Malibu Barbie. It's not a huge surprise she only wants money. I wouldn't be surprised if a ransom note turns up and when he pays it, she takes off with a fortune."

"Jesus. You really think she's faking all this—like, that she'd do that?"

"Maybe." Roxie shrugs. "Come on. Didn't your mom marry Tom for the money? Don't they all?" she says, and Sasha feels a surge of adrenaline rush through her. She didn't even know Tom had money until well into the relationship, *you little twit*, she thinks but doesn't say, of course.

"I never thought about it," Drew says. He deflects but doesn't exactly stand up for his mother.

"I mean, no offense," Roxie adds. "Just sayin'. Must be nice to be a hot chick and get whatever you want." Sasha hears an awkward pause in the conversation.

"You don't think you're a hot chick?" Drew asks, and as offended as Sasha feels by where this conversation has led, she also feels a little inner cheer that Drew sort of knows how to say the right thing to a girl. She's never seen him interact with one before, so it's all a little surprising, and a bit weird.

"Oh, shut up," Roxie says.

"No, you are. You shouldn't doubt that," he says.

"Yeah, whatever," she giggles insecurely, and from where Sasha is listening, it sounds like Roxie's standing up now, so Sasha inches back a little bit farther in the hallway.

"I gotta get back before she reports me missing," she says.

"Ha-ha," Drew says. "Later."

"Later," Roxie repeats, and Sasha sees the back of her as she walks to the front glass doors, pushes them open and disappears into the dark parking lot. She's about to go over to Drew, but something makes her stop. She peers around the corner and sees him dropping some crumpled ones onto the table for tip money, taking one last bread roll from the basket and shrugging on his coat.

Sasha doesn't hesitate—she just slips out the side door and into her car, which is parked inconspicuously by the dumpster near the back kitchen entrance. Then she watches him. She watches him get into his birthday-gift car and back out, and as soon as he pulls out of the lot, she is right on his tail.

As he makes his way to the main road, Sasha stays a few car lengths behind and follows him. It's not like him to go home before curfew and he has a little time, so where *will* he go? She follows him, nervous, palms sweating.

He takes a left on Crestridge. Okay, he's probably headed home. After a while he passes the turn for home and keeps driving east. Then, he takes a quick right onto First Street. She tries to think where he could be stopping. First Street leads to the interstate. It heads out of town. There are very few undesirable establishments in Cloverhill Lakes, but this weird stretch of road leading out of town has a liquor store, a sex shop, some bail bonds places and also a few beat-up gas stations. She watches Drew pull in and park under the awning of a closed-down burger joint called Hefty's. It's dark and abandoned. What the hell could he possibly be doing there?

She pulls into the gas station across the street, drives up to a pump and turns her car off. She opens the camera on her phone and zooms in until she can get a clear view of him. He sits in the car a few minutes, but then he gets out and looks around, side to side, with an incredibly paranoid expression. Then he knocks? For some godforsaken reason, he *knocks* on the door of a place that has boarded-up windows covered in graffiti.

Her heart just about stops as she sees a figure open the door. Someone is in there. Why? She doesn't see any more than the side of a hood and an arm, but Drew talks to the person for a moment. Then she watches Drew take some money out of his pocket and hand it to the figure, who counts the bills. Then the figure hands Drew a bag—something the size of a small backpack, but it's hard to really make it out clearly. It just looks like a dark mass. It's all she can glimpse before Drew tucks it into his coat, gets back in the car and drives off in the direction of home.

Fuck.

CHAPTER SIX

Andi

Knowing she's out there, covered in painting cloth while everyone is looking for her—while my kids sit a few hundred yards away on the living room couch watching *Cobra Kai* and eating pretzel sticks—is a surreal and indescribable feeling. This whole day has been like living in hell, waiting for darkness to fall and for the kids to go to bed so I can do something. I need to move her, but I'm trapped right now.

I sat on the porch most of the afternoon, watching, making sure nobody went past me into the back property. I think about George coming to trim the weeds and water the garden on the west side of the house like he does every week, and I imagine him going out to the back shed for supplies, but of course he doesn't come on Saturdays. I know I'm letting myself get worked up into a state just thinking of any reason anyone might go back there today. Angela sometimes picks fresh flowers when she cleans the house, but that's on Mondays, and it's October, so there aren't any flowers left to pick. I need to be rational. Nobody will go back there before I have a chance to.

I don't leave the porch, though. I have Rox bring me tea and tell her she can go meet her friends at Blanc's later if she brings home dinner for Dez, and he's perfectly happy watching TV all day without being nagged to do something productive. Even though he's missing his friends' play, he seems just fine with the trade-off of junk food and video games. I told him it would look insensitive for us to be out to dinner and a play with the rest of them when his stepmom is missing. In reality, maybe it would look better to be there—less guilty—but I am not leaving my post for anything. So I sit, trying to make plans in my head about how the hell I'm going to do this. About what the fuck I'm actually doing.

Then, after a mercifully uneventful day, I get a text from Regan just as dusk is setting in. A photo from the play. I think it's a joke at first, but of course, she'd never joke about her late husband. She wouldn't do anything to appear less stable than people already think she is. No one blames her for being that way, they coddle and protect her, actually, but she is aware and tries hard to keep things buttoned up. There's no way she'd send a joke about this, so I ask her WTF, Regan? and she doesn't know what I'm talking about, and after I tell her, I hear nothing back. I can only assume it was a stranger who just looked like Jack or it was dim lighting or a fuzzy photo or a combination of all of that. Maybe I shouldn't have said anything. It probably really upset her, which I only register after the fact.

But I let it go for now because I'm just a few hours from

making a move—the most abhorrent, disgraceful move of my life—and it's taking all my energy and focus to appear even halfway normal in front of the kids. I've avoided them most of the day but now it's after seven and so I take a deep breath and go inside.

Roxie wants to go hang out with Drew at Blanc's for a while before she brings sandwiches home—the Drew thing is . . . new, but a relief. The less I'm around the kids today, the less chance of them remembering how odd I was acting at this particular time in history. As hard as I try to hold it together, I know I'm not doing a great job. I give Roxie the keys and she leaves. I notice Dez is not in front of the TV where I expected him to be.

"Dez," I call up the stairs, but he doesn't answer. Then I hear the rumble of the automatic garage door lift. Holy shit. Is Carson back early? Why would he be back? I'm so screwed. I whip open the door off the kitchen that leads to the garage and see Dez with his helmet on, pushing his bike toward the driveway.

"What are you doing?"

"I'm gonna ride dirt bikes with Jason," he says with a confused look.

"No," I snap.

"You said we could do whatever we want today. I'm not leaving the property."

"No," I repeat, even more harshly. "It's almost dark. Back inside."

"Mom, for real. He's already coming. We're meeting at the shed," he says, and my heart lurches. I can feel a shooting pain in my head—a cluster headache beginning to form, tapping at my temples like an ice pick at the thought of what he just said. *The shed.* It's not unusual for them to meet there and take the dirt trail around the woods, but I hadn't even thought of that as another thing to worry about—another way someone might go out there before I have a chance to hide what I've done.

"Call him and tell him you can't," I say as calmly as I can possibly muster.

"Just till dinner, come on. So embarrassing. He's already coming. Why?" he whines, and I try to think of a quick reason he can't refute.

"Imagine what your dad is going through. If they find something—if he needs us or the police have more questions—I can't be out in the woods looking for you. You need to stay here," I say, my hands shaking, my breath shallow. All I can think of is Jason Hillier out in the woods, pulling the paint cloth off Tia's body. It's so overwhelming, I sit down on the garage step for a minute so I don't pass out.

"Fine." He drops his bike and starts to walk past me.

"Call him," I say again, and he sighs, rolls his eyes, then pulls out his phone, holding it to his ear for a few moments.

"He's not answering. Can't I just—"

"No. Go inside and play *Halo* or something until Roxie's back. And text him not to come," I say, sitting on my trembling hands, waiting for him to stomp inside, and as soon as the door slams, I run.

I run barefoot across the cold, muddy grass over the dirt clearing and into the trees, as fast as I can. Jesus, this kid cannot get close to the shed. She's right there. I stop and rest my hands on my knees, catching my breath once I reach the shed where they planned to meet. No Jason Hillier in sight, thank God. Okay, okay. Calm down.

I look over to the low wooden fence, which has cans and old beer bottles scattered beneath it and some shattered glass in the dirt from the times we hit the target over the years. And like a nightmare I can't wake up from, she's there, still there—a shape under a drop cloth that seems so unreal I can barely wrap my head around the reality of it all. I think about dragging her into the shed but then I think about DNA. I only know what I have seen in shows, but that is enough—they can trace anything.

I stand there, undecided, with my heart pounding, and then I decide to text Dez. He'll think it's weird, and I am trying hard to appear like I'm acting normal, but I can't risk Jason fucking Hillier riding around on his bike and seeing her. I know exactly the path the kids take from the house into the woods, and they would go right past her. Probably they wouldn't notice a blob of drop cloth. The property is huge. There are a couple sheds, woodpiles, a heap of limp pool floaties next to the shed, some tarps over the firepit. Why would they think twice about what was underneath a cloth? But I can't take that chance. I have to know before I move a muscle.

Did you tell Jason not to come? I text Dez.

?? yeah. He went home. Why are you texting me?

A flood of relief washes over me, but I don't respond. He'll be lost back in a video game in a minute and forget all the rest of it until Roxie arrives with food. I wait a little longer until it's fully dark and I'm convinced he's not coming, and then before I walk back up to the house, I look over at where Tia lies on the ground and whisper, again, that I'm so sorry. And now the tears are coming and I have to work even harder to walk into that house looking like I have it together.

I sit at the dining table in dim light, nursing a cup of tea and thinking about how I get out of this, about what to do so I don't get caught and destroy the lives of everyone around me. I hear the muffled sounds of the TV from the living room. The kids have eaten, Dez is asleep on the floor and Roxie is scrolling, mindlessly, on her phone from the sofa. I have to make my move once I know they are both in their rooms, asleep. I can't make one wrong step.

The boat is the best way. I can use the tarps to wrap her so no DNA is spread around. I'll wear gloves. Tia's small, so I could easily drag the weight of her in the tarp down to the rowboat. It's tied to the dock and we rarely use it—Ray used to use it to fish, but Carson is a devout animal lover and vegetarian who thinks fishing is barbaric, so the boat just sits there mostly unless Dez talks Carson into a trip across the lake for fun.

I could row out to the deepest part and just let her peacefully slip into the water. Jesus, God, I'm a monster. What am I doing? How is this my life? My phone rings and I shriek and hold my heart.

"Mom?" Roxie says from the living room. I see the number is local but I don't recognize it. I answer as Rox appears in the doorway with a concerned look. I make a waving gesture telling her I'm fine and she raises her eyebrows at me and then goes to the fridge for a soda.

"Hello?"

"Ms. Bennett?" a man's voice asks.

"Uh, yes. Who's this?"

"This is Detective Morrison from the Cloverhill Lakes Police Department."

I freeze. I try to speak but I choke on my words and have to clear my throat and try again.

"Sorry, hi. Yes. What can I— Did they find Tia?" I think to quickly ask because that's probably what a non-guilty non-psychopath person would ask.

"No, ma'am. I'm just calling because I'd like to ask you a few questions."

"Me? I . . ." I stutter.

"Just standard stuff. If we can find a time to meet, that would be great. You were one of the last people to talk to Tia, we've been told, and we want to get a general statement from you," he says, and then silence hangs in the air between us.

"Of course," I say.

"Great. I'll stop by, then. At your house after the community search party finishes."

"The what?" I ask.

"Some of Tia's family have coordinated a search party tomorrow morning."

"Oh."

"I think Ray is coordinating it," he says, a little uncomfortably. "I guess speak to him if you'd like to pitch in and help."

"Yeah," I say before hanging up the call. I feel a fist of pain in my chest and a wave of nausea as I immediately poke at Ray's number to call him. Being left out of the town goddamn search party will not be a good look, and he didn't even tell me.

"Hello?" he answers, and his voice is small and hollow, so I quickly remember he's a victim and not a hated ex-husband in this immediate scenario. As I'm about to reflexively yell at him about not including me in this event, it hits me like a punch to the throat that I'm the reason for it all—for the entire town searching for Tia, for Ray's pain, for this whole sickening, devastating horror show.

"Ray, hi. I just— Um, I heard a group of volunteers are getting together tomorrow, and . . ."

"And what?" he says impatiently.

"I didn't know about it. I'd like to help."

I hear him scoff. "Well, you already are. I gave them permission to search our property, so expect a crowd tomorrow." I'm suddenly so lightheaded I have to sit down in the kitchen window seat.

"Sorry?" I croak out.

"Tia's mom coordinated most of it. We're meeting at the top of the lake in the town square. Half the folks will be combing the woods down the west side. The plan is to search the mile of dense trees surrounding the lake all the way around and all the properties in between. I'm heading up the search on the east side including our house, and everyone else in the area is cooperating."

I just sit in stunned silence, because how could I not "cooperate." Even if I wanted to look like some pariah in the situation and say no, I'd have no choice. Ray's name is still on the house because of a long, drawn-out divorce that ended in him not buying me out and waiting to cash out until I sell, like it's an investment or something, because of course he doesn't need the money. He bought a house across the lake. It was better for me financially after it all shook out, but now he has a say, and a mob of people will be digging around the property tomorrow. I could vomit.

"Why didn't you tell me?"

"I don't know, Andi. I might be a little preoccupied. It's not like they're going inside, for God's sake. Why? Do you have something you need a heads-up about? Anything to hide?"

"Jesus, Ray," I say, standing, feeling tears prick my eyes.

"Sorry," he says. "I'm just—"

"Of course, sorry," I say, cutting him off. "How—how can I help? Is there anything else we can do to help?" I stutter. I hear silence for a moment, then a sob that he stifles and tries to quickly recover from. He can't speak.

"I'll be there in the morning. I'm so sorry, Ray. I . . ."

"Yeah," is all he manages and then the call ends. I have to hold my phone with two hands so I don't drop it, my hands are shaking so violently.

Then I see Roxie still lingering in the door frame. I want to scream and beat the walls with my fists, but I just stand there like a statue and blink at her so I don't snap or start bawling uncontrollably.

"You should head to bed," I say in a measured tone.

"That was about Tia?" She comes in and sits on a stool at the breakfast counter. I nod. I'm still clenching every muscle and trying to stay calm even though my mind is reeling.

"It's so weird," she says. "Like, she might really be missing. Are we gonna help look tomorrow?" I nod again and offer a tight smile because it's all I can muster.

"They're doing a shoreline search tonight," she says, and I feel a new rush of adrenaline course through me.

"What does that mean?" I ask, going to the fridge to rummage for a bottle of water so I can keep my back to her.

"Dad called a little bit ago. He and some other guys are going out on boats around the shoreline 'cause he thinks the only explanation is that Tia somehow slipped and fell like on a trail by the lake—some of the banks are kind of high and rocky in different places. He says it's the only thing that makes sense. I guess maybe this is actually real," she says, and I can see the fear in her eyes. The usual snark she has when she talks about Tia is absent, and she looks scared.

"Well," I say, "all we can do is pray and try to help out with the search."

"Can I go out on the boat search tonight?" she asks.

"No, it's not safe. Try to get some sleep and we'll go first thing with everyone else." I walk over and kiss her on the head, ever so briefly, so she doesn't notice my trembling. She nods and puts her soda can in the sink before heading up to her room.

A red-hot panic sears through my entire body. The whole town will be poking around our property tomorrow morning and there's a group going out on the lake tonight. My plan is destroyed and I have no other plan. I'm done. I'm entirely fucked. Think. I have to stay calm and make smart decisions right now. It's not the time to fall apart.

Maybe I should just turn myself in right now. Maybe I should have not panicked to begin with, but it's far too late now. If they wouldn't have believed it was an accident if I'd called 911 immediately, imagine where waiting over twenty-four hours to confess will land me. I have no choice but to try, because if I'm found out, I am a goner either way. I have to try.

I think about the meat freezer in the garage. It's a crazy idea because it's right next to our cars—the kids lean their bikes up against it—but since there's never been meat in it, it just sits there. For a while, Ray kept his handgun locked inside for lack of a better place to secure it, so there's still an old padlock hanging from the metal clasp where it closes. For a couple years we plugged it in for the kids and there were a couple boxes of freezer-burned Popsicles on the bottom, but it hasn't run in years. It just sits there, unplugged, dead, hiding in plain sight.

And that's why it's an option. An appalling and horrifying option, but nobody will look there. Certainly not the kids or Carson, and it's not like the police have a warrant to search the house. I just need to get Tia off the land and hidden away somewhere they won't find her. Nobody in the family will notice if the padlock is locked or not since it's just been hanging there for practically a decade. It's a fixture we all look past. It's the safest thing I can do right now even though I feel like an absolute barbarian thinking of hiding a body close to my kids. What other choice is there?

I sit in the silent living room, waiting for when I'm certain the kids are asleep. It's after eleven thirty when Roxie's light finally goes dark. I wait another half hour to be sure and then I pad softly up the stairs and crack her door open to check. I whisper her name, no response. I walk across the hall to Dez's room. He's fallen asleep with his bedside lamp on and an episode of *Adventure Time* playing on his phone. I turn off the video, click off the lamp and cover him up before tiptoeing back down the stairs.

There's an old parka in the back of the closet I've been meaning to send to charity, and I pull it on. Then I take a pair of winter gloves from the drawer in the mudroom and slip my feet into rain boots to navigate the wet ground, and I walk out into the cold night air.

When I reach Tia's body, I crouch down next to it and pull back the cloth. A sob climbs up my throat as I see her pale skin in the moonlight and the dried blood covering the side of her head. *Why?* I want to scream at her. *Why were you here! If you had just left things alone this would have never happened.*

I feel like nothing less than a vile, immoral monster as I pull the blue tarp from the shed—the one Carson used to protect the bed of his truck when he brought the Christmas tree home last year, and I wrap Tia and the paint cloth carefully inside. I take duct tape from the workbench and tape up the edges so she is sealed as thoroughly as I can manage.

It's too easy to drag her small body through the trees, into the clearing and across the woodsy side yard to the garage. I pause, then walk up onto the back deck and listen for anyone, any movement from the kids, and when there is none, I pull her inside the garage and close the automatic doors. The motor kicks on, and I watch the doors slowly slide down their rollers and cables until they meet the concrete and I am safe inside. I exhale.

Tia's wrapped body sits in front of the freezer, and I have to hug her to my own body and heft her up with all my strength. I heave and use my knees and back to lift until I can force the weight of her over the lip of the freezer and then push the rest of her body up with all my might until I hear a hideous crack against the ice chest interior and she falls inside. I lean my hands on my knees and fight back tears. I feel like I'll hyperventilate, so I try to breathe. *Just stop and breathe. You didn't do this on purpose. This is just a terrible accident and you have no choice,* I say to myself silently. I look down at her body in the cooler, and then I hear something—the creak of a door opening.

"Mom?"

I slam the cooler closed and whip around to see Dez standing in the door frame that leads from the garage to the mudroom. He's in his *Avatar* pajamas and hugging his arms around himself against the cold.

"What are you doing out here?" I snap, and I see his face fall. I try to control my tone—control my fear and terror—and start again. "I mean, is anything wrong? Why are you up?" I ask, standing in front of the meat freezer as if my body can conceal it.

"I heard a sound. I thought there was a robber," he says.

"Oh, honey. I'm so sorry. It was just me. I'm getting some firewood for the fireplace."

"It's late. Why are you making a fire?"

"Oh, uh. I can't sleep. But let's get you back to bed, hon. Do you need something to drink? Will that help?" He nods and turns to go inside. I quickly hook the padlock on the freezer clasp and click it locked. I have no idea what the code is and will probably end up using wire cutters to get it back off, but I'll figure that out later. It's all I can do right now.

After he's inside, I quickly take off my coat and gloves and drop them onto the extra sheet of painter's cloth I brought in from the shed. Then I pull my boots off and drop them onto the pile as well. I'll leave it all there until after I get Dez back to bed.

He sits at the counter and drinks a box of strawberry milk.

"You can't sleep 'cause you're worried about Dad. About Tia, huh?" he asks. I pick up the kettle I'm heating on the stove, pour myself a cup of tea and turn to him.

"Yes, I think everyone's a little worried right now, but it'll be okay," I say.

"Jason's mom said you killed her," he says out of thin air, and I spit my sip of chamomile out involuntarily and gasp—to Dez's shock, apparently, because he looks terrified. I put my mug down and stare at him, shaking off the tea that's dripping down the front of my shirt.

"What did you just say?"

"I thought you would say that was stupid or call her a twat or something the way you do with Tia. I didn't mean to make you mad," he says, and I immediately console him.

"Honey, no, I'm not mad. It's just—that's a terrible thing for someone to say and of course . . . Tia's probably . . . fine." I force the last word out even though I feel like a psychopath telling my child this when I know the truth. It's for his own protection, I tell myself.

"Jason told you his mom said that?"

"Kinda. When I messaged him not to come over, he said his mom wouldn't let him anyway and that he heard her on the phone with one of her friends saying it had to be you who did something to Tia." I stand in the dim kitchen with absolutely no idea how to respond to this—how to handle this. It's already starting—the finger-pointing, the whispers, the blame I knew would lie on me before anyone even knew Tia was really gone. I had to do what I did and it's even clearer now.

"His mom's a twat anyway, though, right?" Dez asks innocently, and I'm ashamed at how freely I've used these words in front of him.

"No, baby, Mrs. Hillier is a very nice person. I'm sure Jason misunderstood the conversation. Look, let's get you back to bed. We have an early morning tomorrow."

"Okay." He comes over and puts his arms around my waist. "Don't worry. It'll be okay," he says. Then he turns and heads up the stairs to his room.

I don't have time to waste. I feel like Detective Morrison could show up at my front door at any second if he wanted to, that Carson could pull up in the dirt drive at any moment, a fucking SWAT team could have the house surrounded for all I know and I just need to move. I throw my rain boots into a trash bag and carry it out to the garbage bin at the side of the house and push it down to the bottom, making sure regular house trash is on top. Then, back inside, I wrap the coat and gloves I was wearing as tightly as I can into a ball.

After I shower, I put the clothes I was wearing under my coat into the washing machine, just to be extra safe. I go out to the back deck and throw logs onto the fireplace. When I'm satisfied that the fire is strong, I take the wad of wrapped-up coat and gloves and place it on the flames. I stab at it with a fire poker until I see the edges catch, and then I sit on the sofa across from the fire, the exact place I was sitting when Carson talked me into shooting the goddamn stupid gun in the first place, and I watch it burn.

CHAPTER SEVEN

Regan

When I arrive at the meeting spot in the town square for the search, it's a sea of venti macchiatos and Lululemon. Through the puffer coats and ponytails, I spot Sasha sitting on the concrete steps in front of the fountain, and as I get closer, I see Andi, standing next to her holding a cup of coffee and looking . . . shockingly pale and, frankly, terrible.

"Morning," I say, knowing Sasha probably thinks I've lost it after running out of the theater, and Andi doesn't understand whatever sick joke she thinks I was playing at with the selfie I sent her. They look surprised to see me. I don't even know what I'm doing here. I should be in Windsor Locks pounding on every door looking for Jack, but really, where would I begin? Nobody will believe it was him. Do I even really believe it?

"How are you feeling?" Sasha asks, which is probably code

for, did you have to check yourself into a psych ward last night—or what stage are we in of your mental breakdown exactly?—but she's far too nice to express any of that.

"Fine," I say, then change the subject. "Is that Drew and Roxie?" I ask, nodding across the square where the two teens sit by the fountain—Drew is wearing a backpack, and Roxie is next to him, holding a folder of papers they seem to be going over together. That's unusual. I know there was an attempt to shield the kids from this, but of course, by now, the whole tri-state area knows about Tia. There's no more keeping the kids from it, but they certainly can't be part of searching for . . . well, at this point, a body in the woods, because that's really why we're here. I guess if I had a teen, I wouldn't know whether they should be involved or locked in their room until this was all figured out. I'd want to protect them from the trauma of it all. But it's impossible to know how to handle any of this.

"They wanted to help," Sasha says, and Andi just nods. She looks like she got hit by a Mack truck. I guess she's taking all of this harder than I thought. I watch her eyes flick, almost manically, back and forth from a circle of women talking by the fountain to the Pilates girls handing out whistles and flashlights in case folks need them. I see what she's seeing. She's not just imagining the quiet accusations; they come in glances over shoulders and in the whispers between friends, but the message is loud. People wonder if she did something to Tia. If anyone knows what unspoken judgment feels like, it's me.

But Andi doesn't address it. She casts her bloodshot eyes to the ground, and I feel so much goddamn heartache for what she's about to go through if Tia isn't found safe—an innocent person guilty by the court of public opinion. She already knows it. Poor thing.

"So what the hell was with the photo you sent?" she asks, still looking down, poking at the gravel with the toe of her Burberry sneakers.

Sasha looks at me—a look that tells me she wants to know as well, but is too polite to ask. Instead, she offers a tight, sympathetic smile, but her eyes tell me that she's worried about me. I know I scream "unstable" and need to explain.

"I'm sorry I left like that," I tell Sasha. I pull the hood of my coat up against the crisp air and sit down on the steps in front of them.

"What happened?" Sasha asks, and I take a deep breath before I speak. I hesitate. I've thought about whether I would say anything, but I have to tell someone. I contemplated going to the cops last night. But there are a lot of reasons I can't do that yet. It's a small town and the police department is all-hands-on-deck with the missing person search. They also think I'm unstable and won't take it seriously. Jack was friends with most of the department, and they all attended his funeral. His actual fucking funeral. Everyone was there, witness to it, so they know he's not hanging around the back of a community theater in Cloverhill Lakes.

So I could report what I saw and appear wildly unhinged . . . and at the end of the day, what will they do? What *can* they really do? Jot down some notes on a form they call a police report between inner eye rolls? No. Not the route for me to take right now.

I did wonder about my meds. I know at least one of them can cause hallucinations, but I feel like I would know. I sat up in bed last night looking at the names of each one and googling side effects. I told myself I would stop going down that rabbit hole, at least when Hallie is home, because it can send me into a full-blown panic attack. But I just feel like it's not in my head.

I took acid in college once and saw six elephants having a tea party in my backyard. They morphed into giant anteaters and sucked up all the grass and trees and the house with their snouts and then they sucked me up and I was in their belly swimming around with all the living room furniture. It was a hoot. Never laughed so hard. But I was aware that I was hallucinating. I think I would know if I was just having an average day and out of nowhere started seeing things. I would know.

So I decide to say something, and if Sasha and Andi don't believe me, I don't know what the hell I'll do next. The heaviness of the depression I can't claw my way out from under feels so heavy and oppressive, I can't bear this alone. So I blurt it out.

"I saw him. It was him."

Andi snaps her head up. She gives me a look of utter confusion while Sasha's expression is something closer to pity.

"You freaked out because you saw some guy who looked like him after I pointed it out. A lot of guys have sandy hair and square jaws. It was dark, Regan. Come on," Andi says.

And then before I can defend my position, Sandy Milroy starts speaking into a bullhorn to get everyone's attention. She's Tia's aunt, I think, or maybe just her mother's friend, I'm not sure, but her name has been all over the organization materials as a contact. We stop talking and begin moving closer to the fountain, where everyone is beginning to congregate in order to listen. She thanks everyone and gives some safety instructions, and then she explains the search. The lake is just under ten miles around. Folks are assigned to a side, and I see Roxie and Drew purposefully walk over to the side away from us, which I guess is a teenager thing to do, but it still strikes me as a little odd. Then she gives us printouts of maps of the woods and the route to take so we can spread out correctly and ensure the dense wooded areas that span for miles in some places have a cutoff point. We're mostly just focusing on the manageable portion that's more residential and meets the houses and lake. That way, nobody can get lost.

Andi says she wants to take the west side so she can end at her house because she has a meeting this afternoon, so we grab our walking sticks and whistles from the supplies table that Sandy has neatly put together and begin our descent into Bramble Thicket, the three of us together.

The air is heavy with a mist that threatens to turn into rain, and it makes everything more unsettling—more eerie—as we make our way through the hazy air, poking at wet leaves and branches with our sticks and listening to the hum of melancholy conversations from the groups in the distance.

"There are black bears out here. Why would she jog these trails? Does she carry pepper spray or anything?" Sasha asks. She's probably just filling the dead air and at the same time trying to make sense of what we're doing, but Andi snaps.

"How would I know?" We both look over at her, but she keeps her gaze away, tapping a tree with her walking stick and letting out an exasperated sigh, as if she's inconvenienced that her whacking didn't yield Tia to somehow materialize. She looks almost like a teenage boy with her small frame swimming in a vintage hoodie and no makeup on.

"So who was the man?" Andi asks, taking the focus off herself.

I don't respond. I suddenly feel pathetic telling them something that sounds so outrageous, and it's not the time anyway. Maybe I'm starting to doubt it myself. I was there, of course. In the front row of the church, which was so cold that day. My mother wrapped her coat around my shoulders. She had to help me stand up from the pew when it was time to go. I remember it in nightmarish fragments and blurs—the reception held at Grady Watkins's house—everyone was drinking scotch and singing along to Jack's favorite Van Halen songs because "that's what he would have wanted," but it all felt wrong. I drank tepid coffee out of a small white mug in an armchair in a corner and stared at the wall, still in utter shock and denial. I wouldn't talk to anyone. I remember it like yesterday. It's when the darkness started to set in, and I've never been the same since.

So now, the voice telling me to be rational, telling me that the funeral was real and Jack is dead . . . is just a little bit quieter than the voice screaming at me that I saw him with my own eyes boarding a train to Windsor Locks. It makes me feel crazy. Andi's and Sasha's reactions make me feel deranged. Maybe I can't trust myself. Maybe the pain is still too blinding to see it all clearly and I'm just seeing what I want.

"Holy shit." Andi stops cold and of course so do Sasha and I, at first thinking she found something, but she's looking at me with a hand on her hip. "You legit, like, really think it was him," she says.

"Let's just keep walking," I say. I'm freezing.

"Like, you weren't just traumatized or something because you saw a guy who looks like him and it brought it all back . . . You think it really *was* him?"

We've all stopped now and are standing by an ancient fallen

tree that smells like damp earth. Sasha puts her hand on my shoulder.

"Is that what happened?" she says with so much compassion, I think I'll burst into tears.

"You're the one who pointed it out," I say to Andi. "You thought it was him, too."

"I didn't understand at first, though," she says. "I mean, for a second that's what I thought, and I just reacted and texted you . . . but of course I thought about it for two more seconds and felt terrible that I even said anything. It was just a shock. I . . ."

"What photo?" Sasha asks, looking from Andi to me. I pull out my phone.

"You never met Jack. You can be the judge. The selfie we took last night," I say, opening my photo app and turning the screen around to show her. She squints at it.

"Okay," she says, not knowing what she's looking for.

I point to the figure in the background. "That man," I say, then I quickly scroll to a photo of Jack from a few weeks before he died. One of my favorites. We're in Martha's Vineyard sitting at a seaside restaurant and he has Hallie on his lap. They are both wearing lobster bibs and smiling for the camera. I turn the phone around to show Sasha.

"I know the theater photo is dark, but I know what I saw. I know my husband," I say, my voice cracking ever so slightly. Then I see something very unexpected. Sasha's reaction. She tries to hide it, but I see her squint at the image and look very perplexed for a moment. She studies it and then shakes her head ever so slightly.

"What?" I say, snapping back the phone from her hand. She looks up like she's just been snapped out of a trance.

"Nothing," she says.

"What? What's wrong?"

"Nothing," she says again, shaking her head and taking a deep breath. "It's just—I'm very sorry for . . . your loss is all."

Andi cuts her off. "Well, half the women in the Cloverhill Elementary Facebook group have already told the story about how you ran out of the theater calling after someone, but nobody saw a man."

"But you see him. There." I stab my finger at the photo.

"It looks a lot like him," Sasha says.

"It sure does, I'll give you that," Andi says. "But, Regan—"

"What? But what?" I snap.

"Nothing. I have no idea how to explain it. I don't know what to say," Andi says.

We start to walk again, looking out into the misty trees, trying to fulfill our task, although I don't think any of us expects to find something out here. I'm not surprised there's already talk, and I'm not surprised Andi is skeptical; that's her way of protecting me. I've known her long enough to know that. What I can't shake is Sasha's reaction. I watch her peering into the thick brush and holding her Starbucks cup with one mittened hand. What the hell was that? It was like she recognized him and it gave her a shock.

"He ran," I say, and they both stop and turn to look at me.

"What do you mean?" Andi asks.

"I followed after him. I chased the taxi he got into. I followed it all the way across town. He ran from me. He heard me call his name and he kept going and got on a train. Who takes a train? And especially, who takes a train directly from a community play? At intermission?" Sasha and Andi look at one another and then back to me. I hate it. I hate what they're thinking and how I can tell they think I'm off my meds or something. I take out the paper train schedule from my pocket and unfold it, shoving it toward them. Sasha takes it, and Andi moves in to look at it over her shoulder.

"Wait. You . . . literally chased the guy to the train station?" Andi says.

"It makes five stops before ending in Windsor Locks. He could be anywhere," Sasha says, and Andi gives her a look I can only interpret as "don't encourage her."

"I did. What would you have done?" I say softly, beginning to feel completely defeated—not heard. I take back the paper schedule and fold it into a neat square. I make a just-drop-it gesture with my hands, and I sigh. I begin walking ahead of them, blinking back tears. I hear the caw of a crow circling in the gray, empty sky above us. The sound is hollow and the air is wet and cold and I desperately want to be home.

"You could post his photo on social media sites in these cities. Every town has different Facebook pages from some community group or another," Sasha says. "There are a lot of places you could post his photo since you have it narrowed down to a handful of cities. Ask if people have seen him. Give your contact info for any leads. It's not that many places. They aren't huge cities, either," she says. Andi raises her eyebrows at that.

We all stand looking at one another under a canopy of dead trees in these eerie, dense woods where we have been tasked to ensure Tia's dead body hasn't been hidden by a psychopath or mauled to death by wild animals, and it's all so surreal, it's dizzying.

"That's not a bad idea," Andi says, breaking the silence, and then we walk. Quietly now, more intent in our search, focused as we trek the last couple of miles to the halfway mark, which is a lakeside pub just past Andi's house where Sandy has arranged for one of the church buses to take folks back up the shore to where their cars are parked. The team that started at the bottom of the lake will be about an hour behind, so by the time they make their way up, the bus should be back to collect them.

I think of Tia's poor mother and wonder how she even had the wherewithal to plan all of this in her state. I suppose it's like the mother who can lift a car off her trapped baby in a forced moment of superstrength when their child's life hangs in the balance.

I think we are all incredibly relieved when we arrive at the last stretch, out of the woods and into the clearing by the lake. We walk the trail behind Andi's house and onto her property. There is a group of five that has been keeping pace ahead of us who arrived first, and I see them poking around in Carson and Andi's woodpile and inside the shed they have next to a small wooden fence, lined with cans and bottles for shooting practice. It could be a photo of anyone's yard in anyone's home in the county. Nothing odd, except Andi.

She stops cold, pulls the hood off her head and squints to see something. I look to where she's looking and see the garage door open. Inside, Carson is there, and I see a police car parked in the dirt clearing and an officer standing inside the garage with Carson, and they're . . . I don't know. It looks like they're moving a freezer together, one on each side.

Andi cups her mouth with both hands and her face drains of the little color it had. Her eyes roll back in her head as she passes out cold and hits the ground with a hard smack.

CHAPTER EIGHT

Sasha

Sasha sits by Andi's side as she lies on the sofa in the living room. Regan is in Andi's kitchen making tea—a weird quirk she's noticed about Regan, who defaults to putting on a kettle of tea every time something even slightly stressful happens, like she's in some British novel. Andi is out cold, and Carson is beside himself interrogating Sasha and Regan about what the hell happened. Of course, they have no idea. Andi was there one second, and on the ground the very next. The officer's name is Morrison, and he got on his radio to dispatch an ambulance to the house, but now he's outside on the front lawn, waving folks to keep on going and head to their checkpoint at the lakeside pub in a "nothing to see here" tone.

Everyone obeys, *but God help me*, Sasha thinks, *this will have them talking even more.* What's going on inside that house? Why is there an officer? Did they find something? Then, suddenly,

Andi comes to, violently sitting straight up and gasping, holding her hand to her heart, looking around with fear in her eyes. She tries to stand, but Carson rushes over as Regan comes in with a tray of tea, and Andi holds out her arms as if in self-defense like we are circling her and about to attack.

"I can explain all of it," she says, tears welling up in her eyes. Carson takes her hand and sits her back down on the couch.

"Hey, hey. It's okay. You need to sit," he says. "What happened?"

Regan sits on the coffee table and puts a hand on Andi's arm while Sasha dutifully pours cups of tea on the tray without knowing why she's doing it—just fueled by anxiety and confusion, she supposes.

"It was all an accident," Andi says.

"What was?" Regan asks. "You fainted. That's all."

"You're okay," Sasha consoles, placing a cup of tea on the coffee table in front of her.

"Where's the detective? Is he taking me in?"

"What?" Carson says. "No—"

"And what the hell are you doing here?" she says, cutting him off. "What the hell are you even—why were you in the garage with a detective? Why were you moving the freezer? I . . ."

"Andi, stop," Regan says. "What day is it?" she asks.

"What?" Andi snaps.

"Who's the president?"

"I don't have a fucking concussion. I don't get what's happening." She looks so fearful and red blotches bloom across her chest, and Sasha can't wrap her head around exactly what's going on.

"I told you I'd be home midday Sunday. It's after one

o'clock," Carson says, a little annoyed that she seems unhappy he's home, but still holding her hand, clearly understanding that she's had a fall and maybe a bump on the head.

"Oh," Andi says numbly, her eyes still darting around the room.

"And the detective said he called you and was gonna meet you here to ask questions about Tia. He's asking all of us. It's not just you. Do you remember talking to him earlier? Did you hit your head?" he asks patiently, but she snaps back her answers.

"No. Goddammit. I saw you in the garage with him moving shit around." Everyone in the room exchanges furtive glances at one another, wondering if she really does have some sort of concussion.

"Yeah. My tire is low. I was getting the air pump off the hook on the wall when he pulled up and startled me."

"What does that have to do with anything? Why are you telling me that?" she asks. Regan is now perched on the arm of the couch next to her, feeling around her head for bumps, as Andi mindlessly swats her away.

"It fell behind the giant-ass freezer we still have for some reason. He came into the garage and we chatted while we waited for you, and he helped me scooch it out a few inches to get the air pump. I mean, jeez. Is there any other detail you'd like to know? Or can we maybe get to what the hell happened to you? Are you okay?"

"I'll get an ice pack. You have a goose egg," Regan announces, then disappears into the kitchen.

"I think she's just under a lot of stress," Sasha says.

Andi stands abruptly and goes to the front window, looking out at Morrison, who's still directing stragglers toward their checkpoint. "He's not . . ."

"What? Jesus, Andi. Can we just—can you just lie down and rest? Let Regan get the ice and just . . ."

"He's not arresting me?" she asks, her mouth gaping open and eyes wide.

"They don't arrest everyone they want to question," Carson says with annoyance in his tone that only makes her panic more. "You have to understand you're the ex. You saw her the day before. They'll have questions. That's it. Everyone knows you were not involved. Shit, if it makes you feel better, we can go through the Ring footage to prove you were here. I told them you were here. Nobody legitimately thinks you did anything, babe. People are just freaked out."

Somehow during Carson's speech, Sasha clocks Andi's eyes expanding and glossing over at the words *Ring footage*, and then she watches Andi sit down quietly on the couch. Andi doesn't say anything else until the ambulance sirens can be heard coming up the dirt road, and then she whispers an almost inaudible "Oh, God" under her breath.

Once the medics come in, it feels like a too-many-cooks-in-the-kitchen situation, so Sasha decides to take the church bus back to the town square. She squeezes Andi's hand before she goes and promises to call and check in later, but she's relieved to be out of there if she's honest. The weight of it is too much. A whole town searching an eerie forest hoping not to find a dead body, and at the same time hoping to find something. It's really an indescribable thing to witness—watching them all balance their usual meaningless chatter about soccer practice and the new *Love Is Blind* season, then remembering where they are and what they're there for and morphing back into the somber, melancholy version of themselves they're supposed to be at such an occasion.

But Sasha has secrets of her own to deal with, and she's made a promise to be somewhere. Tom has made the two-and-a-half-hour trip to the Manhattan restaurant, the way he does every other week to check in on things, see his brother, attend some meetings or whatever else goes into owning a few restaurants. Sasha doesn't much care for the mundane details about bookkeeping and bottom lines and barbecue smoker prices and any of it, really. She pretends to be interested and of course does genuinely listen when Tom chats to her about work, but she has other things on her mind each time he makes the New York trip or whenever he works late.

She's arranged for Drew to watch Chloe—she tells him she has "margarita book club" tonight. She assumes Tom might have a few pints with his dad at the restaurant bar anyway and come home in the morning, or if he does come home tonight, it'll be late, so she makes the forty-minute trek to see Raffy, and despite how many years she's been going to see him, she still feels a pang of guilt twisting in her gut—she knows keeping this from Tom is a betrayal. It feels practically criminal after ten years, but that's the thing about white lies . . . they snowball. There is nothing inherently wrong with seeing her ex-husband, because they coparent Drew, if you can call it that. But Tom has been so understanding despite all the baggage she came with, which makes her feel extra guilty for not being honest about this.

Raffy lost himself to the bottle a long time ago, so when she stopped by to drop Drew off when he was younger, Tom knew she had to stay and supervise, because who the hell could predict if Raffy would even be vertical let alone able to be responsible for a young son? Drew has wanted less to do with Raff as he's gotten older. It seems like his visits are fueled by pity when he does go, and Sasha can't make him have a relationship with his dad. She's glad he doesn't, if she's honest, because watching his father slowly kill himself isn't something she'd like Drew exposed to. But she still goes.

It just sort of happened and then became a habit—to make sure he was okay, take out the trash, open a window, check his meds, and then somewhere along the line, she realized it was secretive—that Tom wouldn't approve of her going there alone although he probably wouldn't say it. He's too kind. He wouldn't forbid her or try to control her. He'd just be very hurt, and how could she blame him for that?

But she can't abandon Raffy, not after what he's done for her. So she drives up, always with a mix of anticipation and a visceral sense of dread to see his face, wondering how bad things will be today. She winds her way up the steep road and onto the long dirt drive of the first house they bought together, where *Rafael and Sasha Carro* is still written on the mailbox at the end of the drive where it meets the road. Only her name has been rubbed off and is just a faint imprint now. Back when Raff was doing well, so, so long ago now, he was buying up real estate in Mexico and renting out beach bungalows. They bought this cliffside fixer-upper, in cash, and renovated each room, from the Spanish bath tile to the walnut floors. It's not big or fancy. They thought about expanding, turning it into a showstopper, but they wanted modest and cozy. Good thing, she supposes, because he's let the place go to such an extreme—the wood floors long ago rotted from dog urine from a Jack Russell he had a few years ago; the walls are covered in mold from bad ventilation when he went through a paranoid phase and closed off all the vents and windows; and the list goes on.

When she pulls up to the front door, she squeezes her eyes closed, sighs and hopes for the best, but when she walks inside, she is immediately hit with the overwhelming, acrid smell of vomit. She opens the window next to the front door even though the temperature outside is in the fifties and it's already chilly in the rooms Raffy rarely pays to heat. She sees through into the living room where he is passed out on the couch. From the looks of the puke, he probably passed out last night and is still asleep, which is a good day for her because he'll be able to have a coherent conversation after she wakes him up. Talking to him with a hangover is always better than after he's already started for the day.

She covers her mouth and nose with her scarf and sits down at the edge of the couch in front of his frail body, and she strokes his hair for a moment and fights back tears—she feels like she should be used to it but she somehow seems to be mourning his loss like it's brand-new every time she sees him like this. She kisses his forehead and then gently shakes him awake.

"Hey, Raff. It's me," she says and watches his eyes flutter open. He jolts a little when he becomes aware of her and then the vomit down the front of him, and the late hour. He looks at himself for a moment like a frightened child who wet the bed.

"Just give it to me," she says, and he looks so fragile as he pulls his shirt over his head and hands it to her that she can barely stand it.

"Can you get in the shower?" she asks him, and he doesn't speak, just shakily stands and disappears into the back hall and then she hears the water running. She throws his shirt in the washer and starts a load. She walks around the kitchen and living room with a Hefty bag, dropping all the empty bottles inside, and cleans a few surfaces with a disinfectant wipe.

When he returns, he's wearing a hoodie and sweats. He opens a Heineken to stop his hands shaking, then sits across from her on the couch, where the indented cushion and pile of blankets tell the story of a man who has scarcely left that spot in many days.

"How's Drew?" he asks—always the first thing he says.

"Good," she says, because she hasn't decided if talking to him about what she found would be helpful or set him off in some unknowable way.

"He never comes up. He said he would when he got his license," Raff says.

"He will. It's been a little chaotic," is all she says, because he won't know about Tia or the school bomb threat or anything else. He thinks he's being spied on by the government through his cell phone, so he refuses to turn it on half the time. Or maybe it's all a show and he does it so Sasha will still come up to see him in person.

"Your fridge is empty," she says. "I ordered Instacart. Nothing healthy, don't worry. Promise you'll make something later," she says. Even though she sees a flash of embarrassment in his eyes, it's never enough for him to change. There's not enough shame in the world to pull him out of the depths of his addiction.

"Sure, Sash. Thanks," he says, and then she suddenly can no longer stand the stench of bodily fluids mixed with disinfectant and she tells him she needs some fresh air and goes out to the back and sits on one of the Adirondack chairs that circle the firepit they used to roast marshmallows in a hundred years ago. He pops another beer and puts on a coat and follows her out. He throws a few logs on the fire. As he fiddles with lighter fluid and kindling, she sees glimpses of the man he once was. Until the day that changed him.

On one rare occasion when Drew was young, Sasha left him with her mother and accompanied Raff to Mexico, where they stayed at one of the renovated beach properties for a much-needed getaway. At the airport on the way home, they got tipsy on rum punch at the airport bar and almost missed the flight. As they rushed to the back of the dwindling line to board, there was a man, practically in tears. He said he'd lost his passport and it was his grandmother's first trip to the US. "Marta," he said, pointing at a small woman sitting in the wheelchair in front of him, and asked if we could help her onto the plane and keep an eye on her. "She's ninety-two," he said. "She'll be so scared but has to get there for a funeral." They agreed. Of course they would help, Raff said immediately.

There had been some tip-off, of course, and that's why the guy was trying to get rid of the bag in the poor woman's wheelchair. He vanished. She was unrelated to him and clueless about what was happening. Sniffer dogs came, police. Sasha and Raff were both arrested. The only reason they let Sasha go is because Raff, after hours and hours of interrogation, took the blame to protect her because he knew it was over for him whether she went down or not, and he'd never let that happen.

Three years in a Mexican prison, and he turned into someone else, someone who would never recover from the trauma. They tried. But at some point, she had to do what was best for Drew and let Raffy drown in his own pain. If they didn't have Drew, maybe there would have been enough therapy and time and love and hope in the world for him to have survived it, but he didn't survive. Not really.

She just could never bring herself to explain this to Tom. She wishes she could forget it herself. Maybe she's still in some eternal denial that it all happened. Sometimes she has trouble understanding how she could possibly live this whole other life so separate from the life she lived with Raff. Some days it seems impossible.

"I wanted to show you something," she says, pulling a 5x7-size piece of paper out of her bag with a photo printed on it. She printed it only because she knows he won't look at her phone like a normal person. It would turn into an argument, with her begging for him to "just fucking look, for God's sake," she knows. Cameras, Big Brother watching, electronics bugged—the conversation would take a paranoid turn, and she needs him to focus, so she just printed it and shows him Jack Hoffman's face. "Does this person look familiar at all to you?"

He squints at it, then takes it from her as he sits back down, still bent over, poking at the fire with a stick with his free hand. He holds it back out to her.

"No. Should it?"

"I don't know . . . I saw it and . . . I just know I've seen him before— Like, I'm sure."

"Okay?" Raff says.

"He's dead," she adds.

"Oh," Raff says. "Am I supposed to know what you're getting at here?"

"No. I just wondered if it's someone you used to know, maybe, and I'd only met him in passing. I just can't put my finger on it."

"Sorry." He hands it back. They sit together for a long while. Raffy steadily drinks until his eyes are hazy and his trembling has subsided, and Sasha makes small talk about a television show they both like and about Drew trying out for basketball and about winter coming, and then the sun has sunk behind the red maples and dusk sets in. Raff places his hand on top of hers, resting on the arm of the chair, and she feels the warmth and weight of it and lets it be. And they sit some more, saying nothing at all until it's almost dark, and then she goes into the house and collects the grocery delivery from the front step.

She makes him a pot of pasta and puts a loaf of parbaked garlic bread in the oven and tells him not to burn the place down and that she set a timer. He's back in his well-worn spot on the couch with a blanket around his shoulders. She almost leaves, but then she sits and waits the ten more minutes because she doesn't trust that he won't forget and burn the place down. She slumps next to him in her big coat and they stare at an episode of the Carol Burnett show until the lonely, hollow ding of the timer pierces the air from the kitchen, and then she gets up and fixes him a plate and places it on the coffee table in front of him.

"You don't have to do this," he says. She doesn't respond. She kisses him on the top of the head, leaves some cash on the countertop, then quietly exits the front door and drives home.

She tries to put him out of her mind the way she does each time she leaves him, and she keeps the radio off and just sits in the silence as she drives.

When she arrives home, she hears video game noises from the living room. She thought maybe she'd ask Raffy's advice about Drew at some point, but she couldn't, and she knows she needs to confront the situation. She hears the game pause, and she pulls off her coat and puts her bag on the counter. As she heats up some water to make tea, Drew comes into the dim kitchen and takes a soda from the fridge, then leans against the counter.

"Hey," he says.

"Hey. Chloe get to bed on time?" Sasha asks.

"Yep," he says, about to go back to the living room.

"Thanks," Sasha says, and then, "Hey . . . Drew." He pauses and looks at her. She has rehearsed the best way to ask him about this without making him shut down completely. There is really no way. It will sound like an accusation even though she'll frame it as a question that could have a reasonable explanation.

"You were at that closed-down restaurant, Hefty's, the other night and I happened to pass by and saw you . . . talking to some guy . . ."

"Oh, you happened to be passing by?" he says with a humorless little laugh.

"First, I'm the mother in this situation and you won't talk to me with that tone. If I want to follow you everywhere you go every single day, I can do that. Second, I saw you give some guy money and he gave you something, and I could have leaped to every conclusion and grounded you and jumped out of the car like a lunatic embarrassing you. I could have taken your phone, yet here I am, talking to you about it calmly. So try again," she says.

He sighs, swallows. "So was there a question in there somewhere?" he asks.

"What were you doing giving a stranger money at an abandoned building? Yes. That's a question."

"Post Malone tickets," he says, flatly.

"What?" she asks.

"That's a person. Like, music. A concert. Tickets were sold out and so I bought some off this guy from school," he says.

"I know who it is. Why would you be getting them late at night in an abandoned building?"

"I don't know. That's where him and his friends hang out—take girls. Probably drink and cause trouble, too . . . before you ask, but I was just there for the tickets," he says, and if he's lying, he's good at it. He didn't know I saw him, so he has to be making this up on the spot, and what's unsettling about that is it came to him so quickly. The details. There is no way that guy was a classmate. He had to be thirty at least.

"I saw a small backpack. You need a bag for two tickets?" He stumbles a moment at this. Then just shakes his head.

"It was dark. Maybe that's just what you thought you saw," he says. Okay, he's gonna play games. Sasha won't take the bait.

"So where are the tickets?" she says instead.

"Gave them to Roxie. They were for her," he says, looking at the floor.

"That was nice of you," she says, turning to take the kettle off the stove, pouring the hot water into a mug and dipping her peppermint tea bag. "You don't have to hide things from me, you know. Like if you're in some kind of trouble. I saw construction paper in your room—red circle cutouts the same shape as that school bomb threat," she says, turning to him. He puts his soda down and his mouth hangs open.

"Are you actually serious? Now you're going in my room? For your information, I was making pumpkins and blood-shot eyes and all that other crap with Chloe you asked me to help her with. You wanna talk about who's hiding stuff from who?" he says, being sure to keep his tone in check because taking his phone or car away are real threats he knows she'll follow through with.

"What does that mean?" she asks, incredulously.

"It means why do you enable him?" he says.

"What are you talking about?" she asks, still playing dumb.

"How's Dad? Did you make sure to leave him money that you tell yourself he'll buy food with when you know the truth?" he says, and she did not expect this.

"There's a fine line between enabling and keeping him alive," is all she can bring herself to say, because she's shocked that he knows this and also feels protective of Raffy and equally protective of Drew. She doesn't want him involved in adult matters, but he's noticed things. He's a smart kid.

"Okay, Mom," he says.

"You should go see him next weekend. He asks about you," she says.

Drew purses his lips and gives a small nod, then disappears back into the living room, where Sasha hears the dramatic music and gun sounds from his video game. She takes her mug and begins to make her way to check on Chloe before she takes her long-awaited hot bath.

After she turns on the water, she realizes she left her phone on the counter. Halfway down the stairs, she can see into the kitchen over the open banister, and there's Drew walking in and then stopping and staring at her bag on the counter. He cocks his head sideways and looks at the paper printout of Jack that's sticking out the top. He has a puzzled look on his face.

Then she watches him glance left and right, and he goes

over and plucks the image out of the top of her bag. He stares at it a minute, then folds it roughly, shoves it into his pocket and quickly leaves the room. What in the hell would her son want with a stranger's photo—a dead man's photo? Unless that man is not a stranger at all. Or not dead.

CHAPTER NINE

Andi

A thunderstorm has rolled in, and I'm sitting in the garage on top of a Yeti cooler and staring at the meat freezer. Carson is getting the kids ready for Hallie's birthday party this afternoon, which, despite the weather, Regan didn't cancel because she didn't want a hysterical ten-year-old on top of all the rest of the chaos, I assume.

Carson told me to rest while he made the kids get dressed and sign Hallie's card, while he found a bottle of wine to bring to the party, and all the rest of it, and I'm grateful for that because I can't seem to bring myself to calm down and act normal. I take a moment, in my Dior dress and peacoat with a wrapped gift balanced on my knees, and try to take a couple of breaths before my family comes barreling out and piling into the car. Ring footage. I thought I was done for in that moment, because I hadn't thought of the Ring camera, but when I went to look through it, I realized we hadn't changed the batteries that went out months ago. We said we should, but we live in Cloverhill Lakes, so who needs cameras? At least, that was the case only days ago. But thank God.

The lightning flashes like a strobe light through the window, and thunder cracks and startles me to my feet, speeding up my heart even more, and I stand and pace the garage floor. I guess I'm keeping watch over the damn thing to make sure nobody comes near it—I need to make sure everyone gets in the car, out the door and back home to bed before I do whatever it is I come up with next.

Morrison thought it would be better to talk to me tomorrow considering my "fragile condition," and buying time is fine by me, but how the actual fuck do I do this? How do I move her? How do I walk around and appear normal and not at all like a murderer—a monster? I can't conceive of how a person could pull this off, but I'm forced to figure it out. I have to.

I hear the sound of Carson telling everyone to get a move on and that I'm waiting in the car. I slip into the passenger seat before they all come bounding out the door and wonder what the hell I'm doing. I don't even know what I'm doing. I'm making it a full-time job to keep a neutral expression across my face and say normal things. That's what I'm doing. If we canceled going to Hallie's party, that would look strange, and I can't do anything but appear routine, normal, innocent.

As the kids buckle in, Carson reminds me that it's Monday and the dads will be watching the game in the media room with the rest of the husbands when he gets there, and who plans a party during a Patriots game? And I tell him a single mom who doesn't give a crap does and Dez asks if he's allowed to say the word *crap* since he's not allowed to say *shit* and before I can answer, Carson backs the SUV out of the garage and there is a deafening bang, crack.

"Crap!" Dex yells, and Roxie screams. I'm holding my chest, trying to absorb what just happened. I leap out of the car, realizing he's backed up into the meat freezer and it's fallen over onto its side with a metallic crash so loud my heart is still in my throat.

"Damn thing never got pushed back against the wall," Carson immediately starts to say, thinking I'll blame him and instinctively absolving himself from any liability. "Who put the emergency brake on, for Christ's sake?" he asks. Although it happened so fast, I could see he was trying to push the gas and the car wasn't moving and when he released the brake, it jolted back. Unbelievable. Nobody answers, and he knows it was Roxie because she's still learning.

"I got it," I practically yell in a panic, rushing over to the freezer. "Just pull up," I say, desperately trying to distract him. He stands outside the driver's-side door with the car running and looks at it. To my absolute horror, I see the impact has broken the lock and the tarp Tia is wrapped in has tumbled out ever so slightly. I kneel next to it and try to push the tarp back in, telling him to just pull up and around, for God's sake.

He can't tell what's inside, but if he comes closer, maybe he'll try to help or ask questions.

"Fine, jeez," he says, getting back in the car, but Dez jumps out and comes right up behind me before I even know he's there.

"Barbies," he says matter-of-factly, pointing to a lock of silky blond hair that has poked out the crease in the tarp.

"Jesus," I say. "Get back in the car. We're late." I'm holding back tears, and a full-blown panic attack is threatening to take over.

"I wanna see," he says.

"It's just old toys I stored in there—I meant to bring them to Goodwill. Please get in. We're going." My whole body is shaking from the surging adrenaline, and I try to keep my back to him and not panic. Dez shrugs and gets back in the truck while I push the heavy tarp back inside the freezer with trembling hands and hook the broken padlock back around the metal clasp. "Shit, shit, shit," I mutter, my mind reeling, silently pleading for Carson not to exit the car and come over. It won't lock now, but it will keep it closed at least. I rush back to the passenger seat and Carson backs up, pulls around the fallen freezer, and drives off, closing the garage door behind us.

He's clueless. Thank Christ. He's just flipping radio stations and asking if Dez is excited for cake. I try to breathe and keep my eyes out the passenger window, focusing hard on the falling rain in a bid not to start bawling my head off.

"We should call and get that thing hauled away. It takes up too much space and we don't even use it."

"Yes," I agree too eagerly, and he gives me a side glance and then raises his eyebrows in an "okay then" expression. "I'll call tomorrow morning. Just park outside tonight," I say, so grateful it was his idea to get rid of it and not mine—not some suspicious thing I did. He just casually thinks we should get rid of it. Yes, fuck yes, we should. I will move Tia after everyone is asleep and tomorrow we'll have the freezer eliminated as evidence.

The drive is uneventful. Carson explains to Roxie that she doesn't need to put the emergency brake on when she's parked in the garage on a flat surface and then lets it go and hums to a Journey song. Roxie is on her phone. Dez is asking if he can have soda *and* cake, and I'm thinking about how little time I have to fix this so I don't end up spending the rest of my life in prison.

How can I move her without being seen? Everyone has a Ring camera these days. I can't just drive her somewhere in the middle of the night—it would be completely out of character and suspicious no matter what story I came up with. Everyone is paying attention to my demeanor because of my relationship to Tia. Of course they are. I can't make one misstep.

Carson works from home half the time, which makes it harder to plan because I never know his schedule, and he doesn't always know where he'll be working—whether he'll be called into a client meeting or can work from home—sometimes until that morning. But somehow, I have to find a window of time when the kids are at school and he's gone, and then what?

"Do you go into the office tomorrow?" I ask him.

"Well, I don't know if I should. Will you be okay?"

"I'm completely fine. I was just asking because maybe you could drop Dez at school if you are," I say. I'm hoping the little push will make him offer—that would give me some certainty of a space of time I can be alone.

"Don't know yet. I have a lunch with some bigwig buyer who hasn't confirmed a time, so I might need to prep at home until they let me know. I can take him, though," he says.

Shit. I need more than a forty-minute school drop. A client lunch is usually long and boozy when Carson calls them a "bigwig," so maybe I can do it then. If I can push Morrison off a little longer and he doesn't show up at the house. God, this is crazy.

"Thanks," I say quietly, and then Carson makes a turn onto the charming covered bridge that I have always marveled at, with its weathered spruce timber and metal gable roof, and as we cross over the Connecticut River, something is set into motion.

There is a picnic area on the bank below the bridge, and I remember last time I was there—that cookout a couple years ago. All of our friends were there, friends of friends and some I didn't know, and I'll never forget it because that's when I should have known. I sat on a picnic table with a checkered cloth and drank a glass of prosecco while the kids threw a football and the guys stood around the grill poking at hot dogs and talking about gold or some boring thing, and I saw Tia go and fix herself a drink from the mimosa bar Kitty Wilson insisted on setting up on a folding table down by the water. That was the moment: when Tia passed Ray at the grill and touched his back, her hand lingering, as she asked him if he wanted her to get him anything. He said "No, thanks," but her hand remained and then gave a little intimate squeeze before she made her way to the bar. I didn't clock it then.

But none of that really matters now. What matters is I know exactly where I need to go. I know how to get rid of a body. By the end of the day tomorrow, this will all be over.

CHAPTER TEN

Regan

"A birthday party from hell, poor kid," one of the caterers jokes as they try to maneuver food trays and equipment through the pouring rain and safely into my kitchen. They have to dodge Hallie as she spins in her birthday tutu, unperturbed, and still over the moon that all of her friends are coming even though the bounce house had to be canceled.

I give the caterers an apologetic look and tell them where they can set up the bar and chafing dishes. Then I take advantage of the short amount of time I have before guests brave the weather and start trickling in. Kids' birthdays are equal parts squealing ten-year-olds and tipsy parents. Most of us hire an attendant to run the games and cake patrol so we can take photos and enjoy the moment, and once you experience the luxury of this particular approach to kids' events, it's hard to go back. So I let Kathy "the party princess" deal with all the work and duck into my bedroom.

First, I check inside the en-suite medicine cabinet to make sure I've hidden all my prescriptions and none of the moms can come snooping in here. I can just see Vicky Wallen snapping a photo of all the shit I take and posting it to Instagram. That's probably unfair, maybe I'm just paranoid, but I worry every day that Hallie could be taken from me if I can't keep this panic under control, if I can't manage this depression enough to keep getting out of bed and at least going through the motions so she doesn't feel the weight of any of this.

Once I'm satisfied everything is secure, I sit at the edge of my bed, open my laptop and check one more time if anyone has responded to my many posts on message boards from Wallingford to Windsor Locks—and any surrounding areas I could find with community boards or social media pages with local groups that let me join. Any site where I could cut and paste my plea to anyone who has seen Jack—with a photo of him smiling at a gastropub in Jersey we went to once. I don't remember why I took the photo, but he looks happy in it. I click around, looking at Nextdoor.com pages, Facebook and even a page Andi told me about on Craigslist called "Missed Connections," which is a terribly sad place where people who met someone at a concert or an outlet mall or Tom Thumb post a short appeal, hoping that random person they wished they connected with will think to look at this bizarre place on the internet to find them back.

Just when I think to myself again that it's the stupidest thing I've ever heard of and the last place anyone would reunite with someone, I get a notification. My heart skips a beat as I open the message. It's from a woman named Beatrice who lives near

Windsor Locks and has a profile picture of herself in a purple crochet hat holding a ferret. I click to open it.

Dear anonymous woman, it starts, because I didn't leave my name, only an encrypted email they can respond to.

> I'm such a hopeless romantic that I usually check the *chance meeting* section and the *missed connection* board every day in hopes that some handsome prince out there might have seen me reading on a park bench somewhere or maybe lost sight of me just as the bus doors were closing . . . or something else romantic like that, and sadly, I have not yet found my knight in shining armor, but I did see your post and I recognized the man.

I scroll down and see she's attached a photo. Of Jack. Oh, my God. I don't believe what I'm looking at. She goes on.

> I snapped a photo of him this morning after I saw your post. He's sort of turned away in the shot, but I didn't want him to think I was stalking him. Been there, done that. Anyway, I work at the Bluebird Café and he comes in all the time. Orders coffee. Cream no sugar, and an apple turnover.

I stop reading and clasp my chest at the utter shock. That's him. That's his coffee order. Apple turnovers are his favorite. What is happening? I finish reading.

> I asked if his name is Jack and he said no, but he looked freaked out by the question and has never

given me a name even though I've asked once or twice before. He just changes the subject and that's why I started calling him Apple Turnover when I see him come through the door. I get a good chuckle out of it. Anyway, how romantic. I hope you find him. He usually comes between eight and nine in the morning, when he does. Please let me know if you find him and fall in love.

Electricity buzzes between my ears and I feel lightheaded and enraged all at once and I think I could almost faint but simultaneously feel like punching the drywall on all of the walls into dust and screaming until my throat aches, but I can't do any of that or even respond back to this very kind but lonely-sounding woman because the doorbell rings and I hear Hallie calling, "Mom, come on," and I have to go put on an act for at least an acceptable three hours before I'm allowed to fall to pieces.

Once things are in full swing and Kathy has exhausted a balloon dance party and painting activities, the kids have moved on to running around and screaming, hopped up on cake sugar, I guess playing some form of tag. The parents poke toothpicks into cocktail wieners and stand around with wineglasses, although most of the men are out on the deck watching the game on the big TV or playing pool. Andi looks like a ghost across the living room sitting in an armchair. Sasha sits next to her stirring a martini and hollering at the pack of wild-eyed ten-year-olds chasing each other around the coffee table to "take it to the rec room" . . . which they do, the hoots and squeals disappearing down the hall.

I perch on the edge of the coffee table opposite Andi and place my hand on her knee. "No word about Tia yet?" She shakes her head and looks out the window at the fingers of drizzle streaming down the glass.

"No one's blaming you," Sasha says, even though word is that Tia wouldn't have gone on that run if she wasn't blowing off steam from the argument with Andi that the whole world apparently knows about now, and some people probably are sort of blaming her.

"Obviously, she'll turn up," I say, but I don't know that at all. I didn't think Andi would be in this much despair over Tia. I mean, of course it's human decency to worry about someone who's missing even if you hate them—you don't want them dead or anything, but Andi's barely functioning, it seems. Having your name in people's mouths is very unsettling.

I'm sure she's most worried about how it affects her kids, but we're talking about Cloverhill Lakes. The crime rate has to be near zero. Until recently, of course. Still, surely Tia will turn up.

"Yeah," Andi says mindlessly. We all sit in silence and listen to the sound of small talk from the folks mingling and the cheers from a football audience muffled through the glass doors. I stare out at Carson and Tom, clinking their beer bottles together at what I imagine is a touchdown. I think about how Ray should be here and wonder where he is exactly? Driving around hopelessly, bawling his eyes out at home, drunk somewhere. My heart aches for what he's going through. And then I think about how Jack should be here, too, and usually that's when grief starts to take over and I have to excuse myself a moment, and sometimes it happens with bursts of white-hot rage, but right now I'm just very numb from the double dose of lorazepam, and I wish everyone would leave my house so I can process Beatrice and the Bluebird Café and what the hell it all means.

I do think twice about telling the girls about the message until I know more, but I feel like they're a part of this now. It was Sasha's idea to ask around online. I want to have allies and not go it all alone, even if they are starting to wonder if I need to be committed somewhere. I need their support.

"I have something to show you," I say, looking over my shoulder to make sure nobody else is within earshot. I click open the message from Beatrice and turn my phone around for them to see. They both lean in and read it. Sasha scrolls past my initial post and I watch them read the woman's reply.

"No fucking way," Andi says, perking up a little bit. She grabs the phone and zooms in on the photo of Jack, who is turned slightly away, sitting at a café table with a cup of coffee, but you can still tell it's him. She squints at it. "Jesus, fuck, Regan."

"I know," I say. Sasha didn't know him, so it's hard for her to offer much feedback, I'm sure, but she gives a sympathetic shake of her head and hands the phone back.

"How is that possible?" she asks.

"I'm gonna say something you probably won't like," Andi says. "Not to be a total dream-crusher dick here, but . . . we attended his funeral, honey. This is someone who looks like Jack. What other explanation could there be?"

I grab my phone back and sigh. "Something. It's something," I say.

"Reg, he was transported by air . . . by a US consular officer," she says, I guess to remind me that what was recovered of his body was officially chaperoned from Colombia by the US Government. She thinks that should shake me out of thinking his death was a hoax. It's not like he's missing. We were all there. He was said to be unrecognizable so I didn't see his face, but I got his clothes and his watch and his wallet, and I threw a rose on his casket. The US Consulate doesn't bury the wrong guy.

"We'll go with you," Sasha says.

"What?" I say.

"To that coffee shop. We'll go with you. We'll find him," Sasha says with kindness and optimism in her eyes.

"Dude," Andi says. "*If* that's him. Big giant-ass if. Then that woman who wrote you *asked* him if his name is Jack. If it is him, she spooked him. You think he'll go back there if he's on the run?" she asks, and my heart sinks. I hadn't thought of that, but she's right.

"We have to try," Sasha says.

"What a moron this chick is. Fucking Beatrice. She scared him off," Andi says, then feels the need to add, "which is fine because I'm sure it's not Jack."

"Right," I say, pushing my phone into my pocket.

"But you're going, right?" Sasha says.

"Tomorrow after I drop Hal at school," I say, because of course I'm going. They look at one another then back to me with a mix of surprise and either horror or a bit of excitement—I can't really tell. But they don't get it. They don't know that this is the first time in two years I have felt the fog of my depression shift. I can't say I feel it lifting exactly, but something is stirring and maybe I feel something resembling hope for the first time—and if not hope, maybe just a laser focus on the possibility of getting some answers for the sudden downward spiral of my life—and it's fueling me, giving me life right now. Nothing will stop me from seeing this through.

"I'm just gonna say something," Andi says again.

Sasha places a gentle hand on her arm and quietly replies, "Maybe don't."

"I'm just saying. The facts. We wanna keep our heads clear here—be realistic. I don't think pretending he's not dead is the helpful thing."

I see Sasha squeeze her eyes closed briefly and take a breath—a quiet gesture of disapproval of Andi's usual, but not always appropriate, frankness.

"I mean, we know this—someone is messing with you. Facts. *Why* is the question. Also facts. Why would some psychopath do this?"

It's a good question. Who would have a problem with me? A widowed mother from the suburbs with not an enemy in the world I can think of. And it makes me even more sure that somehow it has to be him.

"What if it was genuinely just someone who looked a lot like him?" Sasha asks. "And maybe he genuinely left the play for some other reason and didn't hear you call him? He didn't run, he had an emergency and it wasn't about you . . . and what if all your message-board posting just happened to reach someone who saw him since you did the scattershot approach—you said so yourself—hitting all the sites in those cities? I mean, things like this happen. I saw a photo once on social media and it was two little kids on a beach vacation somewhere. A boy and a girl who met later in life and ended up getting married and didn't know that they were on the same beach twenty years earlier. They each realized they had almost identical old photos of that day. They were strangers who just happened to be caught in the other's childhood vacation picture and now they have kids and live in Tampa. I mean . . ."

Andi blinks at Sasha like she's lost the plot, and I give a small nod in agreement as if a point has been made, and maybe there is some sense in it, but no. It's more than just a coincidence. It's an energy. A feeling that something is brewing. Something is happening.

"It's not him, Reg, come on," Andi says.

"Who's not him?" Tom asks playfully as he comes over, places his empty on an end table and squeezes Sasha's shoulder from behind the couch.

"Nobody," I say, standing, done talking about it with them at the moment and ready for a drink. As I head to the kitchen, I catch Andi asking Carson if they can please go now, which hits me the wrong way because she's always the one who stays long after all the guests have left. She's always the one who has one more joke and one more nightcap to share with me. But not tonight. Andi says her goodbyes and is gone a couple hours before everyone else.

Everyone is weird lately and I don't know if it's just my paranoia or if there's something in the air that's just not quite right.

After the structured games turn into kids screaming and leaping on furniture, and the game comes to an end, folks start to pluck their coats from the pile in the guest bedroom, starting the goodbye process that just leads to small groups of people moving closer to the front door and continuing conversation until they say goodbye for real, and after twenty minutes or so, the place is empty and the caterers are cleaning up.

I pay Kathy and help her collect her boxes of games and paints, and I tell Hallie to get in the bath before bed and that we can go through her presents and write thank-you notes after school tomorrow. We didn't intend on having the party on a Monday—we switched it last-minute when Sunday turned into a town search party—and we were lucky everyone obliged considering the circumstances and I didn't have to crush Hallie completely. But now I'm beyond exhausted and crumple into the chair by the fireplace after the house is empty and I hear the bath running upstairs.

I'm glad I was forced to wait before responding to this strange Beatrice person, because my instinct was to ask a million follow-up questions, but now, after a little space, I think I need to show up and ask her in person—see her reaction for myself. I message back, Thank you. I'll be there tomorrow, and then I think about cleaning up the scattering of balloons and wrapping paper that litter the rec room floor, but instead, I pour the last of a bottle of prosecco into a glass and take a swipe of cake frosting with my finger and begin to head upstairs when I see a text pop up. It's from Janey Beck, one of the moms in Hallie's class who's in my book club.

Did you hear about Tia? it reads.

I text her back, No. What? I know her family is close with Ray and Tia. What has she found out?

As I wait for her reply, I hear something.

It sounds like—I don't know exactly—like something fell. A couple of thumps. I stand and go to the kitchen and stay very still to listen. I think it's probably a parent outside who forgot something and is coming back up the walk. A lot of people had to park practically two blocks away because the Watkinses were also having a party, a football cookout, and the street was full of parked cars.

I put down my glass and hold my heart for a moment when I realize no, it's not outside. It has to be coming from the basement. I was sure I heard water running upstairs. But did Hallie go down there for something? I move closer to the basement door off the kitchen and open it, peering down the stairs, but it's dark.

"Hal?" I call down. Nothing. I hear the ping of a text coming through my phone over on the counter, which makes my heart leap from my chest. I take a second and breathe. And then I hover over the basement stairs and switch on the light to try to see if there's anything down there, and then . . . yes, I do hear movement. Footsteps. I walk down a few steps and it's quiet and I think I am probably imagining things. Breathe. In for four, out for eight. *Don't let yourself get like this*, I tell myself. *At least wait until Hallie is asleep.*

Okay, everyone just left. It's not like I heard a bump in the night. It's fine. All the lights are on, and the caterers are probably still loading their car outside. Lana Murray brought her Pomeranian in her purse. What if it got out? I mean, I need to practice being rational. Not everything is a threat. In for four, out for eight.

I reach the bottom stair and see all of the boxes that were sitting on the shelves along the walls turned over, rifled through, upside down, on the floor—papers and files strewn, snow globes and soccer uniforms and old Barbies dumped. What the hell happened? I don't have more than a second to consider this.

I feel it before I hear it. A crack. A searing pain to my ear—the side of my head. I feel a scream try to escape my throat, but it doesn't have a chance to come out before the shock and an explosion of pain take me over and the world goes dark.

CHAPTER ELEVEN

Sasha

The kids picked at Swedish meatball appetizers and birthday cake all afternoon and said they didn't want dinner and went to their rooms. So it was not the evening Sasha had in mind when she heard the doorbell and saw it was Tom's father, Al, holding a couple of bags of barbecue in the rain and peeking through the front glass to see if we were coming to answer the door.

He brings food over a couple nights a week most of the time in addition to his Saturday outings with Chloe—not every week, but as much as he can—and it's sweet. He hangs out with the kids and lets Chloe paint his nails with purple glitter, and Drew teaches him how to massacre the enemy on some video game Sasha can't begin to remember the name of. He usually lets her know before he shows up, but generally, he's the kind of guy who does whatever the hell he wants, so you never know.

He has so much money that it's a wonder he doesn't have a driver take him wherever he needs to go and hold an umbrella over his head as he makes his way up the walk. But not Al. He drives around in an old Cadillac and does tai chi and plays chess in the park and smokes cigars with some of the other retirees and still finds time to micromanage Tom at the restaurant—or at least that's how Tom sees it.

Sasha was not expecting him tonight, and when Tom decided to go out for a couple of drinks with the other dads who wanted to keep the football game buzz going a little longer and take advantage of the rare occasion their wives were allowing it, Sasha was looking forward to slipping into her fuzzy robe and making a cup of tea and getting cozy on this rainy evening. The last thing she wants is more food and the smell of old tobacco mixed with library books or whatever that scent is that always lingers in Al's clothes. As much as she loves him, it's just not the mood right now.

Still, she sighs and opens the door. She arranges her features into something she hopes looks less disappointed than how she feels before she greets him.

"Al, goodness. Come in, you're getting soaked," she manages.

He stomps the rain from his boots on the front mat and hands her the bags.

"Hiya, Sashi," he says, unbuttoning his coat. He always calls her Sashi, and it doesn't bother her coming from him.

"Hi, Tom's out, hon. Sorry, I didn't know you were coming tonight."

"Eh, well. I was at the restaurant and some asshole never

picked up their baby backs, so I thought I'd just swing by, leave it for the kids," he says, following me into the dining room.

"They're stuffed full of cake and soda, but I'll join you," she says, because she's happy the kids are settled in, supposedly finishing homework but probably playing video games, but she doesn't feel like doing the helicopter thing right now, so she pulls out a couple of plates and offers Al to sit.

They eat lukewarm ribs to the sound of heavy rain drumming on the roof and tapping at the windows around them.

"How's the restaurant?" she asks.

"Eh," he says. "The hostess started dating one of the line cooks, Mason, and then she caught him groping one of the waitresses in the walk-in cooler—which one was it?" He looks at the ceiling as he tries to think. "I think we have three Caitlyns and two Ashleys, so one of them anyway, and then they broke up so she stopped showing up to work and I had to be the hostess myself all afternoon. I can see why everyone quits. It's a thankless job. Pays shit and people are awful. Everyone wants a goddamn booth. There are only so many booths, people! Don't blame the hostess for that. What's wrong with a nice two-topper? The chairs are better to sit in anyway. Those booths wreck your back. Jeeza-lou." He digs into a Styrofoam dish full of coleslaw, shaking his head.

She giggles at this, because it's ridiculous to think about Al wiping down menus and seating people at his own restaurant when he could afford to buy the whole damn town if he wanted to. She doesn't know why he does it except that he says it keeps him young.

"There's nothing wrong with a nice two-topper," she says, then offers him a glass of wine, which he declines. He leans back in his chair and looks around, and she feels a bit awkward, wondering how long she'll have to make small talk and when Tom might be home because she's exhausted but doesn't want to be rude.

"I think Tom will be back pretty soon. He recorded the game if you wanna watch it," she says.

"Oh, that's okay, kiddo. I'll get going, I just . . ." He pauses, and she can tell he wants to say something. It's not like Al to just show up or linger if Tom's not around. Not that they don't get along or have things to chat about—it's just the way things are, probably in most families. But there seems to be something else going on.

"You just what?" she says.

"Well, it's not really my place, Sash, but your kiddo . . . he got suspended from school for a week, I think."

"You think? What do you mean? Why wouldn't I have been contacted?"

"I heard him at Blanc's with his friend he always brings in there—the girl. I think he signed your name to the notice that was sent home, and I think the school office has his girlfriend's number on file instead of yours. Pretty slick, I know. I don't know how they pulled that off. I just—I'm not his grandpa, technically, but I still feel like I am, so I felt like I needed to tell you."

Sasha feels a prickle of heat climb up her back. She pushes her plate away and shakes her head in a moment of stunned silence, because what the hell is really going on with Drew? How deep is he in whatever it is he's gotten himself into?

"What did he do?" she asks.

"That I don't know. I woulda said somethin' to him directly. But I don't know. I like the kid. I just wanted you to . . . not be in the dark is all," he says, and then he stands and pushes his chair back. "That's all."

"Thanks, Al. I really appreciate that."

"Yeah, I'm a snitch, but whaddya gonna do?" He shrugs on his coat and glances outside. "It's a bitch out there," he says, changing the subject.

"Yeah. Sure you don't wanna wait for Tom?"

"Eh." He makes a dismissive gesture, and she realizes he came over to talk to her and probably knew Tom was out because they text all the time. She doesn't think she has to ask him not to mention this to Tom because he went out of his way to tell her privately. Still, she stops him just before he exits.

"You don't need to mention it to Tom. I'll deal with it," she says, and he nods and straightens his hat before bracing for the falling rain and walking to his car.

She can't have Tom know because she decides in that instant that she also can't have Drew know she is privy to this information. She won't scream at him or ground him or take away his precious Xbox. That won't help her find the truth. She plans to get to the bottom of it in a more efficient way.

Her first thought is to track his phone and follow him, but whatever he's involved with, whatever the hell he's hiding, he seems to be really good at it, and she thinks if she were hiding a secret or up to no good, she'd probably strategically leave her phone behind or turn it off or something if she were smart. And Drew is very smart. She can't believe she's going to go to these lengths to spy on him, but she has to know. She has to protect him. From himself and maybe from serious danger.

She won't tell him that she knows he's pretending to go to school every morning this week because certainly that's what he'll do if he's already gone this far to make sure she doesn't know. She'll just have to follow him. In the morning, she'll call the school and find out what he did, but rather than confront him, she has a better idea.

She makes her cup of long-awaited cinnamon tea, climbs the stairs, flops onto the bed, and wishes she could just shut out all the noise and sleep for a couple of days and wake up with everything back to normal, but instead, she takes a sip, places her mug on the nightstand and looks up GPS trackers for cars. She is stunned by how easy it is. For twelve bucks on Amazon, she can buy a little gadget that syncs to her phone and shows her where Drew goes in real time. It will be delivered overnight—4–8 a.m. to be exact. Perfect.

Before she can sit and let her mind reel and go to all the terrible dark places it will wander to, wondering what's to become of her son, her phone pings. She reads the text.

They located Tia!

CHAPTER TWELVE

Andi

Fuck! Her phone! How did I not think to look for a phone in Tia's clothing? I barely looked at her, really. I saw the blood on her head and felt for a pulse. I covered her up right away and haven't looked at her or checked her pockets or anything since. I only saw it lying on the concrete garage floor next to the freezer after we got home from the party—a phone I didn't recognize—and then I put it together. Shit. Fuck. It must have fallen out of her pocket when Carson hit the freezer. Tia had a phone. What a stupid error.

I rested easy that she did not have a phone because the cops said that either it was off or the settings for *service location* and *GPS* were turned off, making it untraceable. Most people would think that meant maybe she had an accident and her phone was destroyed when she fell off a cliff somewhere, or maybe she was murdered and the killer turned her phone off or destroyed it. But if you're me, you don't think those things. If you're me, you assume the police would have had the place surrounded if her phone traced to my house.

I don't know what I assumed about her phone. At first, I didn't even consider it. Then when there was news about it not being locatable, I breathed a sigh of relief. I had gotten lucky and really didn't know what the hell happened to it besides maybe it fell into the lake on her run or it died. But here it is. It's on. There's no security code to open it. This has to mean that she is the one who disabled her GPS or it would be pinging and they'd find it—find me. Jesus. I have to get rid of it immediately. I need to get rid of her, God help me.

When we arrived home from the party, I made popcorn. Carson and the kids turned on *Survivor* and are all on the couch at the moment. I ducked out. I had to get that padlock back on the freezer, but the fall broke it. I thought maybe it was just forced open and it would still close, but it's useless and I can't lock it. The freezer is lying on its side with bits of blue tarp sticking out the bottom, and for the love of God, I have to at least get it locked and get rid of this phone. Then, tomorrow, I'll find a space of time when everyone's gone to safely move her.

I stare at the freezer in a stunned silence. I'm so absolutely fucked. I have to act right this second. I have to do something right now or that's it. I pop into the kitchen and grab my keys and breezily tell Carson we're out of a few things for Chloe's lunch tomorrow, and when he says she just wants PB&J, I blame it on my period and tell him I'm going to grab monthly things and he stops asking questions.

I take River Road and drive along the wet two-lane

stretch—it should give me ample opportunity to find a clearing where I can pull over to drop the phone into the river, without any record of me going somewhere totally off the grid or out of character.

The rain has turned into a thin drizzle and my windows are fogging up as I white-knuckle the steering wheel, trying not to speed, trying not to hyperventilate. At every stop sign, I scan my surroundings, trying to find the perfect inconspicuous place to slip out, and when I drive past the riverwalk, I see a couple walking in woolly coats and patrons having drinks next to heaters on bar patios on the street. At the next stop sign, I glance around, paranoid that anyone I know might see my car even though right now all I'm doing is driving down the road to a store. Nothing suspicious here.

At the next stoplight I glance to the warm lit windows of businesses and restaurants along the street and see everything I long for. To be fucking normal and not have the world crumbling around me. Just a woman at See's Candy buying a bag of chocolate turtles; part of a couple at Barney's Hardware, looking at a fall wreath in the storefront window; an elderly woman throwing the pigeons sunflower seeds from her purse as she waits for a bus. What I wouldn't give to be any of them right now—to be anywhere else right now.

I pass the riverwalk area and the trees thicken, and after a few minutes, I decide this is as good a place as any. I pull over to a parking space at a scenic overlook. There are only three spots and of course nobody is here in the dark and the mist, so I step out of the car and clutch the phone in my hand. I brought Clorox wipes in my pocket to get rid of any fingerprints on the phone before I drop it. All I have to do now is hurry.

I get myself to the rocky overlook and pull out a wipe. My hands are trembling. As I'm trying to wipe the phone clean, I start to lose hold of it. The mist and the alcohol cause it to slip from my grip, and as I fumble and catch it, to my horror, I realize I must have hit a button, because it's calling the last number dialed. Jesus Christ. Tia's phone is calling Ray! I click it off, hold my heart and almost scream from sheer shock.

Then I fling it. I panic and just fling it toward the river. I watch it hit a protruding rock below and snap and then . . . blip. It drops into the river and washes away. I race to my car and speed away as fast as I can.

My mind reels as I drive, nervously thinking about our world of cameras and tire-track forensics and cell towers. There will be evidence now that her phone pinged off this tower. Even if the tracking and service location are all off and untraceable, I'm sure that changes once the phone is in use. Fuck!

I shakily pull into CVS, and I know I'm on camera and I think about all of the shows I've seen where the idiot criminal is caught buying duct tape and bleach at a Walmart and I don't know if buying a padlock looks bad. Will Carson notice the new padlock and ask about it? Then I'd be screwed anyway. But what choice do I have? I buy some random items I scarcely even look at—throwing KitKat bars and face scrub and Gatorade into my basket, casually looking for the aisle that would have padlocks. I spot them next to office supplies. Just a small section with a few notebooks, tape, pens and tools.

I don't know what makes me do it—perhaps I'm just overcome with adrenaline—but I purposefully drop the small plastic package the padlock is in onto the floor. Then I reach down and, in a moment of insanity, think it's a good idea to drop it inside my fuzzy UGG boot and walk out with it so they don't have a paper trail of me purchasing it. It's not like it's a shovel or zip ties, but I know I'm under suspicion and I can't take any chances.

I feel sweat forming under my coat as I walk to self-checkout. I scan my items. A small line forms behind me. The machine gives instructions and with each item it seems to unnecessarily shout at me. Put your CHEWY CAT TREATS in the bagging area. Put your MAYBELLINE EYE CONCEALER in the bagging area, announcing to everyone around each item I purchased. Then, of course I bought tampons in case Carson were to notice, which he won't, but still. So the machine yells, please put your TAMPON PEARL in the bagging area, and I see Mr. Whittiker from the PTA in the other checkout line, and I feel a prick of embarrassment as if that matters one freaking iota right now, but still, I notice my face flush.

I feel the padlock inside my boot. I think for a second that maybe I should lean down and pick it up to scan, but I can't have PADLOCK screamed across the store. I just can't. I insert my card, steadying my hands to do so, and then I take my plastic bags of items, silently chiding myself for not remembering my reusable bags and wasting plastic. Again, a ridiculous thing to be concerned about in this moment, but nothing is rational right now. Everything is louder and brighter than it should be, and I have to get out of here.

I pluck my receipt from the feeder and hurry out the front automatic doors. I pick up the pace to my car, feeling the hard plastic of the padlock package digging into my skin. I try not to look like I'm panicked, but then I hear a voice behind me.

"Ma'am?" It's the clerk. She's followed me out. "Ma'am," she says again, and I pretend not to hear. I walk even faster, trying not to break out into a sprint, but she's right behind me. I think of getting arrested and going to jail and Carson finding the freezer unlocked, the body inside, while I'm being arraigned for theft . . . and then they'll find out what I've really done. Oh, my God. I start to run.

"Ma'am. Stop!"

CHAPTER THIRTEEN

Regan

I hear howling—the sobs and shrieks of my daughter, standing at the top of the stairs, too afraid to come down, afraid I'm dead. It's her screaming that wakes me up. I blink my eyes open and wonder how long I've been out. Hours? Or maybe only seconds; maybe Hallie was already on her way down when she heard the noise. I see broken glass. The egress window is shattered from where the person must have escaped. I'm dizzy, still piecing together what happened, but I have to console my baby. I push myself up from the floor.

"It's okay, honey. Hal. It's okay. I just—I must have fallen. I'm okay," I repeat, but I don't feel okay. I'm lightheaded, nauseated and fucking terrified. I slowly steady myself on the wall and hold the rail. She holds out her arms, still hiccupping with sobs, and I carefully make my way up to the top of the stairs and hold her. She wraps her arms around me.

"I thought you died," she cries. "I heard a noise. There was a man," she says. I pull away, holding on to her shoulders, and look at her.

"What?" My fear turns into fury as I realize she saw this intruder who came to . . . look for something, it appears, or hurt me, maybe? I don't even know, but the fact that she witnessed this outrages me, and I'm feeling helpless to protect her from all the crazy things that have been happening.

I should probably go to the hospital. I could have a hematoma and/or brain swelling. I've read about "talk and die syndrome," where a person seems totally fine after a blow to the head and then, in an instant, is gone. I try not to panic or show any fear in front of Hallie. I think about calling my parents. I should. I talk to my mother almost every day, and not telling her about the Jack thing or this feels very wrong, but somehow I just can't drag them into it. As much as I want the unconditional support they always give, I can't burden them right now.

I settle Hallie down on the couch with a blanket and *Para-Norman* playing on the TV. Then I go to the kitchen and call Andi. Maybe she can come and stay here awhile so I can go to the ER. No answer. I call Sasha and she graciously arranges to have Hallie sleep at her house while she takes me to the hospital. I hesitate. I feel bad for thinking it, but there is just something . . . not quite right about her son, Drew. I should give him the benefit of the doubt—he's shy and standoffish, which is why he seems off-putting to me. Maybe it's all the school shooters who seem to look kind of like him, and although I am ashamed for making such assumptions, still a small part of me wonders what's up with him. I also can't help wondering why Sasha acted strange when she saw the photo of Jack, but all in all, it's likely just my frazzled nerves and paranoia creating problems where they don't exist.

I go and sit next to Hal on the couch, and more calmly reiterate that I just fell and the guy was one of the caterers coming back for some things. I tell her everything is fine but I should get checked out, so she can sleep at Chloe's. I see a smile tugging at the corner of her lips at the idea of a sleepover on a school night—even though she's tired and probably at her limit of fun in one day, she can't help herself. She collects her things, and we wait for Sasha's car at the front door.

The drive is quiet, as I know neither of us wants to say anything in front of Hallie, and after we drop her off and make our way to the hospital, Sasha only asks if I'm okay and I tell her I am. She doesn't push or make me talk about it, and I appreciate the space because I'm still in shock. I haven't fully processed what's happened or why.

The ER waiting room is a bleak and haunting place. Sasha brings over two Styrofoam cups of weak coffee and hands me one. I touch the bump on my head. There's no blood, just a giant raised knot and pounding headache. I've already replayed what happened and thanked Sasha a million times over for her help, and now we wait. The hollow feeling inside pokes at my ribs. The grief. The emptiness that is only made worse by fluorescent lights and the smell of disinfectant. I notice I'm trembling. I take a Xanax from my purse and slip it under my tongue; it works faster than Ativan. I wrestle down the familiar thoughts—I don't want to be here anymore. I don't want to live feeling like this. But then my love for Hallie pushes into the dark thoughts and they dissolve into guilt and that's how I distract myself for a while until the cycle starts again, usually only minutes later. I sigh and bury my head in my hands. Sasha puts a hand on my back and speaks softly.

"What did the police say? Why didn't they call an ambulance?"

"I . . . haven't gotten that far yet," I say, sitting back up, trying to keep it together.

"Wait, what? You didn't call the police?" she asks with her mouth hanging open in disbelief.

"I will. Of course. But I had to get Hallie somewhere safe first—I could not put her through that. Maybe that's stupid of me, but the guy is gone, and I haven't touched or moved anything that could be evidence. It's Hallie's goddamn birthday, and she's been through enough. As soon as I find out I'm okay, I will call the police and meet them at the house. It was already over—nothing they could do in the moment—so a few hours can't hurt."

"Yeah," Sasha says, "makes sense." But the look on her face tells me it makes little sense and I'm crazy. She changes the subject.

"I heard they found Tia," she says.

"I got that text, too. From Janey Beck . . . the town gossip, so I wasn't sure what to think. I haven't had a chance to respond to her. Do you know if it's true?" I say.

"All I was told," Sasha says, "is that Tia called Ray. Like there was a call from her number to him that only rang twice and ended. But the phone was untraceable before that, so he thinks she's alive."

"Oh, my God. But they still don't actually know where she is?" I ask.

"I guess not, but it seems like good news. I think they can find where the phone pinged from," she says.

"Man. I was starting to think she really was . . . dead, you know? With all the weird stuff going on, probably murdered by some lunatic. Andi must be relieved," I say, placing my coffee on a metal side table.

"I can't get ahold of her," Sasha says.

"I guess we wait for the whole story," I say. "From what Janey texted, Ray was a sobbing mess in their living room when this call came in—he's close with her husband, Darren—and then when he didn't answer her call in time, he was even more of a mess. But apparently they're with the cops now," I say, and then a nurse comes out through the metal doors across the room and calls my name.

After some imaging and other tests, I'm released with pain meds and instructions to rest and not drive for a day or two. Sasha is really a saint for staying with me the whole time—the ER is the last place anyone wants to be, especially late at night when we're exhausted already. She drives me back to her place and says I should take the guest room so Hallie can sleep.

"Oh, heya, Regan," Tom says when we come in through the front door, sitting up from where he was clearly asleep on the couch in front of the TV. He stands.

"You should sit. God, are you all right? What did they say?" He motions to the couch, and I sit.

"I'll make some tea if you want," Sasha says.

"Jeez, you probably want something stronger than that after what you've been through." Tom pours a glass of port from a little dry bar in the corner of the living room and holds it out as a question.

"Sure," I say. I've never had port before. It's really sweet, but I pretend to like it because I would indeed like something strong right now.

"It's a Quinta das Carvalhas," Tom says.

"She doesn't care, sweetheart," Sasha says, kissing him on the cheek. She's already told him I'll be staying, and he brought fresh towels and things into the guest room for me, she said. Their kindness is touching, and I know I'm not showing enough gratitude right now.

"You hungry?" he asks. Tom's dad brought barbecue.

"Tom was an Italian grandmother in another life. Always pushing food on everyone," Sasha says, perching on the arm of the couch.

"Or brisket. You know we always have brisket," he says, switching off the TV and picking up his phone from the coffee table.

"She probably wants rest," Sasha says, giving him a gentle "get lost" look if I'm reading it right, and so I smile in quiet agreement.

"Night." He kisses Sasha on the head. "I'm really glad you're okay, Reg," he says before climbing the stairs up to their room.

"Will you be okay?" Sasha asks. "I can stay up with you."

"I'm fine. Thank you, God, so much, for everything. I think I just need a little time for my nerves to settle."

"I'm right up there if you need anything," she says, giving me a hug. "Night."

"Night," I repeat. And then the house is silent besides the sound of the ticking clock on the wall, which unnerves me because the sound of time passing always feels wrong. I sip my port and stare around the dim room. I click off the lamp and lie back, covering my legs with a fuzzy throw, and stare up at the ceiling, cupping my port. I need to calm my mind. The police will take a report, but with the assailant long gone, it will do nothing to alleviate my fear. The security alarm wasn't armed yet because people had just left. The person must have known that, because the alarm is always on otherwise. Should I feel safe knowing I have an alarm on every door and window moving forward? Or should I just burn the goddamn place down? Because that's tempting right now.

Suddenly, I hear something in the quiet house. A soft tapping. Then I see that it's a figure coming down the stairs. When he walks past a sliver of moonlight coming through the front window, I see it's Drew. He doesn't see me; he must not know I'm here. He very quietly opens the front door, expertly slips out, and closes and locks it with silent precision. And then he's gone.

I sit up and stare at the door a moment and wonder if I should tell Sasha, but something makes me . . . hesitate. I don't need one more thing right now, and I decide not to involve myself. Instead, I rinse my glass out in the sink, then quietly make my way upstairs to the guest room. Second door on the right. But before I go into my room, I see Drew's door across the hall cracked open. It's so, so very none of my business, but what other chance in a thousand years would I have access to this strange kid's room? I know he's gone and know he has to be hiding something, because he snuck out wearing a hoodie, looking guilty as sin as he disarmed the house alarm. That's not normal. I push the door in with one finger and look up and down the hall.

His room looks pretty unremarkable. The glow of the computer screen is the only light, and I poke around at Drew's desk in the semidarkness. It's nothing other than textbooks and crumpled notebook papers. I open his bedside drawer and see some chargers, earbuds, a single sock—nothing. I feel under his mattress, and nothing. He seems relatively normal if you only have his room to go on. I can't see well enough to dig into the recesses of his closet, and so I decide to try one last place—a backpack slumped on a chair in the corner. It's unzipped, so I quickly rifle through the folder inside but it's just math homework. I'm about to give up when I feel the corner of something thicker and smaller than the rest of the papers. I pull it out to see what it is, but before I can even squint in the dim light to look closer, I hear a door down the hall open. A light is turned on. I panic. I should hide—I can't be caught in here like some sort of unstable, I don't even know, pervert—because why would I have reason to be in this kid's f-ing room? Oh, my God. I decide in a split second to leap out into the hall. I shove the object under my shirt and in one quick motion, slip out the door and close it behind me, and when I turn, there is Sasha, directly in front of me. My heart is hammering in my chest. She looks confused but doesn't say anything right away.

"I thought it was the guest room, I'm so sorry. I didn't wake him up. Sorry. Definitely not the guest room, then," I blather nervously, and it's not totally a lie because I did not, in fact, wake him up. I see her face soften. She laughs.

"It's okay. Across the hall." She points. "There's an extra blanket in the chest, and you can turn the fireplace on if you're cold." She squeezes my shoulder. "I just came out to turn up the heat."

"Thanks," I say, and I can feel my cheeks burning red and hot with embarrassment. I quickly slip into the guest room, close the door behind me and lock it. I sit at the edge of the cold bed and pull the square of paper out from under my shirt, but it's not paper. It's a photo. A photo of . . . Jack.

CHAPTER FOURTEEN

Sasha

Drew slouches over his phone, which he should be grounded from, and eats a piece of toast in two bites while Sasha pours a cup of coffee for Regan and then one for herself. She sits at the kitchen counter, where the girls are giggling over pancake faces—Tom is getting a thrill out of making a show of cooking for them. He has the cuffs of his dress shirt rolled up and engages fully in the impromptu game of breakfast caricatures before he's off to meetings with a prospective new "craft vinegar supplier" so he can make their new sauce even more amazing and perfectly balanced.

Sasha always finds it funny the things he does—like sampling new beer and sauce ingredients in the middle of the day on a Tuesday—compared to most people she knows. Like poor Carson, who is in some sort of corporate sales job that has him traveling and in a constant state of stress and dread about his work. Free steak dinners and booze are the only things he seems to enjoy about it. Sasha's lucky . . . most of the time . . . that she has such a cozy little life, and then she catches herself thinking, *Why is Drew trying to ruin it? Why can't he just be happy?*

She watches him stand, pull his coat from the back of his chair and say "see ya" before making his way out to his car for school . . . which, of course, she knows he isn't going to because she knows he's suspended. She notices Regan watching him exit through the front door and walk past the front window, and she has a furrowed brow—a disapproving look. Odd. But Sasha isn't going to overthink it; Regan's mind is probably just elsewhere.

"Okay, let's get going," Sasha says, hurrying the girls off for their bags and coats so she can get them dropped off and start tracking Drew's movements. In a flurry of putting plates in the sink, grabbing bagged lunches and looking for rain boots, they are out the door and dropping Chloe and Hal off in front of the school within thirty minutes. As Sasha drives Regan home, she wants to offer to drive her to Windsor Locks to look for her dead husband, but she can't. She has problems of her own to contend with, and she probably shouldn't get involved. After all, everyone knows Jack is gone, and whatever Regan is going through, it feels like more trouble no matter how much Sasha sympathizes.

"You sure you'll be okay?" Sasha asks, pulling into Regan's lot, wondering if she'll make the drive anyway, to hell with the doctors or concussions. She probably will, Sasha thinks. She seems fine, medically speaking . . . and very determined.

"Yes. Thanks. I really appreciate all you've done for me. I don't know what I would have done."

But Sasha knows Regan has tons of family she's close to and friends. She's deeply rooted in the community and has the empathy of just about everyone after her loss. Sasha wonders why Regan didn't call any of them before her. Yes, the three of them—herself and Andi and Regan—have been peas in a pod since Sasha moved in, but she's still the newbie. She can only assume this assault makes Regan think the bombing wasn't a prank gone wrong but a very real threat to her life . . . and she's not ready to make that public just yet.

"The police are coming to talk to me, so I'll be fine," Regan says, exiting the car and stepping into the misty gray air. Of course the police didn't find any evidence besides the broken window and strewn boxes Regan already knew about, so Sasha can't imagine going back into that house on her own, police on their way for a chat or not. She offered Regan the option to stay and rest, but she insisted on going home, so Sasha waves goodbye and reminds her that she'll be back by three to pick up the girls and head to Wild Roast Café.

When she's out of sight from Regan's house, she pulls over on the woodsy two-lane road just up the street and opens her tracking app to see where Drew has gone. That absolute shit has driven himself all the way to Hartford. She zooms in and sees that he seems to be stopped at a Carl's Jr. So he's suspended, in some deep, deep shit, lying to her and stealing photos of dead people, but he's popped in to treat himself to some bacon fries at a fast-food joint. She's seething as she white-knuckles the steering wheel and gets on the freeway, headed into the city.

The gray and drizzle are relentless. The extended forecast hasn't a speck of sunshine in sight, and the constant gloom is mirroring Sasha's mood as she becomes more and more certain Drew is turning unknowable and slipping further away from her into something dangerous. She keeps the radio off and lets her thoughts bombard her as she tries to play out worst-case scenarios and potential solutions—because there must still be a way out for him. If he made a bomb threat or even . . . if he—she can barely stand to let herself think it. She's been repressing the thought, staying in denial so it won't really be a possibility in her mind, but it niggles around the edges, and then there it is. The question she hasn't wanted to ask herself. What if Drew planted that bomb in Regan's car that killed someone? Will Sasha be visiting him in prison for the rest of his life? Maybe she'd be able to protect him if he would just confide in her—because then she could believe it was an accident, a joke gone wrong, that he thought it would be a prank and never conceived it was powerful enough to really blow up. Or . . . she doesn't know, but there has to be a reason. Drew isn't a monster.

When she gets into the city, she looks at her tracker again, and he's just outside downtown. His car is parked in a lot, and she doesn't know the area, but she's not far away, so she drives too fast over wet, cracked streets and her tires dip into potholes as her heart speeds up, wondering what she'll find. What could he possibly be up to?

When she spots his car, it's at a Dave and fucking Buster's. She can't believe she's letting him get away with this when he should be grounded with his phone and computers locked up for a year. At minimum. But she is certain this is a better strategy if she actually wants information. So he's playing pinball and dicking around, and she just has to swallow down the absolute fury over this Ferris Bueller shit and wait it out.

After an hour, she finally decides to walk over to the Starbucks across the street and order a cup of coffee. She keeps her eyes on the parking lot where his car sits just a couple rows over from hers, and watches even though she has the app. There is still a tiny part of her that hopes—what? She doesn't even know—maybe that his friend took his car for the day and Drew is at the library studying and feeling guilty for whatever it is that got him suspended. She'll call the school about that later this morning to find out. She dreads that, too.

She drops her coffee when she spots him. She's mid–Stevia pouring when she takes a glance out the window and sees him walk to his car with the hood of his sweatshirt up, looking shifty as he keeps his gaze down and hurries to his car. She apologizes for the spill as she runs out the glass doors in time to see his taillights glowing in the dark haze of the day, turning onto Sixth Street. She jogs back across the road, almost slipping on the wet pavement, pissed off and breathless from the unexpected spring, and then she jumps in her car and goes. She opens the tracking app because she doesn't want to tail him too closely, and anyway, he's already too far ahead.

The next time he stops, it's at a smoke shop called Vapors. *Great, now I probably have to deal with vaping on top of everything else*, she thinks, but she quickly brushes the thought away and tries to stay focused. She sees his car parked in the small gravel parking lot. The place is a brick building with no windows and a metal door. It has a hand-painted sign with a poorly illustrated pink pot leaf on either side of the shop name, and it all looks as shady as it can possibly manage.

She parks next door at a Mexican grocer so her car won't be recognized, and she doesn't see him anywhere. He must have already gone inside. She is trying to imagine what he would drive all the way to the city for if all he wanted was video games and vapes. There's plenty of that sort of thing in Cloverhill Lakes. He's not in there more than fifteen minutes, but when he does emerge, it's from the side door of the building. An older man stands in the door frame and they shake hands—the man stands very close to him, saying something, holding Drew's elbow with his free hand and leaning in like whatever it is, it's something very important. She even sees the older man look around, subtly down the street right then left, to make sure nobody is around. Then he pats Drew's arm a couple of times, and Drew gets in his car and drives off. Sasha doesn't notice him carrying anything—she can't detect a look of distress or fear. It's like this is a totally normal thing to be doing. Once Drew is long gone, she knows what she has to do. She has to find out who these people are and what they want with her son, because he didn't come all the way here for smokes. She needs to get to the bottom of what he's involved in, and that means finding out who he's secretly meeting and why.

She tries the front door and fully expects a little bell to ring indicating a customer and to be greeted by sickly sweet tobacco scents and a young, stoned cashier, but none of that happens. The door is locked. She planned to pretend to be a customer and ask some casual questions to see if she could garner any information at all, but it's closed—it looks as though it's often closed and probably a facade for something far more sinister.

She walks around the side door and climbs the three brick stairs to the steel door and tries to pull it open. To her shock, it swings out at her and throws her a little off balance, but she steadies herself, already a little rattled, and steps inside quickly and closes the door behind her, then freezes in the dark hallway she finds herself standing in. A few yards in front of her, she sees stairs that lead down to a basement, where there's a light on—and she hears the rumble of men's voices talking. To the right is a closed door that leads into the vape shop, which is dark inside. To her left, there's a dark hallway that looks like it leads to a small office or supply room as far as she can tell.

What could he have been doing here? Sasha can't understand it—she can't even come up with one scenario that makes sense. Maybe if she can silently move down a few stairs, she'll be able to hear what the men are saying and maybe then she can figure out what's happening, who they are, what this place really is.

She tiptoes down the first stair and strains to listen, but before her foot touches the third stair, suddenly, she can't breathe. She can't scream. Someone has grabbed her from behind and covered her head in a plastic bag, and she can't even gasp for a breath. The plastic sucks into her mouth and nostrils and she's never been so terrified in all of her life. She claws and kicks, but the man who has her in his grip is strong, and no amount of fighting is helping—it only rips the small amount of air she had left in her lungs out of her more quickly, and then she starts to see stars and her body feels tingly and weak. Just a fraction of a moment before she loses consciousness, the bag is pulled away and she drops to the floor in a heavy thud.

"Wanna tell me what the fuck you're doing in here?" a voice asks, and she sees three men she doesn't recognize standing over her. She opens her mouth but nothing comes out because she still can't catch her breath to speak. She tries, but he asks again and she only makes a small squeak, and then she lets out a gasp as tears run down her face.

Then one of the men lifts his booted foot and smashes it

down on her hand so hard she actually hears the bone in her pinky finger crack. She finds her breath and a guttural scream of pain and terror escapes her mouth. She curls up into a ball on the floor, holding her head, protecting herself for the next blow, knowing this is the end. This is how she'll die.

CHAPTER FIFTEEN

Andi

I'm losing it. I'm fucking losing it. The woman just wanted to hand me a bag of tampons and KitKat bars I left on the self-checkout station, and I ran away like a nutcase. Good job making sure I don't do anything to make people think I'm acting odd and paranoid. When I got home last night, nobody even looked at me. They were so absorbed in their show. So I went into the garage and locked the freezer with the new padlock, and now I wait.

It's Tuesday and the kids are at school and Carson is lounging around the house in socks and boxers, returning emails on his phone and drinking a third cup of coffee. I have to get him out of the house.

When I asked if he was going into the office, his answer was "Maybe." I know he has a lunch meeting, but that's an eternity to wait. God help me, I can't wait another minute without losing it. I text Roxie and tell her to watch Dez for a little while after school because I have errands to run. I'll leave a paper trail. That's what I need to do. I need to leave my phone at home, because turning it off will look suspicious—so will leaving it, because nobody does that anymore, but not as much as turning it off on purpose. I could at least argue I forgot it in a rush. Turning it off is deliberate and suspicious.

I'll stop at a few stores and do normal-person stuff so if it's ever looked at—my movements and whereabouts—it might not be an alibi, but at least people will see me looking completely normal with the right amount of melancholy due to the tragic situation, of course, and with all my spaced-out store receipts, when would I have time to dump a body? I have to plan it down to every last detail.

I'll just go about my routine—getting the Girl Scout uniforms from the cleaners for the troop like I said I'd do before handing them off to Regan for the event tomorrow. That's perfect. I'll pick up some donuts to send along, too, and get receipts for everything before I execute the plan—the only plan I could really think of.

The river. It's my only way out. Of course, I can't just drive over there during the day and stay anonymous, because they can track that, with everyone's goddamn house cameras and surveillance everywhere you turn. I have to—God help me, it's so hard to really be thinking these terrible, horrific thoughts, but I have to—I have to sink her into the Connecticut River. It's deep, and today it's very calm, but the current will pick up with more heavy rain coming in, and Tia will be far, far away from here—even if she is found, she'll be washed up somewhere way downstream, so it won't connect to me. I watched a movie once where a girl's body caught on a tree limb on the bottom of a river and wasn't discovered for years. Plus, what are my options? It's not like I wouldn't be missed if I drove far away somewhere by myself to find the perfect lake or well or something. Where would I bury her? How? How long would it take to even dig a grave by myself? A long time, I think. A gruesome, harrowing long time. It has to be the river.

There's a Halloween Superstore up that way. I can say I'm going to pick up the kids' costumes and some decorations for the yard, because I actually promised them I would. Going all the way to that specific store might seem a little strange, but I could say they had the better Freddy mask Dex wants at that location. I could justify going up there by saying Costume World didn't have it in stock.

I move around Carson, trying to carry on with the things I would normally take care of in the morning. I cut up potatoes and vegetables and put them in a Crock-Pot; I load the dishwasher; I pick up everyone's socks and plates around the living room from last night that they promised to clean themselves, and then I make a couple of calls to organize the rest of the year's Girl Scout activities—Jeanie Baker is hosting a STEM outing and Karla Schneider is going to head up the Christmas craft event, and I volunteer to organize the organizers and get everything on the calendar and running smoothly.

It's definitely normal stuff to be doing today, so I put on a cheery voice and offer some ideas for papier-mâché snowmen and Advent calendars and then, sometime after 2 p.m., Carson finally puts on pants and heads into the office for a few hours. Then I get to work.

The freezer is still lying sideways on the garage floor, and when I open the padlock, Tia's wrapped body slides halfway out and rests in front of me, a shapeless mass. The smell of her hits me like a punch in the face. I turn away, almost gagging, but I have to keep moving. I've already begun mumbling tearful apologies as I pull her out the rest of the way and open the hatch of my car. She's a small woman—maybe a hundred and fifteen pounds—but she's still a lot to lift even though I'm inches taller than her and not out of shape. Still, the only way to get her up from the ground is in a series of labored efforts to hoist her, in a bear hug, and get enough of a grip to leverage her the few feet off the ground and into the hatch. When I have her just at the edge, I get a hold on her legs, bound in tape and painting cloth, and use my knees and back to lift and push at the same time as hard as I can, finally managing to get the weight of her into the car. It will be much easier the other way when I'm just pulling the weight.

Once I have her in the back, I cover her in the blanket I keep in the car for weather emergencies and then I push a few tarps on top of that to try to keep the smell contained, which helps. Then I close the hatch and try to breathe. *It was an accident, it was an accident, you're not a monster,* I repeat in my mind over and over again with each horrific action I am taking. I start the car, back up, and call Jerry's Junk Removal and schedule a pickup to get the freezer hauled away tomorrow. I drive the two-lane road into town, where I will create a little paper trail and make sure to be seen here and there so I am remembered in this moment as being in town in good spirits if they ever track this time frame to the dumping of her body. It can only help, even though I really have no fucking clue what I'm doing and do not have the luxury of googling anything or researching to find a better way. I just need to keep moving and get rid of evidence.

In town, I park in a vacant spot in the town square near all the cute shops and restaurants, and I check my locks three times before I go in and pick up the Girl Scout uniforms from the cleaners and shove the receipt into my pocket. I toss the uniforms into my back seat, lock the car again and nervously, shakily, walk over to the Wild Roast Café to pick up donuts as planned. Then I'll drive out to the river. There's an area that gets pretty woodsy and rural ten miles north, and there are places I could pull over unseen. My hands are trembling at the thought of this, so I shove them into my pockets while I wait in the line at the bakery counter.

I hear my name called and turn around to see Regan and her daughter in a booth, with hot chocolate and pastries. She waves me over. Shit. I force a smile and make my way over to them.

"Join us," she says. "Table service is faster anyway. Melinda Campner just ordered like seventy-five caramel macchiatos, so it could be a while." But the only thing I see are the contusions and bandage on the side of her head. I sit across from her, next to Hallie.

"What the hell happened to you?" I ask, then look at the ten-year-old next to me and apologize for my language. She giggles.

"I'm okay," Regan says, and the look on her face tells me she doesn't want to discuss it in front of her daughter. "We were supposed to come here with Sasha and Chloe after school, but she never showed up. She was supposed to pick me up, but after a day of rest, I feel totally fine, so we are having cocoa and cookies as promised." She cheerses Hallie's mug.

"Peppermint cocoa, even," she adds.

"You're okay, though, you sure?" I ask again.

"Yes, but I'm glad you're here because I need the uniforms."

"Oh, I have them. I can bring them in. I was just grabbing some treats for the event, but they've had enough sugar, so no need to spend an hour in line," I say as I keep glancing out the front window to keep an eye on my car across the street and simultaneously trying not to seem nervous.

"Did you kill that missing lady?" Hallie asks out of nowhere. I see Regan cup her hand over her mouth.

"Hallie!" Regan shrieks, and a couple of people look over. Hallie shrinks in her seat and turns red.

"Sorry, I just heard it at school."

"I always tell her it's polite to always ask and never assume. She was just— Sorry. Nobody really thinks that." Regan is trying to cover, but I know they all do. I feel something rising up inside me at that moment. All this time I have lived in a mostly numb and shocked state, but now the tingling in my hands and lightheadedness are pushing in and I can tell a panic attack is coming. I quickly excuse myself to the bathroom, which is mercifully right next to the booth we are sitting in.

Inside the tiny single-occupant restroom, I lean over the sink and try to calm my breath. Tears are streaking down my cheeks and I am hyperventilating, which is causing me to see stars. I have to keep control, because there is only a thin wooden door with a flimsy hook latch between me and the rest of the café, and I can't have anyone hear this. Shit, I need to pull it together. "It's okay, it's okay," I mutter to myself. I sit on top of the toilet seat and rest my head in my hands.

I can hear them talking right outside.

"Sorry, I didn't know," Hallie says.

"It's okay. Here. How about you go get in line and get Auntie Andi those donuts and I'll go grab the uniforms from her car, and we'll get going," Regan says, and it takes a second to register that the keys I hear her pick up from the table are my keys. My car keys. By the time it all makes sense, I'm storming out of the bathroom door, but it's happened so fast. I see her out the café door already. Hallie in the bakery line with a twenty in her hand, watching me run past her and out the front door. Regan is almost to my car.

"Wait!" I shout, running after her. "Stop!" But like something out of a nightmare—almost as if it's happening in painful slow motion—I see her beep the key fob. She doesn't hear me or turn. She clicks open the hatch to my car and it automatically begins to open. The hatch is all the way open and she's peering inside as I scream.

"Are you crazy?" I catch up to her and fling myself at the hatch, pushing it forcefully closed. "Stop! What is wrong with you?" It clicks closed and my face is flushed and wet with tears. She didn't move anything yet, thank Christ. She didn't see. Panic and relief swell inside me.

"Oh, my God, Andi. What—I was . . ." she starts to say, but I snatch back my keys, push past her. I lunge myself into the driver's seat and screech out of the parking lot, leaving Regan standing there with her mouth hanging open and a half a dozen other witnesses to the bizarre scene that just happened.

It's almost dusk by the time I get out of town and onto the rural road leading to the part of the river I'm looking for. I can't slow my heart rate after what happened in the parking lot. I can't stop my hand shaking or the thoughts racing. What have I done? Really, what the hell have I done to my life—my family? I suppress the urge to scream until my lungs bleed. I'll never get away with this, especially after what just happened.

The moon is dim behind the clouds and an endless mist

makes it hard to see where the clearings are in the dense tree-lined road, but I don't have much time. I need to just do it. It's been a while since I've seen headlights on the opposite side of the road, so I know I'm getting into the woodsy area I'm looking for where I have the best chance of avoiding a car passing. If I pull into a clearing in the trees, I can turn my lights off and hurry. I can . . . My thoughts stop cold when I see red lights flashing behind me. Then a siren.

CHAPTER SIXTEEN

Regan

Everyone is staring. I finally pick my jaw up off the ground and go back into the café to collect Hallie and go home. I thought Sasha going MIA when she promised to pick me up was very out of character, but this . . . Something is happening beyond Jack and beyond whoever broke into my house looking for something very specific, and it can't all be a big coincidence. This all has to be connected somehow, and I am dead set on getting to the bottom of it.

The police plan to add extra patrol on my street, and I already have a beefy alarm system with cameras in the house. I just hadn't had a chance to turn the system on yet before the break-in, attack—or whatever it was meant to be. But I have a sneaking suspicion that the person was there looking for something. The more I really think on it, if they were there to hurt me, why didn't they have a gun? They seemed caught off guard, panicked, and attacked me with the handle of a shovel that was leaning against the stairs, and then they had to break a window to escape. That couldn't have been the plan.

He had gloves on, and there's no blood from a cut or anything around the window he broke. It seems pretty impossible the police can do anything more than file a report. So what can I do? I was too scared to go into the basement all day after Sasha dropped me off. I just slept and slept. It had been a few days since I'd been able to sleep at all, so it all caught up to me, and the pain pill they gave me at the hospital helped. Now it's time to take matters into my own hands.

"Did Aunt Andi go crazy?" Hallie asks from the back seat, jolting me out of my looping thoughts.

"No, she's just . . . under a lot of stress."

"If you say so," she says with raised eyebrows.

"She's going through a lot—we need to be a little understanding."

"I know, but . . . do I have to go to Dez's pizza night next week? I don't wanna go. No one does."

"Who's no one? Why not?" She doesn't answer. "Hal, why? He's your good friend."

Hallie nods and shrugs and stays silent. After a few moments she looks up at me and I meet her eyes in the rearview mirror.

"We're not safe," she says as I pull into the garage and park. She gets out of the car and slams the door.

"What?" Her words have caught me so off guard that I don't have any other response. I hesitate and she runs off.

She doesn't want to talk about it, so I don't force her. After a couple tries, I let her lie to me about not having any homework and allow her to eat in her room and watch TV.

Whatever she needs today is fine by me. Kids talk and rumors gets embellished. That's all this is.

I double-check the alarms and doors before making a pot of tea and sitting on the armchair near the fireplace. I scroll on my phone to find Beatrice from the Bluebird Café and send her a message. She seems all too eager to offer any gossip she can, so maybe she'll keep me informed since I couldn't get there myself today.

I hesitate, though. I think about forgetting the whole thing. Depression can be funny like that. On one hand I'm fueled by this quest—it's the only thing giving me life right now—but on the other, I question myself every other second, wondering if I'm actually mad. Have I lost my mind? Everyone else thinks so. I see the way they look at me. It's not a self-pitying thing when I say it; I actually do wonder if I had some mental break and all of this is in my head. Maybe I went into the basement on some hallucination-filled rage from the meds and took to the boxes with a baseball bat and imagined it all. It's not impossible. Except that Hallie saw someone, and unless my overwhelming paranoia is rubbing off on her, there is no way we can both be wrong.

I could just go to sleep and forget about all of it—escape life completely for the next ten hours. Then I could drop Hal at school and sleep for six more. That's mostly what I've been doing since I lost my job. Our savings was already plenty to live on, and with the life insurance, I could sleep all my days away and only pretend to be alive for Hallie. Evenings and weekends. That could be my life. It's tempting. But there is something else tugging at me—something telling me to get up, wake up. Follow this through. Something that feels a little like hope. Maybe just for closure so I can move on with my life. I feel like I have to know or I'll rot here, under all the grief.

Hello Beatrice, I type. I was hoping you could tell me if Jack was at the café today? You didn't tell him about our conversation, I hope. It takes only a couple of minutes before her reply comes through.

> Girl, I was looking for him to pop in all day. He always comes on Monday. He did look pretty pale when I asked if his name was Jack though, so maybe he's scared off. How mysterious. I'll message you when I see him next. Don't worry, my lips are sealed.

I close my eyes and seethe at this comment. If her goddamn lips were sealed, he'd be there getting his "usual" and I would have some hope to see him, to figure out who the hell this really is. I have to go there anyway—I have to see the place he goes so often—to see if there are any clues that will help me understand.

Once I check on Hallie and see she's sleeping, I turn off her TV and cover her with a jack-o'-lantern quilt, then I go downstairs to face the basement. I stand at the top of the stairs with my heart pounding. The memory of last night flashes back, flitting across my brain, telling me there's danger, but the danger is gone and I have to look through all of the fallen bankers boxes that sit in a pile on the concrete. Would a normal person be doing this? I find that I ask myself that question a lot lately, but if I waited to feel safe, I'd never make a move. And if I waited for someone else to save me or offer answers to all these questions, or unearth the truth, I'd probably just go on waiting forever. No one is coming to save me. I have to save myself.

I prop a chair inside the door to the basement, paranoid it could close on me. I triple-check that it's secure, and then I make my way down. The police offered to board up the broken window until a replacement could be arranged later this week, and it's that kind of thing that makes me feel grateful to live in a small town. It's still freezing and damp and smells faintly of mildew at the bottom of the stairs, and I don't want to be down here, but why did this man rifle through our things? There has to be a reason. I hadn't been down here since last Christmas and even then it was only for exactly five minutes while I grabbed some storage containers of decorations. The only things here are old tools and boxes of photo albums, suitcases, Jack's golf clubs, boxes of receipts from home repairs and KitchenAid manuals—stuff like that. What in the world would anyone want? Maybe nothing. Maybe they were just lying in wait to try to kill me, but I go over and over that, and they would have done the job if that were the case, not panicked.

I pick up a few of the boxes and straighten up the contents. One is kids' craft supplies—pipe cleaners, cotton balls, markers. The next is stuff that should probably be in the locked file cabinet—tax stuff and expired passport and mortgage documents. The last box I pick up is heavy, too heavy for paperwork and fingerpaints. I peer in and see a safe box. The kind that feels like it's made of lead. It's only about twelve by fourteen inches, but it feels like it's over twenty pounds. It's solid as a brick and locked.

I have never seen this thing before in my life. And then it

hits me, stealing my breath when I put it together. The key I found in the glove compartment of Jack's truck. Holy shit. What if this is what it opens? I hold the safe in both hands and take the stairs up two at a time, breathless, shaking. I put the safe down on the kitchen counter and start to fish in my handbag for my keys. I examine the small brass key for a moment and then say a little prayer as I fit it into the lock.

Click. It opens. It fucking opens. My hand flies to my mouth involuntarily as I stare down at its contents, in anticipation, but when I register what I am looking at, it's not a gun or a million dollars or whatever the hell else I thought it might be. I didn't have enough time to really think about it, I guess. It's just an ID. A driver's license and social security card, actually, but it's not Jack's. It's just some guy's. A stranger's. Someone named Patrick Finch. Who the hell is Patrick . . . Oh, my God. I pick it up and stare. I stand up and place my hand on my chest to calm my racing heart. What am I looking at? It doesn't add up.

It's Jack's photo next to the name "Patrick Finch." A very, very young Jack on an ID that expired years ago. *What?* What does this mean?

I throw it back down on the counter and stare at the wall, my mind reeling, trying to understand. Then I go to the sofa where my laptop sits, and I google the name Patrick Finch. Lots of people come up, but none of them have Jack's face. There was no LinkedIn or social media to speak of that long ago, so if this man—Patrick Finch—vanished over twenty years ago, who the hell is Jack Hoffman? Who did I marry? And which one is dead?

I feel my phone vibrate in my pocket and I jump. Then I

take a deep breath and place both hands on the table for a moment. *Get a grip. Calm down. There is an explanation. There must be.* I look at my phone. It's a text from an unknown number with a local area code. I click it open and gasp when I read what it says.

Jack is dead. If you don't stop, you'll be next.

CHAPTER SEVENTEEN

Sasha

When Sasha comes to, she can't remember where she is for a moment. She blinks open her eyes and finds herself lying on a concrete basement floor. The air is smoky and heavy with the cloying scent of tobacco. She hears men's voices talking nearby. The searing pain of her broken pinky almost makes her cry out, but she bites her cheek and holds back terrified tears as she pushes herself to sit.

There are three men across the room, sitting on metal folding chairs at a card table. One is smoking a cigar and they seem to be arguing about something, but her head is spinning and she can't really put it all together—what's happened, what they would want with her.

"My son," she says in a hoarse whisper. The men look over, and one stands and comes over to her, peering down. She presses against the wall behind and shakily pushes herself up using the basement doorknob as leverage. She doesn't take her eyes off the man, calculating the distance—could she run up the stairs before he reached her? She's not bound or locked up. Why not?

"What are you doing here?" the man asks, standing directly in front of her, holding his cigar and blowing the smoke sideways, not moving toward her like he plans to attack, but she doesn't know what to expect. Her heart pounds. She grips the doorknob of the open basement door with one hand and the brick wall behind it with the other, feeling cornered and paralyzed with fear.

"My son," she repeats. "What do you want with him? Why was he here?" she asks, more desperate than ever to protect Drew. The man's expression changes into a smirk.

"The kid. That's what this is about. Jesus."

"We don't want nothin' with that kid, lady," one of the guys at the table says, but he's not even looking at Sasha. He's drinking a beer and focusing on the cards in front of him. She feels her phone buzzing in her pocket again and again.

"Is he in trouble? Does—does he owe you money or something? I'll pay. I can—"

"He already paid," the guy with the cigar says, smoke billowing out the sides of his chilling smile. "Stay out of it," he says, and Sasha feels a cold sweat forming beneath her coat and the broken bone in her finger throbbing and her head aching and she wants to be home and she hates that all of this is happening, but she can't possibly stay out of it. It's her son. He's been through enough. She won't let him ruin his life or get himself killed. Who the fuck are these people? What do they want?

"Told ya she wasn't police," another of the men says.

"Paid for what? Please. I need to know if he's in trouble. What do you—why was he here? What do you want from him?" Her phone buzzes in her pocket again—Tom worried sick about her, no doubt.

"Not a thing," the man with the cigar says, turning his back to her and walking over to the coffee table, where he sits with the other two beneath the swaying single lightbulb that hangs above it and casts dancing shadows around the basement. She cradles her hurt hand in the other and looks down at it completely confused, unsure what to do next.

"That was just a little warning, from me to you. You were never here. And if you forget you were never here and tell someone . . . well, that won't go well for you. Or Drew." When he says her son's name, Sasha feels a wave of nausea so strong, she actually cups her hand over her mouth, briefly thinking she could vomit. The pain, the confusion, the fear . . . it's all so overwhelming.

One of the men who has remained seated gets up as if he's suddenly annoyed and rushes to Sasha, who backs up and falls, catching herself on the stairs.

"823 River Ridge Lane."

"What?" she stutters.

"Are we clear?" the man says, slamming the door closed so she's sitting in the dark basement stairwell realizing they've let her go and are not, in fact, planning on killing her or breaking the rest of her bones. It was all a warning. She jolts to her feet and runs up the stairs and out the metal side door and just like that, she's outside. She's free. Her car is there. She scrambles, almost tripping over herself to open the car door, and once she's safe inside, she understands what has just happened. Not all of it. But 823 River Ridge Lane is her address. If she goes to the police, or even tells Drew or anyone, she supposes that means she's dead. Or worse, one of her children will be dead.

She screeches away from the empty parking lot and onto the main road, too numb to cry, glancing back in the rearview mirror at the nondescript smoke shop that has a secret identity. It's a front for something and she can't believe she can't figure out for what. She tries to think about what she will tell Tom. How did she break a finger? She looks at the clock and it's just after 5 p.m. Tom might not even have noticed she's been gone. He's in New York and was going to have a busy day. She looks at her phone and he hasn't called yet. Thank God. Just a text that says, love you, I'll call after the dinner rush.

There are five missed calls from Drew, and a voice mail. She calls him immediately, no answer. She listens to the voice mail. It's the school returning her message, explaining that Drew was suspended for punching another kid in the lunchroom, but there is no more detail, just the office school counselor's number to call back. She calls Drew again and he picks up.

"What's wrong?" Sasha says before he can speak. "Is Chloe okay? Did she take the bus? I was supposed to pick her up. I . . . Jesus." She remembers that she was also supposed to pick up Regan and go to the café. Shit.

"Dude, where've you been? She's fine. She called me to pick her up. She's right here. Jeez. But I've been calling all afternoon, though. What the hell?"

"Oh, thank God," she says, and even in this heightened state, she still has to put him in his place. "Don't call me *dude.* We've talked about this."

"Sorry," he mumbles.

"I just . . . I slammed my hand in the car door by accident and broke it. I had to go . . . to the hospital. I texted you to tell you to make sure she was picked up but there must have been no reception at the hospital—looks like it didn't go through. So you're all okay?"

"Dandy," he says.

"Put me on speaker," Sasha says. She can practically hear Drew rolling his eyes at this, but he does as he's told.

"Chlo, I'm so sorry."

"It's okay," she hears her daughter say, and she can tell by the squeaks and laugh track of some annoying teen sitcom that she's half distracted and probably over it already.

"Drew is gonna watch you tonight and you guys can order in Chinese," I say.

"K," she responds.

"Thanks for asking if I had plans," Drew says.

"I decide when you have plans. Use my Grubhub log-in and get what you guys want for dinner. I have one more thing to do and I'll be back late."

"Fine, but . . ."

She hangs up on him, relieved they're safe and uninterested in further conversation about his ruined plans to sit at Blanc's with Roxie when he'd probably really be off doing . . . God knows what. She can't even think about what he's involved in. What the hell could those men be taking money from him for? Drugs are the only thing that makes sense. And then she lets her mind go to other sinister places. Or maybe guns . . . or bombs.

She pulls into a Stop-N-Go to get bandages for her finger, a bottle of water and something to eat because she feels her stomach twisting in hunger and she needs energy to hold together all the parts of her crumbling life. She sits in the parking lot, under the glow of a single streetlamp in the otherwise empty gas station parking lot and sees the rain starting to fall again in the cone of light—a mist that seems to never end and only accentuates the fear and misery she feels. She takes a bite of a prepackaged egg salad sandwich and then puts it on the seat beside her and starts sobbing. She lets the tears come. She pounds the steering wheel with the heel of her hand and lets out a guttural scream. It's all too much.

Then she sits in the ear-ringing silence for a moment and starts the car and heads to go and see Raffy. It's time to get him involved, and maybe the police. If she only knew what Drew was involved in, she might know if involving them would mean helping to protect him or helping to indict him, but she doesn't know. She needs Raff's help on this. She needs him to pull himself together and be present for once, goddammit. It might be futile, but she has to try.

When she pulls up, she can already tell it will be a drunk visit and not a buzzed one, but that's to be expected. She has to catch him fairly early in the day for any hope of a semisober interaction, and even then the fog and hangover aren't really that much better to deal with. Now she can see Raff has fallen asleep in a camping chair next to the firepit and the rain has put out the fire, so he just sits with his head hanging back and his mouth open, getting poured on. It might be the saddest thing she's ever seen.

She sighs as she turns off the ignition, pulls her hood over her head and carefully guards her damaged hand as she opens the door and readies herself for this dreaded interaction.

"Raff, get up," she says, poking him in the shoulder.

"Huh?" He stirs and sits up slightly, squinting in the darkness to make out what he's looking at. "What the hell, Sash. Leave me alone."

"Get up. Fuck, Raff. It's raining on your face, for God's sake. Get inside. I need to talk to you."

"What happened to you?" he asks, looking at her hand. She would be pulling him up and forcing him inside if she were able, because she doesn't have all night, but thankfully, he starts to stand on unsteady feet and stumble toward the back door.

"Nothing. Don't worry about it," she says, following him inside. He flops on a chair at the kitchen table and rubs his eyes. She sees his head bob like he'll pass out at any given moment, so she gets to the point.

"Drew is in trouble. I know he hasn't visited you in a while and you're pissed about that, but have you talked to him at all? Has he said anything to you?" she asks. He lays his head on the table and groans.

"Raffy!" she yells, and he startles and sits back up.

"I don't know. God, Sash, how would I fucking know? I haven't seen him in weeks. Months, maybe," he says. He stands up and tries to walk toward the fridge—for a drink, she knows—but he stumbles and holds on to the table, waiting out a dizzy spell.

"Come on," she says, putting her good arm around his waist and getting him over to the sofa. She goes back to the fridge and twists off the cap to a Heineken and brings it to him. Enabling. That's the word Drew used, and it flits across her brain every time she does this. She can't help it. Even after all these years, she sees the man she used to know when she looks at him—the man who put his coat around her shoulders walking down a busy city sidewalk after dinners at Lucino's, the trips to sunny beaches, drinking from coconuts and planning their bright future, the happiness, the love, all of it. And then she thinks about how it was stolen from him—his freedom, his future, his dignity, his confidence, his whole life. She just hasn't been able to blame him or hate him for ruining them or crumbling under the weight of the trauma. She just can't.

She grabs a towel from the cabinet and sits next to him, pushing the wet hair back from his eyes and drying his face. She sees tears in his eyes that he blinks away, and she gives him a moment to get the alcohol back in his bloodstream before she explains what's happened. Then she tells him about the construction paper, the man he handed money to, the men at the smoke shop, his suspension. She doesn't tell him about her encounter with the men in the basement. That would be too much.

"He's smoking weed, Sash. Don't overreact. I mean, you just laid it out. Handing over money, a smoke shop, a fight at school. The construction paper thing seems like a giant leap, so I would just punish him like any other kid caught smoking weed. I think you're really going off the deep end here over nothing," he says, and on one hand she really wants him to be right, but on the other, she knows he's not. If it is drugs, it's way worse than weed; she knows that after what she just encountered.

She's not sure what she was expecting from Raffy. Maybe she just needed someone on her side. She doesn't want Tom to know. She wants Drew and Tom to be close and not for Drew to be a delinquent that Tom can never connect with. She doesn't want a pieced-together family. Shit. Coming here was useless. She knows every time she comes that she will leave with a stone on her chest and an emptiness in her gut, but each time, she just hopes so badly that something will be different. That she'll see the face of that man she used to know. Just one more time.

But now, Raffy starts to nod off, and the bottle in his hand spills onto his lap as his grip around it weakens. She takes the bottle and places it on the table and then gets up to leave.

She uses the front door on her way out but just before she opens it, she sees something on the bench next to the front door. Drew's new school backpack. Drew, who Raffy hasn't seen in months.

CHAPTER EIGHTEEN

Andi

"Do you know why I pulled you over?" the officer asks after I've handed him my license and insurance card. I know I'm ghostly white in the driver's seat of my car, and I'm wondering if I should run—wondering if I should just slam my foot on the gas before he can get to his car so I'd have a head start. I could just drive. I could go to Mexico. There has to be a way out. Fuck! I can't answer him because if I do, if I open my mouth, I might throw up, so I just shake my head and he gives me a puzzled look.

I'm sweating and I know the blood has drained from my face. I see it register in his expression that I don't look right. He looks past me at the passenger seat and then glances in the back.

"Can you step out of the car, please?" he asks. I could die. I don't respond. I can't. I don't know what to do. "Ma'am.

Are you okay?" he asks, opening the door for me. I nod and then I slowly unclick my seat belt and step out of the car and stand, leaning against it to hold myself up because if I don't, I'm afraid I might actually faint. My head is buzzing and light and I'm swallowing down waves of nausea.

"Fine," I choke out. And then I'm so overcome with terror and adrenaline that I can't hold it in any longer and I lean over and retch. I vomit so violently that it covers the officer's boots before he can move out of the way.

"Jesus," he says. "Have you been drinking?" He steps back and leans a hand against the hatchback of my vehicle only inches away from where Tia's body lies. I don't say anything for a moment.

"Are you intoxicated, ma'am?" he asks again.

"No, I—I have the flu," I say, but he looks at me with skepticism. He looks at my license and then back at me.

"You live at least twenty miles that way," he says, nodding back the way I came. "Where are you going tonight if you're that sick?"

"I was going to the . . . Halloween Superstore near Walton. For my kids. It just sort of came on suddenly," I say, shaking so badly, I have to keep my hands in my pockets so he can't see.

"Get back in the vehicle while I run your license, please." He waits for me to get in and close the door before he walks back to his car, the windshield wipers squeaking and the misty rain sparkling in his headlights. I wonder if this is the last moment I'll ever know freedom. I look up at the moon trying to peek through the clouds and I listen to the treetops rustling in the wind and I ache. This is it. This is my last moment before I'm locked away forever. I think again about screeching away and trying to outrun him, but there's nowhere to run.

After a few minutes, he returns and hands my ID back. Then he steps back from my car door.

"Exit the vehicle please," he says, and I surrender. I step out. He takes a small flashlight and shines it in my eyes. Then asks me to walk ten steps in a straight line. He points in the direction for me to take and I realize that this is a field sobriety test. Of course it is. I puked on his shoes. I take the ten steps and then he directs me to take ten steps back toward him, so I do. He asks me to move my head side to side while keeping my eyes fixed straight ahead and I do. He looks slightly surprised that I appear sober.

Then, to my shock, he tears a ticket off the pad on his clipboard and hands it to me.

"If you get your taillight fixed in the next seven days, you can get this dismissed. There's a website to go to for that," he says. I stare at him. I think my mouth is hanging open.

"I . . . can go?" I ask.

"I'd suggest going home and getting in bed, not shopping and giving everyone the flu, but yeah. Have a good night." And then he disappears in the glare of his headlights and his car door slams closed and he drives away.

I almost fall to my knees in the wet grass next to my car when he's gone. My nerve endings are buzzing with electricity, and my knees are weak and it's all I can do to keep myself standing and fall into the warmth of my running car and stare out the front window in a stunned silence for a few minutes. I don't move. I can't think. How am I even free? The disbelief and revelation of it paralyzes me.

I listen to the drizzle tap the hood of my car and wait. Wait to make sure he's not coming back maybe, or to get the courage up to finish what I started. But after several minutes have gone by, I realize I haven't seen a car pass. A cold wind has picked up and nobody is out on these wet roads, so I just have to do it.

Thick sugar maples and white oak line the two-lane road for miles and even though I can't see the river from my window, I know it's only a few yards through the trees to my right, so I make my move. I pull as far into the clearing between the trees as I'm able, then turn off my car and lights and wait again in the silence. There won't be a better time. I click my hatch and hear the hiss of the hydraulics as it opens. Then I pull my hood over my head, jump out and peer into the back of my car, and there's Tia's wrapped body. Every time I see it, there is the same jolt of panic and shame, but I have to hurry now. I can't sit with it or second-guess.

Pulling her out is proving much easier than lifting her up into the car, which was a nightmare. I grab onto the band of duct tape at her feet and she falls easily from the trunk onto the ground with a crack that makes me want to sob.

"I'm so sorry. I'm so fucking sorry," I mumble to her again as I pull her through the rotting leaves and underbrush. I hadn't thought about the marks the weight of her body would leave through the mud and I'll have to cover it on the way back, which sets my mind reeling. Twigs snap under my feet and the cold bites even through my coat as I pull and try to keep my grip on the slippery tarp, straining and heaving the weight of her. I have to stop and catch my breath a couple of times. Even though it's a short distance, it's so much harder than I thought, but I'm fueled by fear and adrenaline and so I push through the pain in my back and my burning lungs until I meet the water's edge.

Then I stand with my heart pounding. The rain drums on the treetop canopy and rinses my face and Tia just lies there, impossibly lifeless and still. God help me for what I'm about to do. I pull a couple of rocks loose from the mud—they're the size of footballs maybe, and I push one under the folds in the tarp. Then a second and a third. I'm praying the extra weight helps. And then I do it. I close my eyes and I push her body into the rushing water and when I open them, I see her sink gently as the powerful current washes downstream.

And then I fucking run. I run as the rain picks up; it's already covering over the drag marks her body made and I'm so grateful for this I could cry. I run, ducking branches and pulling the weight of my heavy rain boots. I try not to let out the scream that is crawling up my throat and I force myself to keep running, gasping for breath and aching until I reach my car and I pull away as fast as I possibly can and drive home, breathless, tears blurring my vision and my lungs blazing. I don't look back.

When I pull into the garage, I see Carson standing in the door frame leading from the garage to the kitchen. He's waiting for me, which makes my heart speed up. He looks behind him and then closes the door and stands on the concrete step waiting for me to park. When I do, he slips into the passenger seat and it's so unexpected I just stutter over my words. I can't run or clean up all of the mud and smeared makeup. I just look at him.

"What?" is all I manage. "What's wrong?" because I first assume something has happened with the kids maybe.

"What's wrong?" he repeats, looking me up and down. "What the fuck, Andi? Tell me what's going on. What did you do?" he asks with a look in his eye that I've never seen from him before—a mix of concern and . . . disgust.

"Regan called me, checking on you because you weren't

picking up. She wasn't even the one who told me about your breakdown in the town square parking lot. What the hell? I was calling you. I . . ." He stops as if seeing the state of me for the first time. It's not just the mascara under my eyes and my boots and clothes covered in mud. My wet hair is also flattened to my head; my eyes are swollen from crying. I'm pale as a ghost. He pushes himself against the passenger door, backing up to look me up and down.

"Jesus Christ. What's happened?"

"Oh, God," I say, and I am not built for this. The tears just come. I never meant for all of this to happen. I don't know how to hide it. I sob into his coat. I couldn't tell him because he'd have forced me to tell the police and he wouldn't understand all the reasons I could never do that. But how am I supposed to carry this alone? Maybe it's time I tell someone. He pulls my shoulders back gently and looks me in the eye.

"Have you done something, Andi?"

I look back at him, but I can't speak.

"Tell me."

CHAPTER NINETEEN

Regan

Is it a warning or a threat? Jack is dead. If you don't stop, you'll be next. It's all I can think about since I woke up this morning. Sasha messaged me last night apologizing for standing me up—said she broke her hand in the car door and had her son pick up Chloe and just blanked on our plans. So she's picked up Hallie and is doing the early school drop for me out of guilt, and I'll take it because I need to get to the Bluebird Café.

I drive on the interstate toward Windsor Locks and the words echo in my mind. *Jack is dead.* But maybe Patrick Finch is alive. I don't know what I expect to find at the café, probably nothing, if I'm honest, but whoever frequents the place and looks exactly like my husband exists somewhere and I want goddamn answers.

When I arrive, I find the café on a charming historic cobblestone street lined with restored old buildings housing restaurants and specialty shop storefronts. The rain has cleared but it's still overcast and chilly, and I welcome the warmth of the Bluebird Café after parking and walking the few blocks in the biting wind to find it.

Inside, the scent of roasting coffee beans greets me, and the shop is buzzing with patrons and baristas carrying fancy coffee drinks with heart shapes drawn into cappuccino foam and overpriced biscotti and pound cakes. I'm not sure what I expected. I suppose after talking to Beatrice, not something quite so refined. But there she is. Same purple crochet hat she was wearing in her profile photo, minus the ferret. I stand by the pastry case and wave to her, and she must also recognize me from my small thumbnail photo, because her eyes widen and she places a slice of lemon pie on the counter. Then she taps the young woman next to her, who's wearing an apron and ringing people up, and says something, nodding at the pie and excusing herself.

"Oh, my God, it's you. He's not here. I've been keeping an eye out all morning." I feel my heart drop at this but of course it's what I expected. If he's running from me, why would he come back here when someone outed his real name and started asking questions? I feel a rush of emotion but do not allow myself to cry.

"Did you see him on a train somewhere?" she asks, dreamy-eyed.

"What?" I snap, because I did, in fact, chase him down at a train station and found him here because of the train schedule. But how does she know that?

"Like in those movies where you lock eyes just before the

doors close but you didn't get his information, just his name, and now he's gone forever and you're searching for him. It could be the start to any Hallmark Christmas movie, right?"

"No, I . . ." I don't know how to respond, and her interest, although innocent, catches me off guard.

"Oh, God. No. You're a private investigator and you're trying to catch him cheating maybe. Oh, I hope it's not that. Apple Turnover seems real nice," she says, retying her apron and looking over her shoulder at the line forming. Apple Turnover, I remember, is what she called him before finding out his real name and scaring him off.

"What should I do if I see him again? Citizen's arrest?" she asks, and I might burst out laughing at this if I wasn't so grief-stricken and confused about it all.

"No. He's— It's none of that. He's just—he's missing and . . . Please just message me if you see him. I'm just very concerned is all." It's the closest thing to the truth I can offer. I don't want this woman getting herself even more involved.

"Oh, no!" she gasps, looking again at the long line. "I gotta get back, but I'll keep my eye out. You pick out anything you like," she says, gesturing to the pastry case and pouring a mug of coffee. "It's on me, poor thing." She places the coffee in front of me. I smile and thank her and then spot a couple getting up from a coveted two-top next to the front window, so I wait for them to leave, then slip into the chair facing the door just before any of the other handful of people eyeing it can beat me to it.

And then I wait. He always comes between eight and nine, she said, but not since she asked his name. It seems pretty hopeless, but I'm still shaking and anxious . . . and praying he'll walk through the doors. Even though I would hate him and want to kill him, quite honestly. I would still do anything to see him again no matter what he's done or what he's running from. But when eight o'clock turns into eight thirty, nine, nine thirty, ten fifteen, I start to feel the weight of how pathetic this all is. Jack is dead. I'm a fool.

By noon, Beatrice gives me a sympathetic look from behind the busy counter, and I pull on my coat and walk out into the frigid October air. I take my time, looking at the quaint storefront window displays—an antiques store with bits and bobs arranged on a nest of autumn leaves for the season and an old wagon in front turned flower planter; some café tables under awnings with checkered tablecloths in front of an Italian restaurant, which are all empty due to the cold; a nail salon with a handful of women sitting for pedicures, drinking small plastic cups of prosecco. All things that would have brought me joy, back when I was still alive.

I blink away tears and make my way back to my car. I remind myself to breathe. *Shutter Island* comes to mind. Maybe I've created an imaginary world. Dissociative Identity Disorder. The real world is so frightening that my brain has decided to create a place where Jack is still alive and we could be together—a family again. It's created hope where none exists. Is that possible? Could I be that disconnected from myself?

I think of Sasha and Andi and their encouragement. That was real. Are they placating me? Should I even tell them that I came? Andi has enough problems and probably isn't one to be judgy at the moment. Sasha will mask her concern with a supportive comment but probably secretly thinks I've lost the plot. Maybe I have.

I click my key fob and my car beeps and unlocks as I slip inside Jack's Suburban to drive home. But as I shift the car into

Reverse and look into the rearview mirror, I stop cold. I slam the brakes on and the car lurches. I stare into the rearview mirror with both hands cupped over my mouth.

I can't understand what I'm looking at. It's so surreal, there is a moment I feel like I have floated away from my body and I'm looking at myself from a distance—dissociating, yes. That has to be it, because the shock of it can't be comprehended by my mind . . . I almost jump out of the car and start running, but I don't. I stare, stars exploding behind my eyes, my head light and my heart thumping. Then I scream. It's all my body allows me to do. I just scream at the man sitting in the back seat of my car. *His* car.

Jack is sitting behind me. He seems to be moving in slow motion as he shushes me and tries to shield himself from my hands, which are involuntarily swiping at him, throwing blows. Beating on his shoulders until I can barely breathe. I just continue to scream.

"No!"

"Regan, please. We have to drive. Just . . ."

"How? Who are you? I . . . No!" I don't stop. I'm too traumatized, horrified, but then he halts my wrists inside the strong hands I was never supposed to feel again and looks me in the eye.

"I know, sweetheart. But just please drive and I'll tell you everything, okay? Please. It's not safe here."

CHAPTER TWENTY

Sasha

She waits until morning. Tom will be back in town midday and Chloe can take the bus today, and Sasha can watch her son pretend to get ready for school, but this time she has a plan. She tells him not to be late and that she has a coffee date with Regan in town, and then she waits. She tosses his backpack, which he apparently doesn't miss enough to mention or to go back to his dad's to get, into her passenger seat, and then she goes out to the toolshed in the back of the property and takes a small pistol out of the lockbox under the workbench. She shoves it into the bottom of her handbag, then pulls out of the drive and parks a few blocks down, masked by a thicket of trees, until she sees Drew's car fly past her and she follows.

She grips the steering wheel with one hand, fury boiling inside her, and she stays a few car lengths behind him and starts to realize where he is going. So it's no surprise when he pulls into the parking lot of the same smoke shop she thought she would take her last breath in just the night before, but she still radiates with fear as she pulls in behind him. She screeches her brakes on and slides into the gravel lot, and she gets his attention. Just as Drew steps out of his car parked near the front door, he freezes as he looks at her. He doesn't seem to know whether to run or get back in his car and speed away. He's caught.

"Jesus," he says with a mixture of confusion and anger across his face. "What are you doing here?"

Sasha steps out and starts to walk toward him.

"No. Mom, stop. Let's go."

"Don't even think about . . ."

"You can't be here. There's a diner down the street. I'll meet you . . ."

"Are you out of your mind? You don't call the shots anymore, Drew. You're in deep shit. Get in."

"Mom," he says, looking back at the doors and then to her. "Go. Now. I'm right behind you." He jumps in his car and starts to pull away, then stops and watches to make sure she does the same. That little shit just drove away. She can't believe it, but although she's shocked, she does what he tells her, with her heart racing and hands trembling as she fumbles with the car door.

When she sees him pull into Murray's Diner and go inside, she parks and follows him, so completely bewildered by his behavior but also ready to finally confront all the evidence she's been collecting against him. She decides maybe a public place will be the best option since he can't make a scene or run away. To her surprise, he's sitting in a booth with a pensive look on his face when she gets in the door. He looks out the window and behind him with obvious paranoia. She sits across from him, and they don't speak for a moment. She can't even figure out where to begin—all the facts are swirling in her mind.

Instead of words, she just plunks his backpack on the table. He stares at it but doesn't put it together right away.

"You left it at your dad's."

"I can explain that," he says too quickly. The waitress comes over. Her name tag reads *Kimmi* and her chipperness is incongruous to the weight of whatever is happening, although Sasha still doesn't know what that is. Drew orders two cups of coffee while Sasha sits in a dazed silence.

"You've been seeing your dad. But I don't even think that's the place to start since you've been lying about so many things, so you tell me where to start."

"I thought he could help me with something. Roxie and I—we're working on a research project, sort of, and I had questions . . ."

"Stop. Start from the beginning. You were not getting concert tickets that night, and you weren't getting vapes at the smoke shop. How much trouble are you in? Just tell me what is going on."

"Mom . . ."

"You're caught. I've been following you. I know you're suspended. I know where you've been going. I wanted to see if I could understand it—I don't know—to try to help you, but you have to tell me what the fuck is happening," she says. She's never sworn in front of her kids before, so she instinctively covers her mouth as if pushing the words back in, but Drew doesn't even seem to notice. He has a look of resignation across his face because he is, clearly, caught.

"I can't tell you everything," he starts, and then the waitress places their coffee in front of them and asks if they'd like anything else. Neither answers and the waitress makes a face and walks away.

"I'm not in trouble," he says.

"What were you doing at the smoke shop today? I've already met the gentlemen who run whatever is going on out of the basement, so just tell me the truth." Drew blinks at her. His eyes move from her broken hand back to her face and she can tell he registers it. Something like protective rage mixed with fear flits across his face.

"They find people—find . . . things. They run a sort of business like a private investigator, except they don't worry about stuff like laws—an 'any means necessary' type thing. I paid them to get me some information. You're right. I wasn't buying concert tickets when you saw me at that closed-down Hefty's. Some guys I know hack computers and you can pay them for info . . . but they couldn't help me. Probably because you have to know what you're looking for if you want them to do much . . . and so I thought I'd get further with those guys at the smoke shop."

"What are you looking for?" she asks flatly, trying to stay in control.

"Ally Whitlock. The car bomb. It started there. I saw something that day and I didn't tell because I'm still not sure what it means."

"What? What did you see?" she asks impatiently, cupping her mug with both hands.

"Do you think it could have been meant for you? The explosion?" he asks. She leans back and takes in his question.

"What would make you say that?" She feels like the wind was knocked out of her with the question, so out of left field.

"You both drive white BMWs, and were at the same place. I mean, did it even cross your mind? You're the one with the criminal history. Not Ally or Regan Hoffman. You never even thought that once?"

Sasha holds her heart with one hand and has to remind herself to breathe. How does he know this? She spent her whole life making absolute certain he never found out—never knew about Raffy in prison or their arrest. How the hell has he unpicked all of this?

"Criminal record?" she says, thinking, for a fleeting moment, that maybe he's just being dramatic and doesn't really know.

"Jesus, Mom. You're the one who's caught. It's all out on the table. I'm not the one hiding from something and lying. You smuggled drugs on a plane in Mexico—both of you—and Dad went to prison."

"How do you know this?"

"I found the records, and then I visited Dad because I didn't think I'd get the truth from you. He told me everything."

"Well," she says, feeling the red blotches bloom across her chest, "that was a long time ago . . . and your dad pays for it every single day."

"But did you pay for it?"

"What?" she snaps. "What the hell does that mean?"

"Exactly what it sounds like. I know you didn't do it on purpose, but from the perspective of those drug dealers, it sounds like they think you owe them. Maybe someone is making you pay. I've been trying to protect you—both of you. Some shit's just not adding up, though."

Sasha feels pricks of heat climb her back, and her throat closes up. She doesn't know how to respond.

Drew continues. "Dad told me that he was threatened by someone—an anonymous person—when he got out of prison. They were gonna get rid of both of you unless you paid back the money they lost on the confiscated cocaine—like almost three hundred thousand dollars."

"No. No, that's not true. He paid his debt in prison time. That's . . ."

"Why would these people care if he went to prison? He lost their money. Prison does them no good, does it?" She knows this is probably true, but she's just so shocked at the words coming out of his mouth she can't quite make all the pieces fit—she can't understand how he knows this much, more than her, and now she's wondering if she was a target. Drew was supposed to be the one in trouble. How has this flipped so incredibly?

"He said he's been paying this anonymous person for years. Wired money every month to some untraceable account. Then, a few years back, he stopped. He expected someone to come for him, but he said he didn't care if he died anymore so it was fine. But nobody ever came." Drew runs his hands through his hair and pours another cup of coffee from the pot on the table.

"Nobody came because he lives in a fantasy world. He's delusional sometimes. He probably got things mixed up in his head—it was over a long time ago."

"He showed me all of the outgoing transfers. Years' worth." At this, Sasha feels like she can't breathe. She takes a deliberate deep breath and looks up at the ceiling, trying to absorb what all this means.

"He would have told me that—he would have asked for help and I could have helped him," she says. "No."

"How would you have explained to Tom that you needed a few hundred grand? How could you help Dad?"

"Goddammit. What does this have to do with anything—with you being suspended, the school bomb threat? I don't . . ."

"I think all of it ties together. What I'm telling you isn't even really the point. It's just how all of this started. Once I found out about your arrests and all that, I started doing more digging. One thing kept leading to another. Tia, the car explosion, Dad . . . It's all linked. I just can't prove it yet. But I have a pretty good idea."

"Tia? I just—I don't understand what you're telling me. How is that possible?"

"I have to show you. Me and Rox keep all of it in her desk in her room. Her mom never goes in there, and since you come in mine all the time, we thought it was the safest thing. We have most of the evidence—a lot of proof that there is one person behind it all—but we're still missing something. And it would make things worse if I started making accusations before we had all the proof. You think anyone would listen when the weird new kid starts saying something about some crazy conspiracy? I'm trying to protect you. Us. But the only way I know how is to figure out how it's all linked. I'm close."

"Show me," Sasha says firmly.

"I have to text Rox. I messaged her this morning to fake sick and get out of school and meet me at Dad's, so she might already be on the way."

"Why? What were you going there for?"

"I told you. I have to show you. I'll have to message her and tell her to meet me at her house instead."

"Do it," Sasha says, pulling on her coat and waving to get the waitress's attention.

"You really think we're in danger?" she asks him, looking right into his eyes—feeling maternal and protective and also so confused and in the dark as he is somehow leading the way and knows more than anyone else, it turns out.

"Yes," Drew responds. "And I don't think we have much time."

CHAPTER TWENTY-ONE

Andi

I didn't tell him. I almost let it all come pouring out—all of the lying and hiding. I almost blurted out what I had just done, dropping the body of a poor, innocent person into a river. I wanted to tell him that I'm a fucking monster and should be locked up and he should take me to the station immediately to confess and get it all over with, but I didn't. Something stopped me. Something deep inside would not let me do it even though the words were forming in my mouth and were so close to spilling over and putting all of this to an end.

Instead, I told him how I felt so responsible, so guilty, that I had that big argument with Tia the night she disappeared, and how she would have maybe never gone out to run off steam if that hadn't happened. I told him that I was being petty and should have let it go, but I pushed it and now she's missing, hurt or dead, and I couldn't take it—I couldn't handle what it was doing to Ray and the kids, too. So I went out looking for her. That's where I said I'd been. I freaked out—the weight of it was all too much—and so I just went out to the woods and tried to find her in a blind panic for hours.

I told Carson that was why I was wet and muddy with mascara running down my face. He bought it—pitied me, even. He ran me a hot bath and put on a kettle for tea and had Roxie take my car up to Zato's to pick up Thai food for dinner and got the kids to bed, and I'm a horrible absolute wretch of a person.

I lay awake until close to 2 a.m. second-guessing myself—coming close a few times to waking up Carson and telling him the truth, but by two thirty I took a Xanax to sleep and shut out all the noise and chaos, and now it's almost nine thirty in the morning. Carson let me sleep and took the kids to school. I don't deserve him.

He went into the office and the house is silent and lonely and I almost can't take the deafening quiet right now. I pull on a fleece bathrobe and turn up the thermostat a bit before I make my way downstairs to put on the coffee. I almost gasp when I see my reflection in a glass-framed wall hanging. The dark circles and ghostly complexion look shocking. My eyes are swollen from crying and sleep deprivation. I can't be seen like this. Before I can push Start on the coffeemaker, there's a knock on the front door. No. Fuck. Who could be here? Maybe the company that's hauling away the freezer? Or the police? I think I have a fifty-fifty chance of getting rid of evidence or being hauled off to prison in the next five seconds, but when I open the door, it's Ray.

His face is red, and he chokes on a sob as he stands trembling in the doorway.

"Oh, God, Andi."

"What? What's wrong?"

"I didn't know where else to go. I don't know what to do. God!" He falls into me and wraps his arms around me, crying into my neck, and I freeze for just a moment but then I return the embrace and pat the back of his head, saying "It's okay," over and over again because that's what you do in this situation even when you don't know what the hell is going on. Finally, I place my hands on his shoulders and back away from him slightly so I can look at his face.

"What, Ray? What is going on? Talk to me."

"She . . . They found her body in the river. She's dead!"

"What? What!" I snap. How could that have happened so fast? How was I so fucking stupid?

"Turn on the news," he says, walking over to the sofa and picking up the remote. "I had to go down there this morning. It was still dark and there were lights and police tape. God. I can't . . ." He chokes on his words as he says this. "Some dog walker saw her in the rocks. I was warned the news would exploit it the first chance they got." He turns on the TV and flips through channels until he finds the news. I sit at the edge of the coffee table, my heart in my throat. There's a commercial on, so Ray sits on the sofa and cradles his head in his hands while he waits for the coverage to resume.

"Why! Who could do this?" he cries.

"I don't know—are you sure that . . ."

Then he shushes me as the news comes back on and there it is. Tia's face on the screen in a photo Ray gave them to use in the search. She's wearing a T-shirt and hiking boots on one of their trips to the bougie cabin in the mountains they stay in each spring. The reporter gives the overview.

"We're continuing our coverage on a story we have been following for days now. The body of a missing woman, twenty-eight-year-old Tia Hainsley, was found early this morning washed up on the bank of the Connecticut River about twenty miles south of her home in Cloverhill Lakes."

I stand numbly and go and sit next to Ray. We both stare, wide-eyed and still as the reporter continues.

"There are still a lot of questions to be answered about the circumstances, but all we can say now is there was certainly foul play involved. Hainsley suffered multiple wounds to the back of the head, police say likely bludgeoned with a blunt object. Although she was found in the water, drowning was not the cause of death, and there are no suspects in custody as of yet. More on this as it develops."

"What?" I say under my breath, picking out the word *bludgeoned.* She was shot. How are they not saying she was shot? Before either of us can speak, Ray's phone rings. I see Detective Morrison's name pop up on the screen and he answers immediately. He walks into the kitchen to take the call. I only hear a series of "Okay, uh-huh. I don't know. Okay." Then he hangs up.

"I gotta go," he says, wiping his tears on his sleeve.

"Ray, wait. What did they tell you? She was . . . They said she was beaten?"

"Yes." He hangs his head. "I had to identify her." He hugs me again, as if to steady himself from falling or fainting. I hold his weight.

"It's okay," I mumble. "I'm so sorry. They're sure?"

"What do you mean?" he asks, pulling away and looking at me.

"Well, that seems . . ." I think of all the murder shows I've watched in my life and come up with a reason to bring this up. "It seems so personal. If a stranger robbed her or something,

I would think maybe she'd—I'm just saying, they're sure she wasn't shot? Maybe hit her head to cause those injuries?" He blinks at me, not comprehending why I'm asking this, because it probably is wildly inappropriate. But there is no way she didn't die of a gunshot wound.

"I saw her. The whole back of her head was . . ." He stops. He can't speak the words. "There was no gunshot, no sexual assault. She didn't drown. That's what I was told. I already went through all this with them. Why would someone do this? She wasn't even robbed—wasn't raped. So why? What would be a reason?"

"I don't . . ." I stand with my mouth hanging open, unable to even complete my sentence. He moves to the door before he starts sobbing again. I can tell he's trying very hard to hold it together.

"I have to go. I'm sorry. Don't tell the kids yet—that's all I really wanted to . . ." He swallows the last word and then he rushes out the door. I close it behind him and turn around, leaning my back against it, then slide to sit on the floor. I stare down the front hallway and my mind reels, trying to understand what the fuck is really happening here.

Is this a trap? is the first thing I think—do they know and I'm being set up or something? Tia was shot. I shot her. Oh, my God. What if it's possible? What if someone killed her and left her on the edge of our property and I assumed . . . Oh, God. It was dark. I just saw blood on her face. I'd just shot a gun in her direction. There was no other scenario to consider in the moment. But now the reality of the situation is surfacing in my mind. I wrapped her up in the dark. I never saw the gunshot wound, but I never doubted for a second what must have happened.

I jump up with a racing heart. I need to get the facts firsthand. I need to talk to the detective and know for absolutely sure this is all true. It wasn't me. It wasn't my fault. I just can't absorb this—it just can't be possible. I grab my handbag and coat and go to look for my keys, but they're not in their spot by the door. I check my pockets, purse, drawers, and then I remember Roxie took my car to get food last night and maybe left the keys with her stuff, so I take the stairs two at a time and go into her room, which I don't often do, so it feels a bit like a violation of her privacy, but I need those keys.

I dig around in a couple of drawers and then see them on top of her writing desk. As I move to grab them, I see a paper sticking out the top of a school folder with Drew's name on it. The words I see stop me in my tracks. In Roxie's handwriting, the words *Who killed Tia?* are scrawled across the page. I didn't think my hands could possibly shake any more than they already were, but then I shakily pick up the folder, sit in her desk chair and look inside.

There are pages and pages of handwritten notes and printed articles, and a photo of Regan's dead husband. There are stories about Rafael "Raffy" Carro and a Mexican prison sentence. Who the hell is that? I look at his photo and then stuff it back inside with the papers. There is research on car bombs—and then I see something that makes my heart stop.

I call Roxie, but it goes to voice mail. Probably because she's in class. So I call the school and they tell me she's ill and was signed out. My heart starts to race. I text her to call me—that it's urgent. Then I sit down at her desk and look at her computer. It only takes the touch of the space bar to wake up the sleeping screen, and she stays logged in to all her usual sites, so I see a tab for Facebook and look at her recent chats.

Drew was the last person to send a message, early this morning. Meet me at my dad's today. She responds, what time? and he says, by ten. She gives a thumbs-up. Who the fuck is Drew's dad? I scroll up to see older messages, but it looks as though they purposefully don't communicate over apps. It's all mostly cryptic. A lot of call me instead of conversations in writing. What the hell is she up to?

Drew's dad. I think a minute. His last name is Carro. Sasha took Blanc when she got married, but I never once thought about who his dad was. I assumed he was dead. In fact, I think I asked once and that's what Tom said, or maybe I'm making that up in my head and have no idea. Drew's dad? Shit. Rafael "Raffy" *Carro*. I just read the name. Oh, my God.

I try Roxie again, nothing. I try Sasha. Will she tell me if her ex is this Raffy guy? Does she know what the kids are mixed up in? She doesn't answer. Then I call Regan and fuck if she doesn't answer, either. I text her the photo of Jack and tell her I need to talk to her. I send the other photos of a man, Dominic, whom Jack testified against. I need to get Regan's attention so she calls me back. Where is everyone? I'm starting to panic. I need to ask her why my daughter would know anything about Jack and be researching his whereabouts. It's like the rapture came and everyone has ascended or something.

Roxie and Drew are obviously in whatever this is together and that's what they've been up to—all the whispering and hanging out at the BBQ place till all hours. Nobody is answering, so I grab my car keys, taking the whole folder with me and rushing to my car. I decide I'll just drive to Sasha's house because she's usually home during the day, and I pray.

Adrenaline surges through me as I make the short drive to

her house. There is evidence pointing to one person being responsible for both the car bomb and Tia's murder. There is a long string of facts that all tie together somehow, but I can't tell exactly what it means. But something is very, very wrong. Everything has turned upside down in minutes.

When I pull into Sasha's drive, I don't see her car. I peek into the garage, but it's too dark inside to tell if she's here. I knock on the door and wait. Nothing. Then I walk around to the side door of the garage and squint again to see if there's a car inside. There could be, but I don't know, so I holler anyway. She should be here this time of day. I know her normal schedule.

"Sasha! You gotta be home. I have to show you something. It's important."

Then the side door of the garage swings open, and I jump and hold my heart, startled. I drop the folder in my hand and the papers go all over the floor.

"Oh, sorry. I thought . . ." I stutter, taking a moment to put together who I'm looking at, because it's not who I expected. And then I realize what's happening; the man's face looking back at me is one I recognize. I watch him glance down at the scattered papers and something like fear registers on his face.

"I was just looking for Sasha," I say, taking a step back, not understanding for a moment or two that he has seen something that points the finger at him. He has put together that he is a suspect in these pages strewn across the concrete garage floor, and the only reason for him to react the way he does . . . is if he's guilty.

I freeze, wondering if I should kneel down and collect them or back out the door, or say something. I'm suspended in terror when I see the flash in his eyes, but by then it's too late. He comes at me so fast, I don't even have time to scream. Before I can even think about running, he has his hands around my neck. He shoves me back against the wall of the garage so hard a box of tools falls from a shelf and makes a shocking crash, and it all happens so fast. He's pushing his thumbs into my trachea, and I can't breathe. I can't fight because I don't have the oxygen to move. And in an instant, it's all over and the world goes dark.

CHAPTER TWENTY-TWO

Regan

I drive almost a mile but it's all a blur. Tears and rage . . . and fear fuel me to keep going, to just drive—it's all I can do not to collapse in horror or beat him until my fists are bloody. I just numbly drive until I reach a place to pull off—a scenic lookout where there's a stone bench that overlooks the river valley, a wooden railing along the edge. It's off a two-lane, tree-lined road that doesn't see much traffic, and the pull-off is partially covered by trees, so I take advantage of the privacy to stop and get out of the car, walking over to the railing and trying to catch my breath.

Jack follows. He gives me a moment and doesn't try to touch me, probably in fear I might actually push him over the edge in a fit of fury. He stands next to me as we look over the treetops below. The conflicting emotions and confusion rushing through me are dizzying and I don't know where to even start.

"I know you're . . ." he starts, but I cut him off.

"Don't say you know what I think or what I feel or what I'm going through."

"Okay," he says softly.

"What are we running from? What's so dangerous? Who are you, even? Is your real name fucking Patrick Finch? You're not Jack, you're not dead. So . . . what? Where do I even begin to understand what's happening?"

He comes closer and I push him back with both hands as hard as I can.

"Fuck you!" I scream. "Fuck you."

"I deserve all of that. I know I do. Do you want me to explain? Please, Reg, I'm so sorry it all came to this, but . . ."

"You better start fucking explaining," I say, and it's all so absurd and bizarre that I feel like more should be said between seeing my dead husband and getting right into whatever list of reasons he had for abandoning us. Like I should be allowed months to absorb the fact that he's even here before I have to ready myself for some excuse and find myself driving recklessly, fleeing from what, I don't even know—it's just all too goddamn much. I sit on the bench and bury my head in my hands. I'm desperate to know all of the details of how we've come to this moment, but I'm also terrified and know life is about to change. Again. And I have no control over any of it.

"I was Patrick Finch a long time ago." He sits down next to me. I look at him. The kind, familiar eyes, the wool coat, the nervous blinking. He's the same man I know with the exception of three scars on his face I have never seen before. It's Jack. It's like he never left. I feel sick with anger or grief or something I can't even name. I try to swallow it all down and listen.

"My job took me to Mexico a lot then, before I met you, when my financial consulting was focused on opening some high-end resorts in Costa Maya. I saw something I shouldn't. Some guys were running drugs and using a resort as a home base . . . Americans, some organized crime ring, but small. A family who made money smuggling all kinds of shit across the border. I was in the wrong place at the wrong time and witnessed these guys in one of the resorts—it was still being built and it was supposed to be empty, and I went in one night to check on construction progress because they were behind schedule . . . and . . . anyway. They were . . . punishing some guy who didn't pay them for something, I don't know what, but I'll spare you the details. The guy died is all you need to know, and I witnessed what ruthless criminals these guys were—and they saw me."

He stops his story, and I find that I'm leaning in with both hands over my mouth in a surprising flutter of hope that maybe there is an actual explanation for his disappearance, and also confusion—wondering what this has to do with right now, with the danger he says we're in.

"Okay," is all I can think to say to fill the pause.

"I escaped. I reported it before they could get to me—I got one of them arrested and the other two got away. They have so many fake names and aliases and enough money to flee, so it was impossible to find them. The guy who was caught was a pretty dangerous fucking guy. When I came back home to New York, the police encouraged witness protection, but I decided since I didn't have family and I wanted out of the company I was with anyway, I would just change my name and social—they helped with that, and I moved away. It wasn't a protective program like witness protection would have been, but it seemed like enough. And for a long time, it was. I was Jack Hoffman from Cloverhill Lakes for over a decade. We met and had a family and I thought it was all behind me for a long, long time."

"What changed?" I ask, rapt by this story, which I can't believe I didn't know any of before this moment.

"They found me. I don't know how. When I went to Colombia a couple years ago to do a consultation for a start-up, they must have tracked me. I was walking from the pub to my hotel."

"I remember," I say, tears springing to my eyes, because we were talking on the phone on this walk—the last time I ever spoke to him.

"I was pulled into an alley. I don't want to tell you the details, Reg. If you knew the details, you might understand why I couldn't come back and put you and Hallie in danger, but I can't tell you. It's too grotesque. There was no reason for them to come after you if I was dead, so I decided to be dead."

"What does that mean?" I say, aching for all that's happened to him, for all the things that are too unspeakable to even utter. The scars on his face tell a story of their own.

"I was left to die, but some woman stepping out the back of a bakery for a cigarette saw me and I was taken to a hospital. If they thought I died, you were safe. It was over. There would be no more revenge to seek. I had to. I'm so sorry, I know it's unimaginable, but if you knew what they were capable of . . . It was the only way I could see through," he says.

I stand, taking a deep breath and holding it in my cheeks, looking up at the sky and putting it all together in my mind.

"But your body was sent from Colombia by a US consular officer," I say. And although we were told his face had been beaten and was unrecognizable, so I didn't actually see him, you trust the government when they fly your husband's body overseas and tell you it's him, for God's sake.

"There are people you can pay a lot of money to who can erase you. Stand in for US consulars, offer a new identity, make you disappear and have it look real."

"Legally?" I ask.

"No," he says, and I sit back down again, holding my heart and trying to decide if I can accept this. How am I supposed to absorb all this and process it?

"You left your daughter," I say, shaking my head.

"I don't know how else to tell you that I did it to protect you both. I wasn't eligible for witness protection anymore because there was no proof this was anything but a robbery gone wrong. But I saw the guy's face. I know who it was and I know what danger you would be in the rest of your life if you remained attached to me. I didn't expect to live, Reg, I really didn't, but once I got out of the hospital, I knew what I had to do."

"Then why are you here now? Wait. You sent me a message saying 'if you don't stop, you'll be next.' That was you. What the fuck?"

"There was a short time I still thought maybe they didn't know I was alive and you'd be okay. I was trying to keep you safe. That's all I've ever wanted. Do you know how hard it was to leave you and Hallie? Do you have any idea what it took to do that?" He blinks back tears.

"I heard about the car bombing," he says. "I moved to a town not too far away so I could keep an eye on you, or at least try to. When I figured out the bomb was meant for you, I panicked. I knew that was the end. I started to make plans, but I needed to check on you and Hallie. I came to town so many times, just keeping watch until I could get new papers and IDs in the works, but you saw me. I tried to be careful. I took the train under a different name. I never carried a phone or used the computer. I stayed off grid as much as possible. I never wanted you to have to leave your town, your parents, your friends, and I'm so sorry you ever had to be involved. I'm sorry I had to be involved. Jesus. But they know who you are now and they're after you."

I sit on the bench and lean over my knees, trying not to lose my breath. My head feels light like I could pass out and my hands are tingling. I can't think.

"You don't have to come with me, but I worry the police don't know how to protect you—they aren't really a match for this level of organization, this kind of evil. I just . . . I don't know if they'll take it seriously enough until it's too late. It's hard to prove what happened to me was them. My word should be enough, and maybe they'll help, but serious protection is weeks or months of red tape and paperwork, and we don't have that time."

There is a moment that cuts through all of the urgency and terror of everything I've just been told, and I look at him and realize that he didn't leave us—that he's here, he's alive and he didn't abandon us, and I fling my arms around his neck and hold him, taking in his smell and weeping for all of the stolen time and the grief and loss and just let myself be here with him, without red-hot anger running through me, because I understand now. He holds me back as tightly as he can, but I don't know if I can follow him.

"Maybe it took them years, but they still found you after you paid someone a ton of money to erase you, so they could find you again. They could find all of us, even if we run."

"Yes. But they already have, so what choice is there now?"

How can I leave my family forever? How can I live a life on the run for something someone else did, potentially traumatizing Hallie even more? But how can I not?

"I have a place we can go," he says, and I trust him, so we get into the car and drive.

CHAPTER TWENTY-THREE

Sasha

Roxie is standing on her front porch, crying, when Sasha and Drew arrive. Drew jumps out of the car immediately and rushes to her.

"Rox, what happened? My mom will tell the school there was an emergency if you got busted," Sasha hears him say as she approaches them.

"It *is* an emergency. My mom's gone," Roxie says, shivering and hugging herself inside her hoodie, against the biting wind. She turns around and goes inside, and Sasha and Drew follow. Roxie starts pacing, talking a mile a minute. Sasha thinks about how bizarre Andi's been acting and immediately knows this can't be good.

"She tried calling me and then texted me to call her, and I did, but she didn't answer, so I didn't worry about it at first. She's always at the VA on Wednesday mornings, so I thought it would be safe to come meet you here, but . . . then I realized our folder's gone."

"Oh," Drew says, sitting down on the armchair behind him. "Shit."

"What?" Sasha snaps.

"There's just a lot of . . . everything in there. All our work. Evidence," Drew says.

"My Facebook is open on my computer . . . my last conversation with you that says to meet you at your dad's is up on the screen," Roxie says. "She probably figured out who your dad is from all the papers in the folder. But she wouldn't know where he lived, and even if she did and she was driving there or something, she'd answer my call. I don't know what she'd do when she saw all of this—if she'd go to the smoke shop or any of the other people we investigated for answers—but if she did, she could be in trouble . . . and it's our fault."

"Maybe she found it and went to the police," Sasha says, but then she pulls out her own phone and sees missed calls from Andi, and a chill runs through her.

"I called the police," Roxie says. "I told them I couldn't reach her. She didn't call them or go in, and they told me I have to wait to see if she turns up at least till later today until they'll worry about it or take a report."

"Let's not panic," Sasha says. "The folder's gone. You can't show it to me, so tell me. What the hell did you find that's so scary? You need to explain everything. Now."

Roxie sits on the sofa and buries her head in her hands. Drew looks to her and then back to Sasha. After a moment, he sighs and nods. Then he starts explaining.

"Dad came to the Labor Day cookout thing. When the car blew up. I saw him."

"What?" Sasha snaps. As far as she knows, Raff hasn't left his house in a few years. He's not capable of getting around. He turned agoraphobic, she assumed, or was too lost in his addiction to make any attempt at a life outside of that prison he created for himself.

"He was parked down the hill, and I went and talked to him. I was shocked to see him there. Roxie was with me," he says.

Sasha's mouth is hanging open. She slowly sits on the edge of the coffee table and stares at her son, listening intently.

"He was drunk," Roxie adds, as if the detail was necessary.

"Some guy he knows drove him, and he got out of the car and was crying, saying he'd do anything to get you back. I didn't let him go up to the party. I told him to go home."

"What?" Sasha repeats in a whisper to herself, because this is so hard to imagine from Raff that she doesn't know what else to say.

"I thought he meant *get you back*—you know . . . romantically, but then after the bomb, I thought he meant revenge. That's why I asked you if you thought it was meant for you. He was so blasted that day—like more than usual. Maybe he got some drug from the meth head–looking guy with him, I don't know, but I thought, what if it was him that did it and he got the wrong car?"

"He would never do that," Sasha mutters, but then Drew's question from earlier buzzes in her ears. *Did you pay for it?* After all this time, is Raffy harboring hatred for her because he did prison time and she went and got remarried and still has a life? No. That just can't be.

"The friend was some drunk he met in AA. Ironic," Roxie pipes in. Sasha looks to her, wondering how in the world this teenage girl knows more about her husband than she does. It's impossible they should know any of this.

"Dad was hollering and falling over, and the rando guy helped me get him back into the car and said something to us like, 'This is how you treat him after all he's been through? He did his time, leave him be,' or something like that and I didn't know what that meant, so . . . then I looked him up. I googled Dad's name. I never thought about researching him before for any reason, but then it all came out, so we went out to his house. I felt sorry for him—for what had happened to him. It finally made sense that he is the way he is, and I felt bad."

Sasha holds her heart and tries to understand Raff's behavior. He would do anything to get her back? She's there at his house helping him all the time and he's never said anything like that. It's like an unspoken pact they've made—to never talk about the past. She wonders why he would act like that—leave the house, have a meltdown.

And it's like Drew read her mind, because he says, "Like I said, he was on something—that guy he was with was a total tweaker. Dad told me half the people he knows in AA do drugs instead. I think that's why he was losing his shit and also why I wondered if he was capable of the bomb thing. 'Cause he wasn't himself."

Sasha remembers the construction paper she found, shaped like a bomb. "The school threat," she says, looking between Drew and Roxie.

"That was me," Roxie says, "but it wasn't a threat. It was a diversion."

Sasha stands and walks a few feet away, looking out the window for a moment, in disbelief at how deep these two are in—bomb threats, withholding evidence.

"You both thought creating more fear and chaos was gonna stop people from worrying about the car bomb? That it would change the investigation?" she asks, because even though that seems like it could be teenage logic, these kids are smart and embedded in this. That seems risky and kind of stupid.

"No," Drew says. "It was just to throw the scent off a bit. We thought it might help if they had another thread to pull that led nowhere. I don't know. We figured it might take longer to put it all together, and we needed time."

"To help your father? That's what this is about?"

"Mom, he's broken. He's not in his right mind. I thought I could protect him for a little while—just until we could figure it out. He couldn't go back to prison. Can you imagine? I figured he just didn't know what he was doing, so we came up with a plan." Drew sits down next to Roxie.

"And it kinda worked," Roxie says. "People stopped talking about the Labor Day bomb and thought about their kids—the school thing is all they talked about. Still is. And then we went to work."

"For a short time . . . and then everything became about Tia, but that still gave us more time," Drew says.

"How has it gone this far?" Sasha asks, stunned, trying to absorb it all.

"I had to do something. I mean, if you saw the pair of them—Dad and this guy, I don't even know his name—there's no way they were capable of tying their shoes, let alone building a car bomb."

Sasha turns from the window and looks at both of them.

"You know you've broken the law? You know all these theories and ideas may be nothing and you're in deep shit? Andi might be . . ." Just then Sasha's phone rings and they all leap. Roxie stands expectantly, and Sasha looks at her screen. Then she shakes her head, indicating that it's not Andi. It's Raffy. She picks up.

"Hello?" There is no voice on the other end. "Hello?" she says again. Then the line goes dead. What the hell was that? She pushes the phone into her pocket without telling the kids who it was.

"It wasn't her," she says, then looks to Drew. "How did it get this out of hand? Why didn't you say anything?"

"I thought you might be in on it," he says, and the words steal her breath.

"What?"

"We started to go see Dad, to hang out there, help out a little. We totally decided he wasn't involved, but we were determined to find out the truth now anyway. I asked him not to tell you I was seeing him. I guess he felt like that was one of the few things he could do for me, so he kept his word. I wanted time. Then Roxie found something."

"It's in the folder," she says.

"I wanted to show you. I know this is when I should have gone to the police, but, Mom, I thought I was protecting you."

"What? What did you find?" Sasha asks, her heart in her throat.

"In the firepit in his yard—we'd hang out there sometimes. A few days ago, I saw a scrap of cloth. Orange with a tiny kangaroo on it. I said it looked like Tia's running headband she got in Australia, and then I realized . . . it *was*. It was a piece of it. The edges of what was left were burned," Roxie says.

"Jesus," Sasha whispers to herself, unable to think, unable

to process how Raffy could have Tia's headband. There has to be an explanation.

"But when we decided we needed to turn it in, I finally put together who that guy was in the photo you had in your bag. I thought it was an odd thing to have when I saw it, so I took it," Drew says, and Sasha remembers watching him take the photo of Jack and thinking he was the one in trouble, never considering for a second it was some crazy attempt to protect *her.*

"We figured out it was Jack, Regan's husband, who's supposed to be dead, so we looked up his photo and reverse-image searched it, and we learned who he really was. Do you know Jack wasn't his real name? And did you know he testified and put away some big drug dealer in Mexico at the same time Dad was there? It's all connected," he says, then taps something into his phone. He turns around a photo to show her. "It's even more connected than you think," he adds.

Sasha looks at the face in the photo and all the threads start to unravel. She feels so instantly lightheaded and numb as she tries to make sense of it that she thinks she could pass out. She steadies herself with one hand on the arm of the chair next to her.

"Stay here," she says suddenly, reaching for her bag and heading toward the front door. "Tom is in New York, and the kids are in school till three. Is Carson at work?"

Roxie nods vigorously.

"Wait for the police. I'll be back."

"Mom!" Drew hollers after her.

"Lock the door, and don't answer it for anyone. Do not even think about leaving this house. I mean it. Got it?"

"Mom."

"Drew. Do you hear me?"

"Yes, but . . ."

And then she rushes out the door and jumps in her car and screeches away to race to Raffy's house before the world implodes around them both.

CHAPTER TWENTY-FOUR

Andi

When I open my eyes, I don't know where I am. My throat feels like it's on fire and when I try to open my mouth to cry out, I can feel that it's sealed closed. That's the first thing I notice—the tape on my mouth and how hard it is to breathe through my nose. I immediately recognize that if I start crying right now, I will probably suffocate myself. I force myself not to cry. Where the fuck am I?

My hands are zip-tied and the zip tie is connected to something. I squint in the dark space and see that there's a nylon rope connecting the tie around my hands to the metal leg of a workbench. My feet are chained together but not bound to anything else. Breathe. Breathe. Oh, my God. I can't scream; I can't run. I can't even start sobbing. I have to somehow work out a way to stay calm.

Don't panic. Panic gets you killed. And . . . he didn't kill me. If he didn't kill me already, he probably doesn't want to have to do that. It's the only thing that makes sense. That means there's hope. I try to channel all the years of yoga and find an inner calm that will help me stay grounded enough to think—to not panic. Losing my mind right now will not get me out of this. I'm in a small space and it's mostly dark, but there is a rectangle of light coming in from the gap around the door, so I can see in the hazy light just enough to work out that I'm in some kind of shed.

It's similar to the toolshed on our property. There's a work surface cluttered with dusty tools, empty gas cans on the floor underneath it. The wall behind the work surface has dozens of tools hanging from nails—they were probably neatly organized at one point, but now only a handsaw, some wrenches and a level are hanging up, and the rest of the tools are scattered around the floor and table. There has to be something here I can use. If I slide the rope that's connecting my hands to the workbench leg up, I can stand, even if only partially. The leg stops at hip level, so I'm hunched over, but it's enough to get my head above the tabletop and look around.

My heart pounds so hard it almost hurts and the adrenaline is surging through me. I can't control the shaking, but my mind is focused on getting out. There's a clarity that takes over when it feels like life or death, and I'm scanning the small space for anything that can help me. I see a box of wooden matches just out of reach on the table, and my heart leaps a little. If I can get to it, I might have some hope.

I see a few rusty nails sticking out of the wood at the edge of the workbench and they're close enough that I can just reach them. Tears spring to my eyes as I formulate a plan to get myself free. I try to slow down and breathe. I lean my face against the nail, right where the tape adheres to the side of my cheek, and I try to catch the edge of the tape on the nail. I use the nail to pick at the side of the tape until it starts to strip away from my skin, in small threads at first. Finally, I'm able to get enough of the tape caught on the nail, to carefully move my head from left to right and peel the entire piece of tape off. I suck in a deep breath, my throat still on fire from his hands around my neck, trying to choke out my life.

Then I look around to see how I can get the matches. If there is any way to reach them, I have a plan. Just below my chin on the workbench is a Phillips screwdriver. I bite the handle and pick it up with my mouth, trying to catch the side of it on the matchbox and pull it toward me. I groan as I accidentally push it farther away. I drop the screwdriver. "Fuck." I get it in the right position in my mouth and stretch my neck out as far as I can, then I try again. This time I feel the tip touch the small cardboard box and I scoop it toward me, inching it ever so slightly so I don't lose my grip. Once it falls to the floor, I practically scream with relief. I can get out of here. This has to work.

I sit back down on the floor where the matches dropped. I can use my hands since only my wrists are bound, though there is limited mobility. But I'm able to open the matches, light one, and if I bend my finger down in just the right way, I can get the flame under the nylon rope. I drop the first two matches because it's too hard to contort my hand and hold it there long enough, but on the third try, I steady my shaking hand and hold the match in the right spot to start melting the nylon rope. I can smell chemicals from the cheap material burning my nose—like a mixture of burning hair and plastic. I want to turn my face away from the smoke, but I can't take my eyes off that match, which is burning down to my fingertips quickly.

It takes four more dropped matches until I light one more and get it into position and then finally, mercifully, the rope breaks where I've melted it. Now the only thing left binding my hands is the zip ties. But with my feet bound, I can't climb high enough to get to the spot across the room where I see an X-Acto knife stuck into the cardboard of a turned-over box, like someone stopped opening a package halfway through and left it there. What I can reach is a hammer—I saw one on top of the workbench.

I get up again, but I'm not tied to the leg of the workbench anymore, so I can stand up fully and I can reach out both of my bound hands and pick up the hammer, albeit awkwardly. When I sit on the floor again, I don't think about whether he'll hear me and come out. I can't worry about that because there's no other choice. At least now I have a hammer and if he does appear in the doorway, he won't expect me to have a weapon, and I might get a swing in. So I take the chance.

I pound the length of chain between my ankles with the hammer against the concrete slab the shed is built on and I swing and swing, gasping for breath because it's more exhausting than I thought it could be. At first, I think it won't work because it seems like it's not even making a dent, but then suddenly, one of the links flings off, ricocheting off the slab.

I can't believe it. I can't fucking believe it. I spring to my feet. They're free. I rush to the knife and pull it out of the box. I can't hold it and also cut the zip tie, so I sit down on the box, hold the knife, blade up, between my boots, and thank God I pulled on rain boots instead of wearing my slippers when I flew out the door earlier. I hold the knife tight, then place my wrists in front of it, the blade rubbing back and forth in a sawing motion on the tie until very quickly, it snaps off and I'm totally free. I cup my mouth over my hand. I'm free. Okay. Now, where am I?

I go to the gap in the door frame and peer out. I have no earthly idea where this place is. It looks like just about every other plot of land in the tri-state area. Tree-covered, brush, rural. I see the house and I don't recognize it, then I see a man. The man from the file of papers. Rafael Carro. I watch him walk out the back door of the house. He rubs his eyes as if he just woke up. Then he stumbles over to a chair by the firepit. He looks at the roaring fire in the pit with confusion on his face. What is going on? Why am I here?

All of a sudden, I hear shouting from the house, not clear enough to tell who's yelling or what they're saying. Raffy seems startled by this—and confused, even. Scared, I think. But he pushes himself up and walks toward the house, and then I can't see him anymore. I try to tie all the threads of what I know together. I wish I'd taken more time to look at that file. I looked at it long enough to know some bad shit was going on and I needed more explanation, but not long enough to know how the hell I got here. Someone must know what I've done. Is this revenge?

The sound of a truck engine revving startles me. It's loud and it backfires like a shotgun. Then I hear the truck screech out of the dirt driveway and pull away, and in a matter of seconds, everything is silent. I don't know if I'm alone, but now's my chance to run. When I push the door open to take my shot, I realized it's locked from the outside. I'm trapped.

CHAPTER TWENTY-FIVE

Regan

We take the back roads all the way to the house. I have to pull over and let Jack drive, because I'm trembling too hard to even grip the steering wheel. Everything in the world has been flipped upside down and somehow, I'm supposed to comprehend all of it and make life-altering decisions immediately. I can't. I don't know what to do yet.

"There's a motel thirty miles out of town that takes cash—sort of off the grid. It's a shithole, but it's a good place to stay under the radar until you decide what you want. Of course it's your decision, but I also don't know how I can let you stay—now that they know I'm alive—now that we know you're a target."

"What about Hallie? Is she safer at my parents' for now or should she come right away? Jesus. How do I take everything she knows away from her? Her grandparents, friends, her whole life. How do I explain that? How do we just disappear and let my parents think her daughter and grandchild are dead? It's so absurd—it's . . . How does someone do that?" I ask, swallowing down the tears, my mind spinning as the ramifications start to sink in.

"Because their lives depend on it."

"What if we all band together?" I say, desperate. "We tell my family and we all protect each other—we . . . I don't know . . ." Then I think about the night of the Labor Day party and how my car burst into millions of pieces with Ally inside and how bits of her flesh were found blocks away from the explosion. I think about how it was supposed to be me.

"These people don't usually miss. The fact that some act of God happened and Ally Whitlock, who's never driven your car before, randomly had reason to need it, it's astounding you're here. Either of us. If you'd seen the things I've seen . . ." He stops, leans his head back and blows out a hard breath. "The police are afraid of them. It doesn't matter anyway, because they'll do whatever they want right under the cops' noses. They have such a network of protection, they're not afraid to do it. Kids aren't immune to the danger. These guys don't care who they hurt."

"That can't be true. Hal is just an innocent kid who doesn't know anything about any of this. Why would they . . . This is a fucking nightmare," I say, and I wish I didn't know any of it. I wish I could go back in time and pretend none of this was happening. I suppose maybe knowing is saving my life, but it's all too much to bear.

"Two hours later and it would have been you and Hallie in that car, not Ally Whitlock." I don't have words to respond to this. It's true. And it's not Jack's fault all of this is happening. It's his nightmare, too.

"They wouldn't want you if they had me. Sometimes I think about just surrendering to it all. Since I found out they knew where you were, I've thought about it—that I should just give myself up. If it means you two are safe, maybe it's the only thing left to do."

"No!" I practically scream. "Jesus. No."

I hold my spinning head in my hands and bury it in my lap and just try to breathe. Mafia. That's the word that keeps swirling in my mind. An organized crime ring that I'm caught up in because of something my husband saw by mistake a decade ago. It can't be real. Running and hiding and looking over our shoulders for the rest of our lives—leaving my family, traumatizing my kid even more. This can't be real life.

When we pull into the driveway of our house, Jack stays in the car to keep watch and I go inside to grab as much stuff as I can—Hallie's clothes and favorite things, an overnight bag for myself and the important documents I keep in the safe. I have an eerie feeling like I'm being watched. I move, sobbing, from room to room, shaking, feeling like I did as a kid when I truly feared a monster in the shadows at the ready to reach out and grab me at any moment. But the house was locked and the security cameras are clear.

I pause when I step outside onto the porch with my bags. I look into the thick of trees on either side and down the narrow road in front of the house, but nobody comes out to capture us. Jack jogs up and takes a couple of the bags for me. We push all of it into the hatchback and then we start to drive.

We have a couple of hours before school is out and we

have to decide what the safest thing to do is with Hallie, so we decide to drive out to dinner away from town.

"They won't kill us in broad daylight in front of a crowded restaurant," I say, and Jack glances sideways at me—a look that says "if you say so."

"They shouldn't be looking for us there," is all he says instead, and so we again take the long back roads into the drizzly rural outskirts, and I pray quietly to myself, still not shaking the feeling I'm being . . . followed. Maybe it's paranoia, but ever since we were at the house, I feel like eyes are on me. Could someone have been lying there in wait?

I get a notification on my phone and look at it, but I don't understand it.

"What's wrong?" he asks.

"It's Carson. He said Andi is gone. Nobody can find her. He's home with Roxie and Drew—you know, her daughter, and Drew, Sasha's kid, and they think something's happened to her."

"Who's Sasha?" he asks, and it dawns on me I have this whole life he doesn't know about. Even though it feels like no time has passed, a lifetime has gone by.

"You don't think her missing could have to do with what's happening here? Whoever is after us?"

"You told me everyone thinks she killed Tia and now Tia shows up dead. Town's too small for all of this to be a coincidence."

I think about everything he's told me—all of the timeline and details—and one thing keeps coming back to mind, standing out against the rest of the shocking story.

"That guy—the one you testified against. He's still in prison, you said."

"Yes."

"So this isn't like you owe someone money. It's personal. His family is the one after you for putting this guy away."

"He said on the stand, in front of God and everyone, he wouldn't rest until I was dead. Personal is an understatement. Why?" Jack says.

"The photo. He just looks familiar. Of course I don't know him, don't recognize his name, but . . ." I am scrolling through my social media, looking for a photo from last year's annual Christmas party. Then I turn the phone around and show him. "He looks a little like a friend of mine."

Jack glances over and his face goes white as a ghost. He screeches on the brakes and pulls over.

"Where did you . . . Jesus. How do you . . ." But he's distracted by something in the rearview mirror. He stops midsentence and starts to drive again, but I can see now that he's trembling.

"We're being followed," he says.

"What?"

"A pickup truck."

"How do you know that? Maybe they're just—"

But he interrupts me. "You know that man in the photo? The guy I put away— That's his brother. Part of the family that wants us dead. Regan. My God." He runs his hand through his hair. "That's his fucking brother and you know him? How? God!" he scoffs.

"They moved in a few months ago. To town."

"I don't understand," he says, and then suddenly a deafening pop pierces the air and I realize that it's gunshots. This is really happening.

"Get down!" Jack yells, pushing on my head and speeding

up. I clutch my chest and duck my head down, shaking so uncontrollably I can barely breathe.

Another shot is fired, and I hear the explosion of one of the tires being struck and the clanging of the car bouncing and crashing on the pavement, the smell of burning rubber in the air. Then the screech of metal on the road as our car skids out of control and is forced to stop.

Jack jumps out and tells me to run, but we're in a rural spot, parked in a gravel pull-off with only a stretch of field and prairie grass for several yards before the cluster of trees in the distance. We're targets. I'm too afraid to run. I freeze, but then he yells again for me to run, and he points to the other side of the street at the ravine that leads down to a creek thick with trees, but before I can even make my first step, I see a hooded figure running at us like in every nightmare I've ever had. It's almost happening in slow motion. I leap out of the car, looking for Jack. I see him turn to look behind us and then within seconds the man in the hooded jacket is there. He holds out his arm, aiming right at Jack, and shoots.

He strikes Jack in the chest, and Jack drops to the ground. The man is running back to the truck, and then I hear the engine rev as the tires skid on the gravel before it flies off down the road, kicking up debris, disappearing behind a cloud of dust before it's gone. It's all so fast it feels like a hazy dream as I look down at Jack's body and see the blood blooming through his pale T-shirt. He's motionless.

"No! God, no!" I drop to my knees and scream until my lungs give out.

CHAPTER TWENTY-SIX

Sasha

When Sasha pulls onto Raffy's property, she already knows something is very wrong, because the truck that's sat unused for years in the overgrown grass behind the house is covered in mud, and fresh muddy tracks lead from the main road and up the dirt drive to where it's parked. Raffy had his license taken away years ago after a few DUIs and he also never goes anywhere.

She doesn't believe that he could harm anyone. She knows him too deeply. She also doesn't believe that he has the mental capacity to plan and execute murder, and why would he anyway? He doesn't know Tia or Regan, or the woman who tragically died in the car explosion that was likely meant for Regan. What possible motive could he have? How is he connected to any of this?

She stands next to the car for a moment after she parks

in her usual spot and gets out. There's a fire fading out in the firepit, but no Raffy sitting next to it. She doesn't hear anything. What is she even hoping to gain out of this? The truth, she supposes, before the cops, before investigations, dig up their past. She needs him to put all of the pieces of this mystery together. She needs to be sure he's innocent before she decides what her next move is—why has he been seeing Drew without telling her? She knows why Drew did it, but why didn't Raffy tell her when she pleaded with him, telling him Drew was in trouble?

The headband in the firepit. He has to have an explanation. She'll never believe he has an evil bone in his body, no matter what anyone tells her. Raffy is the love of her life. She can't be that out of touch with reality that she never saw the signs of a psychopath. She closes her eyes and takes in a deep breath and then walks up to the front door to confront him. She prays he's not passed out drunk.

The door is locked, which is unusual, but she has a key, so she lets herself in. When she enters, the house is dark and quiet. It has the familiar smell of alcohol and urine she's used to, but something feels different. She can't put her finger on what, so she stands completely still in the kitchen and just listens.

"Raff?"

Nothing. Where could he possibly be? Her heart rate quickens, and she knows something is very wrong. She calls for him again.

"Raff, where are you?" When there is still no answer, she can't help thinking maybe he's drunk himself to death and/or that there's a medical emergency. She moves quickly from the living room to the small three-season porch at the back of the house, but she stops cold when she sees Raffy sitting there in an old armchair, just staring up at her, wide-eyed, not moving or speaking. He looks possessed, and she's immediately terrified and confused all at once.

"Please leave," Raff says with a flat tone. His eyes are bloodshot and look wet with tears.

"What?" she says, stunned and utterly baffled.

"Sash, please. I'm begging you," he says, looking over his shoulder and then back to her. "Go. Get out of here."

"Raff. What have you done?" she says. He hangs his head.

"None of it's what you think. You have to go. Sash, please, God. You . . ."

"Why, Raffy? What's happened?" Then they both hear a bang. It sounds like the side screen door closing. "Who's here?" She looks at Raff. His eyes are desperate and pleading.

"I met the man who's been blackmailing me for money—the man who set us up at the airport all those years ago. He's back . . . and I think he's gone to a lot of trouble to frame me for Tia's and Andi's deaths."

"Andi? Where is she?" she says instinctively, but as his words sink in, she knows it's too late. She hears footsteps down the hallway and then a figure appears in the door frame. He has a gun in his hand, and he looks shocked and panicked to see her.

"Tom?" Sasha says, and for a moment she's completely perplexed, her mind working to connect all the dots and understand how he is here. Why? And then she sees the crumpled look on his face and watches it drain of color, and she knows in that moment that it's him. It finally sets in. It's been him all along, and her showing up here was not a part of his plan. She looks to Raffy, understanding now that he was warning her, and for the first time notices that he is tied to the chair he's sitting in, which is why he hasn't moved.

"Fuck," Tom says. And then he screams it. "Fuck!"

Sasha doesn't speak. She can't. She just stands there, numb, and stares at Tom, who's shaking his head and pacing, mumbling to himself.

"This was never what I wanted," he says, and she just doesn't understand.

"I don't . . . I . . . Why are you here?" she asks.

"Sasha, snap out of it," Raffy says. "Your husband is the one who put me in prison. The whole family's involved. The barbecue place is a front. The father runs the whole . . ."

"Shut up!" Tom yells, hitting Raff in the side of the head with the butt of his gun—a blow so hard, Raffy moans in pain, and Sasha sees a trickle of blood run down his temple. She screams and takes a step back, still staring, indescribably shocked. Al. Tom's dad. Runs an organized crime ring. It's laughable. There's no way this is real.

"You . . . sent Raff to prison. You were there in Mexico. I didn't even know you then. That's not possible. This is all a mistake."

"It wasn't him that day," Raff says. "It was some cousin or someone who works for them. But it was his doing. All of this is."

"I said shut the fuck up!" Tom screams, raising his gun again.

But Sasha screams louder. "No! Please!"

And Tom backs off. He sits down in a folding chair resting against the wall and seethes. He's caught and he doesn't know what to do, clearly. He didn't expect her to ruin his plans, and now what?

"Tom. This doesn't add up. Please tell me what's happening." He looks at her with defeat in his eyes.

"Why did you have to come here? Goddammit." Suddenly, he points the gun at her, and she holds her hands up and backs up a few steps.

"Tom," she says, fear surging through her body.

"I never wanted to kill you. I saved you, even. I was supposed to kill you years ago and I fought for you." He keeps the gun pointed at her and nods his head for her to move in the direction he's pointing. She backs up and looks behind her.

"Go," he says, and she obeys. She moves down the hall into the bathroom and he comes in behind her and closes the door. When she can't back up anymore, she sits on the edge of the bathtub in stunned silence for a moment. He kneels next to her.

"I never wanted this to happen. I love you, Sasha. You have to believe that. When Raffy stopped making payments to the family, I was assigned to get rid of both of you. But I met you and . . . fuck. Sasha, you . . . It's not my fault I was born into a family of fucking monsters. I never wanted to be part of it. I did fall in love with you when I met you. I did. You have to believe me," he says, pleading, and she simply nods because she wants him to continue and also because she's so astonished, she couldn't even form words if she wanted to.

"I wanted out. I begged to get out. I refused to hurt you, and I paid the family Raffy's debt without them knowing so they wouldn't send someone else to do the job. All I ever tried to do was protect you and Chloe. That's all." When she hears her daughter's name, the state of silent shock turns into rage, and she feels her blood boil. She starts to absorb everything that's happening and knows she needs to escape no matter what it takes. And the words "Raffy's debt" add fuel to her fire, as if he owes them even more. He was set up and did time and they still think the money lost when the drugs got confiscated is something we owe them.

The outrage stirs inside her, but she's smart enough to arrange a look of empathy or compassion across her face—at least, she tries to mask her fury in hopes that appearing on his side might be what saves her.

"So the debt was paid and we got married. Then how has all this happened?" she asks, her voice shaking.

"I bargained with them to get out of the family business. I told you I never wanted any part of it. I was trying to do the right thing. I wanted to be a father—a normal guy. Run the restaurant, be done with all the rest of it—and they said they'd let me if I took care of one last job."

"What job?" she says, impassively.

"It's not important—it just all went wrong. My brother is doing time because of Jack Hoffman."

"But he's dead," Sasha says, scanning the room for anything she might be able to grab to use as a weapon, but she can't find anything of use.

"The family found out he wasn't dead, but they couldn't find him, so they figured if I got rid of Regan, that would punish him. We moved to Cloverhill Lakes so I could find a clean way to do the job. It went wrong. I was never cut out for this. It's never been what I wanted. I'm only telling you all of this because you're here. Because you're in the middle of it now, and the only way out is if you can understand. I did what I had to for us—to get away from the business without getting killed myself. I had no choice. I don't want to hurt you, Sash. Please. If you can understand why I had to do all this, we can still get out. Together," he says. He's holding her knees as he sits on the bathroom floor in front of her, begging her.

Sasha's mouth is dry. She remembers how she recognized Jack when Regan showed her that photo the first time. Once there was a photo up on Tom's computer with all sorts of data, background check–type information, and she jokingly asked him if he was a PI in his spare time. He brushed it off saying it was just a guy applying for a job at the restaurant, but he had a criminal record. She remembers it because of the quick, nervous way Tom clicked off the screen and got up to do something else. What did she tell herself about that behavior—has she been willfully blind about other things like that, other small oddities that should have added up in her mind?

Then she thinks about Tia and still isn't putting all the pieces together yet. She swallows and stutters over her words.

"And . . . T-Tia?" she asks.

"She was a full-time snoop. I'm telling you, Sasha, I'm never left with any choice. I didn't want anything to do with her. She came to the restaurant that night in her jogging outfit and she was trying to flirt with me. I didn't reciprocate and she said something about all men being cheaters and how she'd prove it. I went and got her order from the back and a couple minutes later, I found her at the counter, looking through my phone I left sitting there. I guess it hadn't timed out yet and the screen was still open, so she just fucking snatched it like some entitled whore—she found some things she shouldn't have. She ran out without the bag of food. I had to follow. And it just made sense to leave her at Andi's—she was terrible to Tia. And they both deserve what they got. Tia could have ruined our lives. Do you get that?" he says. And then he puts his head in Sasha's lap, pathetically, and her mind is spinning.

He killed Tia and let everyone speculate that it was Andi, and all the while he's been taking advantage of Raffy's altered state. He's known about Raff, where he lives, blackmailing him for money all this time. He probably planted evidence like the headband in the firepit. Raff has a record, he's unstable, he's easily manipulated. Tom could have gotten away with all of it if I hadn't shown up. Nobody would believe Raff, so there would be no reason to kill him, but Andi?

"You dumped her there. At Andi's. To set her up," Sasha says, putting all the pieces together, numb, terrified.

"Do you understand, Sash? Do you see that my hand was forced in all of this and I was just protecting us—protecting you?"

"Yes. Of course," she says, because she wants to live, and if leaving with him and pretending is the only way, then that's her strategy.

Bang. The silence is pierced with a repeated crash like metal striking metal and then the sound of a woman's cry.

"Help!" and the banging continues. Sasha knows that voice; it's Andi. Tom leaps to his feet with a ghostly look on his face. He rushes out of the bathroom and, before she can follow, swiftly locks her in. She hears him shoving a chair under the doorknob and then the pad of his footsteps running out the back door.

The cry comes again, from somewhere outside on the property. Sasha knows it's Andi, but she can't help her.

CHAPTER TWENTY-SEVEN

Andi

I find a bat at the bottom of a tattered box, so I start swinging it as hard as I can against the doorknob and metal lock until one of them gives. I scream bloody murder as I hack away at the door. I heard the truck come back, so I know someone's here, but I can't see who it is. They parked out of view. I know Tom will hear me but . . . Raffy is there, too. Maybe he'll hear me and save me. He looked perplexed when Tom's voice called him earlier. Maybe he's not involved in all of this but a victim, too.

In that case, there is another person here Tom is focused on, so maybe I can take the chance to escape. But I really have no idea what's happening. All I can do is pray, close my eyes and swing away. When the doorknob cracks, it falls to the ground, and I kick open the wooden shed door and I'm outside. Mercifully, I'm outside. I try to quickly assess where

I am, but I have no idea. I can tell it's a rural homestead on a cliffside. These cliffs run for miles to the east, and I can see through a clearing of trees in the distance where it drops off. But whose house is this? Whose truck, whose shed?

I see the firepit a few yards away, and the fire Raffy was sitting by is just embers now. My bag is there. Clearly tossed in the fire and mostly melted into a clump of waxy makeup and charred leather, but the strap hangs over onto the ground, which is how I recognized it, and there's my phone! It's there. Inside the brick surround of the pit, it lies in the ash away from the fire. It must have tumbled out as it was thrown. A lifeline.

I rush over to it and snatch it as quickly as I can. I stab my finger at the screen and it lights up. The relief that washes over me almost brings me to my knees. The last person I called in the flurry of phone calls I made before I drove over to Sasha's was Regan. When I open my call app to push 911, her number blinks at me, so I just tap on it and share my location with her. Then before I can even begin to dial 911, the phone is soaring into the air and skidding across the muddy grass . . . and Tom is there. He has a hard grip on my wrists, and he ties them behind me again before I can fight back. It's so fast.

Then he snatches the phone from the ground and drops it onto what's left of the burning embers in the fire, and I watch it melt.

"Why?" I scream in his face. "What do you want from me?" He doesn't respond, which is even more frightening. He just pushes me back toward the shed, and I feel desperate.

"I won't tell anyone I was here if you just let me go," I say, because all I can think is that I got in the way. He thinks I know more than I do—those papers hold his secret, which is why he had to silence me, but I don't know anything. The papers were nothing but confusing to me, and if they did point to him, I missed it. And anyway, he has the file now, so why keep me if I have no proof?

"I don't know why I'm here. Whatever was in that file, whatever you think I know about you, I don't. I don't understand any of it. I'm not gonna go to the police, I promise," I plead, but he just keeps silent and when we reach the shed door, he pushes me hard, trying to get me over the threshold, but I'm not going back in there. I resist and push my weight back against his shove as hard as I can, and I stumble forward. Just as he thinks I'll fall into the dark, awful room, I grab the door frame and I don't fall, I fight.

He didn't expect me to be strong; I can tell by the look on his face.

"Don't make me do something I don't want to do," he says, and I lunge at him, swiping at his face with my hand, catching his skin under my nails. He holds his hand up to his face, surprised, and looks at the spot of blood on his fingers when he pulls his hand away. Then he looks at me. He has me trapped with my back to the threshold and no weapon, and I see rage flash in his eyes, so I duck under his arm and I run.

There's a long dirt drive that leads to a narrow two-lane road several yards down a muddy, sloped yard, and I sprint toward that road, without a moment to think about what I'll do if I reach it or how far away any other houses or help might be. I just focus on escaping this psychopath, but he's only a few steps behind me.

I round the side of the house, struggling not to slip and fall in the wet, slick grass, and just before I reach the driveway, I feel his hand swiping at my back. He gets a hold on my sweatshirt, and it stops me cold. I hit the ground, and he loses his grip. I scramble to my feet, but he's already hovering over me, and that's when I see the gun.

He pulls it out from where it's been stuffed in the back of the waistband of his jeans. He doesn't want to use it, I tell myself. He doesn't want to kill me or he already would have. He looks flustered and panicked.

I can't run because all that goes through my head is being shot in the back before I can reach the road. I have to reason with him. I have to believe he doesn't want this.

"Tom, please," I say, inching back, showing my palms in surrender, covered in cold mud and shaking. What else can I do but plead? He seems annoyed at the use of his name, so I change tack.

"Just tell me what you want," I say, and I feel the tears climbing my throat as I think about Rox and Dez, and the fear that I won't make it out of this alive becomes real as I'm staring down the barrel of a gun, having no idea why I'm here—what I did, what he wants. "I'll give you anything you want. I have two kids at home—I have to go home. Please. Anything. Just . . ." And then I make a snap decision that I have to keep fighting, because his face is hard and emotionless and he won't fucking speak, so I have to guess at his next move and his motives and I have to try . . . so I just lunge at him, and because he doesn't expect that, I manage to bump the gun from his hand and it hits the ground and fires.

The sound is shocking, but I don't hesitate. I clamber over to where it fell, just a few feet from where Tom is standing, dropping to his knees to grab it, but I get it into my hand just a fraction of a second before him. He grips my arm and tries to pry it away from me.

I scream in his face. "Fuck you. Let me go, you psycho!" But he bends my arm and it contorts so painfully that I'm forced to drop the gun and then . . . everything that happens after that is a blur of colors and light because it's all so fast, so surreal, it feels like slow motion. Before I can process any of it, the gun is back in his hand and I hear the shot, and it takes a moment to realize I'm bleeding. I look down and see bright red spreading across my sweatshirt. I hold my hands over my stomach in a futile attempt to stop the bleeding, and then everything starts to fade.

Bursts of white light flash behind my eyes and then I feel impossibly cold and calm as I collapse to the wet muddy earth. I feel the blood pooling underneath me, and I know I don't have much time.

CHAPTER TWENTY-EIGHT

Regan

I sit on a vinyl bench in the dark hallway at the hospital, waiting to hear how Jack is doing, if he's okay. When I called the medics, they came fast considering the location, and now I just sit and pray, over and over again, that he'll make it. I just got him back, please, God.

I told the police everything he said—that Tom Blanc is the brother of the man Jack put in prison and the family has a criminal history. I can't prove it was him, though. I didn't see his face and I had never seen the truck before. I was running for my life, so it's not like I stopped to take down plates. It's just like Jack said. They can do something like this and get away with it, but that seems impossible.

All they can do is question him, so they're headed to Sasha and Tom's house now. I tried to call Sasha—to warn her—but her phone goes right to voice mail. I told my mom to pick up Hallie from school, and I didn't answer all of her questions because the less she knows, the better. There's nothing more I can do to protect my family at this moment unless the police find something, anything, and can make an arrest. How likely is that if this family has gotten away with unthinkable crimes for years? Is Sasha a part of this? Does she know?

When my phone buzzes, it echoes down the hollow corridor and jolts me out of my thoughts. I fish it out of my bag and see a message from Andi. I stand up and my hand instinctively flies to my mouth. There's no actual message. It's just a location. It's almost forty miles away near the cliffs in Pine Bluffs. But there are messages from earlier I didn't look at. She tried to call me, saying she was heading to Sasha's. Said she needs to talk to me about Jack and sent a series of photos from her phone. A photo of Jack's real name, a photo of Dominic Terreli, who I now know is Tom's brother in prison. Does Andi know that? She didn't give an explanation . . . just said that it's urgent we talk. Oh, my God. Jack was right. None of this is coincidence. It's all connected.

She's left a voice mail just now. I'd ignored any calls or messages that weren't about my daughter getting to her grandmother's or about Jack, so I just now click to listen.

There's no message. It's just white noise until I hear her in the background. She's muffled, but I hear her screaming. "Why? What do you want from me?" Holy shit. My pulse races. Then there are sounds of a struggle and I hear her say, "I won't tell anyone I was here if you just let me go." Jesus.

I call the police, who tell me I have to call the police in Pine Bluffs. When I do, they tell me the best they can do from my statement is a welfare check, but they need an exact address. I don't have one. I have an area to look in, but Andi's phone didn't send an exact address. Maybe because it's so rural, or because Andi's signal strength wasn't great. And the photos are meaningless to the cops. I babble, trying to tell them how I think this string of events is related, and they tell me to come in to make a formal report. I don't have that kind of time.

I tell a nurse I'll be back in a little while, because there's nothing I can do sitting here right now anyway. What if this is my only chance to catch the son of a bitch? This could be my only opportunity to avoid running for the rest of my life and leaving my family and always living in fear. What if this is the only way out? I could be wrong, but I have to at least try. Is my life more in danger doing nothing and waiting to be picked off? And what about Andi? The police can't send someone out to an approximate location, and they don't know what the fuck I'm talking about when I spout about drug lords in prison from an arrest ten years ago, and they can't exactly act on my conjecture. It's up to me.

I take a taxi the few miles to my house, and when it drops me off, I move quickly. I open the garage and take the Remington 870 out of the safe. Jack's old pickup, the one he always wanted to fix up but never had time for, is still sitting here—I'm so glad now that I didn't have the heart to get rid of it. I shove the gun onto the floor of the truck and screech out of the drive to find the place on the map Andi sent me.

It takes me to a rural road lined in evergreens and boney oaks that have shed most of their leaves. The location she sent indicates this road, but I have to find out where she is exactly. There are only three houses on the whole mile stretch. It's dusk now and a light rain starts to fall, but I can still see down the long driveways as I pass in the afterglow of the sunset, and I can make out the shapes of the houses and see movement.

The first house is 12091 and there is a mother with a baby on her hip closing the car door in the drive and hollering into the house for help with her bags. She looks down the drive at me with something between a scowl and confusion at my presence. Not the one. The next house is dark, so I pull in and creep up the drive with my light off. I see the figure of an elderly man in the front window. The television illuminates the dark front room, and I see his silhouette. He stands and comes to the front door, peering out at me.

"Hey!" he says, standing in his baggy sweatpants, holding a beer in one hand and shaking a finger at me with the other. This is not it. I back up and make my way down to the last house, a quarter mile down the dark, woodsy road, my heart in my throat because I know this one is it. Andi is there. Tom Blanc must be there. I glance behind me at the gun on the floor, anxiously making sure it's still by my side.

When I pull up to the edge of the drive from the street, the mailbox says *Carro* on it, and in the back of my head, that reminds me of something, but I can't figure out what—no matter how hard I think, I don't know who the fuck's house this is. I thought something might make itself clear, but it's just that feeling of something being on the tip of your tongue or the edge of your brain—things aren't coming together. I instantly make the decision not to drive up. I don't want anyone to know I'm here. Whatever's going on, I want to sneak up on it and be prepared. See them before they see me. I pick up the gun and hold it by my side as I walk carefully and quietly up the dirt drive, and when I'm close enough, I see lights on inside the house and my heart almost stops when I see the truck—the pickup truck that followed us. It steals my breath. He's here.

I stand frozen for a few moments, trying to decide how to proceed, but before I can make a next move, I hear something. A small sound like a cry or a faint whimper. I pad silently, gun in position and ready as I inch toward the sound, and when I see it, I have to suppress a scream. I cover my mouth and lay the gun in the wet grass and fall down on my knees next to her. It's Andi. She's hurt. Shot.

"Jesus," I say. But her eyes are closed and she doesn't speak. She only utters a soft moan of pain, and her pulse is weak. I pull off my jacket and wrap it around her waist, trying to add compression to the wound, and then I call 911. I tell them we need a medic right away. I tell them the man who shot her is still on the loose and that he's dangerous.

"Oh, God," I say, stroking her hair. "It's okay, help is coming, okay? You're gonna be okay. I'll wait with you. It's okay." But then I see the back deck light come on and a screen door fling open.

"Who's there?" a man's voice says. Jesus. It's Tom. This is really happening. Why is he here? I don't even know where I am or how Andi got here. It all swims in my head and I stay down on the ground with her, trying to remain unseen. Then I hear the screen door slam and footsteps down the back stairs.

"Run," I hear Andi say in a labored whisper. I turn my attention back to her.

"Medics are coming, Andi. Okay?" I say again so she doesn't feel abandoned, and then I duck into the shadows of the sycamores and move quickly to the front of the house while Tom looks for me out back. I crouch down in the bushes and listen. I hear him shuffling around. Then the shed door opens and closes. He flashes a light around and then goes back inside and the screen door slams again.

Inside, I hear someone crying. A woman. Muffled voices. I plead quietly to myself, praying hard to hear the sound of sirens coming down the road, but nothing. Then, suddenly, the front door swings open and the porch light comes on.

"Hey!" Tom's voice yells. He's heard me but he can't figure out where the sound came from. My truck is hidden behind the trees on the road. I try to stay hidden and wait it out until help comes, but I hear him rush down the front steps and start coming in my direction, and at this point I have no choice. I hold up the shotgun, readying myself, and then I move out from behind the brush I'm hiding behind with the aim of catching him off guard. He's holding out the flashlight on his phone in one hand. His back is to me as he flashes the light toward the other side of the yard, near the parked truck. I see a handgun stuffed in the back of his waistband, his free hand poised to grab it.

I step out, and he hears me and whips around, grabbing for his handgun as he does, but he's met by a shotgun, only a few feet from his face. He drops his gun and holds his hands up.

"Regan?" he says, and I'm afraid of dropping the gun because I'm shaking so hard. I have never done anything remotely like this before, so now that I have control, I don't know what to do with him. I don't want him to run, and it's freezing out here, so while I still quietly beg the universe to let me hear the sirens coming, there's nothing, so I tell him to go inside.

"You're making a mistake," Tom says, but he does slowly walk up the porch stairs and into the house backward, without taking his eyes off me. I follow, and when I'm inside, I see a man I don't recognize sitting in an armchair, bound to it with zip ties. Then I hear banging.

"Regan!" I hear someone yell, and I quickly kick away the chair from under the doorknob and open the door where the noise is coming from. Sasha practically falls out of the bathroom, then freezes when she takes all of us in. I stare at her, taking it all in myself.

"Jesus," I say. "Fuck." I don't know what I expected to see, but not this. "You're part of this?" I ask her. Her face is pale, and she just looks at me, blinking.

"No," the man in the chair says.

"Who the fuck are you?" I ask, but before anyone can speak, Tom rushes toward me, and I don't think. I just close my eyes.

And then I shoot.

"Fuck!" Tom yells, his face red and filled with fury as he looks at his shoulder. I've hit him, but it's little more than a graze. He's bleeding a decent amount but he's not badly hurt. I've only shot this gun once before, at the self-defense lessons Jack forced me to take. I'm not a good shot, but the rage inside me fuels me to cock the gun again.

But before I can shoot, Tom has lunged at me again. This time so swiftly that he's on top of me before I can move a muscle. It's like he's an expert at taking down an enemy with a weapon or something—it's so fast and seamless, he must have been trained to do it. Whatever disarming maneuver he uses, it only takes an instant before my weapon has dropped to the ground and my arm is painfully pinned behind me.

Sasha doesn't go for the gun. She just sits there with her hand on her heart, watching. Is she in on this, or just in shock? Tom snatches my shotgun from the wood floor and pushes me down onto the sofa, pointing the gun at me.

"Goddammit," he screams. Sasha winces. I feel the panic rising inside me. I don't know what's happening here.

"Andi is out there, Sasha. What are you doing? Help her!"

"What?" Sasha says, her eyes flitting back and forth between me and Tom.

"We're gonna get out of here, Sash. Okay?" he says.

I see the fear in her eyes and although I'm still trying to understand how the scene I find myself in came to be, I can tell she's afraid to go with him. I can tell she isn't some monster letting Andi bleed out. She's captive, too. Tom kneels in front of her, but he keeps the gun in hand, knowing I won't move—knowing he can take me down in seconds. He pleads with her.

"Listen," he says softly. "I did everything I did for us—I made sure you weren't hurt when they set out that order on you. I saved your life. I got out of the mess my family put me in. All this—this is the shitstorm that happened because of them. We can walk away," he says, and I think about the cop sirens—how it hasn't even been fifteen minutes since I called and we are out in the middle of nowhere. Will they get here in time?

Tom's leaving means he plans on running, which means there's no reason to kill us, so even though there is a rush of relief that surges through me, I can't help worrying what would become of Sasha.

"We get Chloe and just drive. I have everything we need. New plates for the car, IDs—it would be easy. Just tell me that you understand why this all had to happen, and let's just go."

"What about Drew?" she asks, and then I wonder if she is really considering this or if she's just stalling. I think about Andi outside and wonder how much time she has. I watch Sasha as she looks at Tom intently. He glances down to take her hand in his free hand and in that split second, Sasha quickly makes eye contact with me and then moves her eyes with a slight twitch of her head behind me and down, so that's where I look.

There are two pizza boxes with empty Mountain Dew two-liters strewn on the floor. Empty beer cans and take-out menus and all kinds of shit in the disaster of a front room. I don't comprehend at first, but then, as I listen to him continue imploring her to understand the carnage he's left in his wake, I see it.

On a TV tray near the guy in the chair, there is a half-eaten TV dinner and a Bud Light, and next to it, cutlery. I see the small steak knife and wonder if I can move the four or five feet and get a handle on it fast enough, but there's no way. He'd be on his feet and I'd probably be dead before I could even reach it.

The man in the chair meets my eyes. He holds my gaze like he's trying to communicate something, and then I look down and see that he's stretched out one leg and hooked the side of his boot on the metal leg of the TV stand and he's pulling it, inching it in tiny increments toward me to reach. It's so subtle that Tom doesn't notice. He's locked on Sasha—explaining to her what their new life on a Mexican beach could look like. Cleaning up his misstep about Drew and including him in their grand plans—giving the kid a fresh start at a new school.

Sasha is locked in on him. She doesn't let her eyes flit over to us for one second at the risk of giving us away. Once the TV tray is a couple of feet away, I start to lean, painfully slowly. A cold sweat is forming across my back, and my heart is racing. I keep my eyes on the side of Tom's face as I lean the last inch and grab the knife, gripping it with my fist and leaping to my feet. I hold it over my head and see the spot right between his shoulder blades. I go for that spot, but he's on his feet, and as he raises his hand up to stop me, the knife sinks into the flesh of his palm.

The blade pushes all the way through and the tip of it exits the back of his hand. He screams in pain.

"Fuck!" He drops the gun and stares at his hand in shock before pulling the blade out of the muscle and tissue with a guttural sound that makes me shudder, and in this moment, Sasha gets up. She's sobbing. I don't know what she'll do. The gun is between me and Tom and as we clamber over one another to reach it, Sasha runs.

She gets up and fumbles with the front door for a second and then she sprints into the inky black night and disappears in the trees. Tom tries to get a handle on the shotgun, but he has to make a choice, because the gun is too big to run after her with and he can't let her go.

Then he does something that shocks and baffles me. He takes the steak knife, cuts loose the zip ties from the guy in the chair, and then . . . he runs.

And I finally hear the sound of sirens wailing in the distance.

CHAPTER TWENTY-NINE

Sasha

The rain turns from drizzle to a hard, pounding rain as she hears the sirens howl down the lane. She tries to run toward them, but she can't tell which way that is in the darkness and the thick of trees. She feels Tom behind her. She hears his footfalls on the wet ground and hears his breathing, so she cuts a sharp turn and thinks she's heading west of the house now, but in the darkness she's only guessing.

She hopes that his pursuit of her means Regan and Raff will be able to escape, and if what Regan said is true and Andi is there and if she's hurt, at least help is on the way now. All Sasha can do now is get as far away as she can. Tom has a new life planned for them all—he made an escape and a new identity sound easy. He made it sound like she has a choice, but she knows now what he's capable of and there's no choice. She has to reach the road. She can hear the sirens, maybe only a mile away now. Maybe already on the dirt road leading to the house. She's so close to escaping him and then . . .

There is a hand over her mouth and his arm around her neck. She coughs, gasps for breath and tries to cry out, but she can't; he's caught her. She can't even beg him to let her go or reason with him because his grip is so tight and he's dragging her with all his strength, back the way she just ran from. She realizes she's practically gone in a circle and the dirt driveway is only yards away.

"Shhh, it's okay, baby," he soothes, forcing her into the shotgun seat of the pickup truck in the driveway and getting behind the wheel. He pulls out with a screech of the tires, headed down the wrong way—he's driving into the wooded area on a path made for snowmobiles and hikers, not cars, but it's the only way he can escape the police. There is only one road leading to Raffy's house. Behind it is all woods and cliff-side, so not to risk getting caught, he flies through the forest, branches scraping the glass, the truck bumbling and jolting. Sasha screams for him to stop, begs him, but he only drives faster, more recklessly.

"Slow down. Please, Tom. Stop!"

"You have to trust me, Sasha. I have a plan for us."

"I'll do whatever you want. Just . . . please. You're gonna get us killed. Tom. The police are coming. Everyone in that house just witnessed everything. You can't run," she says, trying to make sense of it all and rationalize it in her own mind, but knowing deep down that if any of the stuff Drew showed her is true, Tom is so deeply cunning and evil. He probably has every step of this planned, an option for any outcome.

"Don't worry about the witnesses. It's all falling into place," he says as the truck hits a low-hanging branch and the window cracks. Sasha screams. She feels like her heart can't take any more. There's blood seeping from Tom's hand and covering the steering wheel and clutch. She feels like she'll throw up. She shakily feels for her seat belt and buckles it, certain he's going to crash into a tree at any moment.

"What's falling into place? What do you mean? The police are on their way to that house."

"Yeah. Good. Your deadbeat ex-husband is taken care of. I cut him loose."

"What does that mean?" she yells over the driving rain and humming motor as she hangs on for dear life.

"His gun killed Andi. I wore gloves. The only fingerprints they'll find are his. I'm sure there are years of his fingerprints on it. Not mine," he says. "Tia's headband was found by the kids in his firepit. I used his truck when I shot Jack. They didn't see my face. Raffy is guilty. I took care of him for you. Even if we'd stayed at the house, I'm sure the police would find all of this verifiable and arrest him. But of course we had to run for our lives. He's a maniac. We were in danger. I told you I'm taking care of this family. I'm only thinking of you. Now we're free. Can you not see that? Jack was my last job. We're out. Babe, can't you see that this is amazing? It's all behind us. And Regan? That's just a happy accident—having the most unreliable and unhinged bitch in town shoot me when it's her husband who committed the federal crime by faking a death? Didn't expect that, but I'll take it."

As he talks and the weight of it all sits heavy on her chest, as each piece of the puzzle finally comes together, she sees the panic on his face before she sees what's coming. The world goes completely silent as she watches his eyes bulge and his foot desperately slam the brakes. The car tires start to skid over the wet ground, but it's too late. Tom can't stop what he's started. The cliffside is close. He can't stop in time.

The truck crashes into the metal safety rail at the edge of the lookout, skidding violently through the steel and over the edge of the cliff. Sasha closes her eyes, gripping the dash so hard she's sure her fingers are bleeding, screaming as her life unfolds before her, and that's really what happens—she sees flickers and flashes of memory: a doll she lost when she was six, a school dance she left crying, a first kiss, Raffy singing karaoke on a cruise ship, Drew's drum set he doesn't know he's getting for Christmas, Chloe's drawing on the fridge—thoughts that don't belong in this terrifying moment.

They soar through the air and her stomach flips and then she hears the crashing metal and her body is smashed and thrust into the dash and slammed back again against the side door, and she knows this is the last moment of her life and she wails for her kids that she didn't protect and for Raffy. And then, when everything stops and finally goes quiet, she opens her eyes and finds she's not dead.

The metal rail must have softened the blow and slowed the skid of the truck enough that it didn't go soaring into the jagged rocks fifty feet down below. Instead, it dropped and crashed only eight feet or so onto a ledge of rock jetting out below as part of the walking trail leading down to the riverbed at the bottom.

The truck has flipped and dangles over the edge of the rock, threatening to drop with any sudden move, teetering on the edge. Sasha tries to take it in—where she is, and how delicate any movement is. She's strapped into the seat, suspended and hanging precariously by her seat belt, upside down, holding her breath, terrified that if she so much as breathes, the car will plummet to the rocks below.

It's so quiet. She looks to the driver's seat, and Tom isn't there. She squints in the dim light from the dashboard, which blinks as it shorts out.

"Oh, God," she whispers to herself. She feels the truck shift and hears rocks beneath it crumble, then tap and knock as they fall the distance down the side of the cliff. She doesn't move. She barely breathes. She hears Tom. He makes a low moan, but he's not in the truck. She was belted in, but he must have been flung from the car on impact. He's close, though.

She wonders if the police will find them and how long she has before the rock shifts under the weight and she plunges to her death. Before she can think about any way she might make it out of this alive, the seat belt squeaks. She lifts her eyes up to see that there's a tear in the belt where the metal clasps meet—damaged from the crash. The material sounds one more warning groan, and then it gives out and Sasha falls from the upside-down seat and crashes onto the roof of the car, which is now underneath her.

She doesn't dare cry or scream bloody murder the way she wants. She holds perfectly still, shocked that the jolt didn't tip the vehicle over the edge. She sees that in the back of the old-model cab, the center window slides over to open, no power required. She has to try. She has no idea what her fate will be if she waits much longer, hoping and praying the truck doesn't fall.

She maneuvers herself into a position to push the back

window open. She grunts, using both hands. It's stuck like it's never been opened before, but she is filled with fury and adrenaline and so she keeps pushing until it slips open with a hard smack. She begins to cry tears of gratitude and relief, but tries to stay calm so she can carefully push her body through the small square, shaking and praying for one more second, just one more second until she can find her feet on the rock beneath her. Then with one more blind thrust, she's through the open window and sobbing at the feel of the rain pounding on her back as she crawls, trembling, out of the truck and onto solid ground. She drops to her knees and tries to calm her racing heart so she can collect herself enough to figure out what to do next. She looks up the cliffside, sharp and steep, and there's no way she could climb it. Then she looks at the steep drop below, and she sees him.

Tom is there, bloody from his hand wound, but also an injury to his head. The blood runs in streaky fingers down his face and he looks even more terrifying than before. He's caught. His jacket is snagged on a flag of metal. There's a safety rail here just like the one they crashed through above, protecting hikers from the edge. Tom must have been thrown from the truck and hit the rail, breaking it—it looks like he's caught on a jagged piece. He's hanging there, only the torn arm of his jacket and the one hand he's gripping on with keeping him up. He can't bear weight on his wounded hand, so he's shaking with the effort. He calls to her.

"Help me," he barks in a hoarse voice. She can see the outline of him only because one headlight from the car is still shining, so she feels her way over.

"Pull me up," he hisses, and she can see his grip slipping, his face red and bloody. She crawls over to him carefully because she has to help him. She can't let the man die, no matter how despicable he is. She's not that person.

"I can't," she cries, because she knows there's no way she can hold his weight, but he's helping by pushing up with one hand and getting a foothold on the jagged rocks below him. The collar of his jacket rips, and he slips down a little farther, feeling for her hand, begging her to help him.

She gives him her hand, and he grips it so tightly it steals her breath. She thinks about Jack and Andi, but mostly she thinks about what this will do to her children, whom she's gone to such great lengths to provide a normal life for—getting Drew away from the dysfunction of Raff back when he was descending into addiction, even though it killed her. This will forever write on the slate of who her children are. It will change them and shape the people they become when they inevitably find out who Tom is, and then she thinks about Raff. How Tom has spent time scouting out his property, setting him up, piece by piece, taking advantage of a vulnerable man after everything they already put him through—Tom and his family took Raffy's life, stripped him of his dignity and future, and then when he became a shell of a man who could no longer cope after so much trauma, after he crumbled under the weight of it, Tom framed him for his own crimes.

But not Raffy. You don't fuck with Raffy. Sasha will protect him to the end. And then she can't tell if it's the rain battering down on them that makes her hand slip . . . or maybe she let go? . . . but in one final tear of Tom's jacket, she loses her grip and Tom falls. She sees him drop from her sight and then she can only hear his cry echoing off the cliff walls as he's swallowed by the darkness. She can't witness him crash onto the rocks below.

She moves away from the edge, panicked, hiccupping sobs taking over her body, and she kneels on the ground, heaving. She tries to catch her breath. She screams for help but only hears her own voice echo in the black air, so she curls up in a tiny ball and, as the rain beats down on her body, she prays to God that help will come.

CHAPTER THIRTY

Andi

Two weeks later

Tia's funeral is on a Friday afternoon, and they want to keep me in the hospital longer, but I insist on being there, so I'm reluctantly sent home with orders to rest. They'll continue to monitor me closely for signs of infection, but after two surgeries, I'm ready to get out.

The early-November cold snap has brought with it a dusting of snow as everyone gathers at O'Malley's pub after the service to raise a drink—a celebration of life, Ray calls it—just like she would want. Inside the warm bar, tables are overflowing with people and pints, winter coats hanging on chairs and a fried-food smell that wafts through the air. There's a sense of safety nobody has felt in a long time now that the monster is gone—there is a sense of peace amongst the mourning for Tia.

I didn't tell anybody what I did. They only know Tom killed Tia. In fact, Ray tells everyone I'm a hero—that my bravery in confronting Tom is what led to the domino effect and set the subsequent events in motion that ultimately ended Tom. I know the truth, though. Does keeping this secret make me the worst person to ever live, or is what I'm telling myself—that this is the best way to protect my family—the truth? Why tell anyone when we found the real killer?

Maybe because laid out in front of me is now a life of shame. I've learned what I'm capable of and, frankly, it scares the hell out of me. I'll be living a lie for the rest of my life.

Footage of Tom's father, Al Blanc, whose real name is actually Murphy Terreli, as it turns out, plays over and over on the news—his dramatic arrest and updates on his charges and trial. The TV is muted behind the bar and nobody is paying attention, but I stare at the clip for the fiftieth time, wondering how this one man with nine alias names and a rap sheet a mile long got away with so much. He's turned my entire life upside down, but he just looks like a guy. Just a regular guy who always brought chocolate marshmallows for the grandkids and liked a G&T at the neighborhood parties. I stare at the close-up of his face—the cold eyes I never noticed in the handful of times I met him—and I shudder.

I don't even need to have the sound playing to know what the next news clip says. A photo of Thomas Blanc along with all his aliases shows on the screen. He was found on the rock ledge of the cliff where he fell, thirty feet below. He suffered multiple injuries, but he's not dead. He's at Mercy General, in a police-guarded room, awaiting transfer to prison once he's well enough to await trial. I'm glad he's not dead. He'll get to pay for all he's done instead of taking the easy way out.

Carson comes over with a pint of Guinness in hand and kisses me on the head, then takes Dez to play pinball in the back room. Roxie brings over a couple of coffees and sits next to me. She slides one my way and we sip on them, watching the news silently together for a moment. We've tried to shield the kids from news footage, although it's hard to keep them from all of it. She hadn't seen this angle on the story yet. Her face lights up and she puts her arm around me and gives me a squeeze.

"Wow," she says, watching the closed captions and looking at me. "You're famous."

I know the story the news is playing by heart: fearless and brave Andi, Regan and Sasha, three women forever linked by tragedy and heroism as they worked together to bring down one of the biggest white-collar organized crime rings in the tri-state area. But I didn't know it was Tom when I stormed over to Sasha's. I'm just a liar who was in the wrong place at the wrong time . . . again. The fallout of a bad situation has dictated my life and maybe that's not how I want to live anymore.

"You're a hero, Mom," Roxie says with pride in her eyes. But the words from the news repeat in my head. *There's a sense of safety nobody has felt in a long time now that the monster is gone.* Is the monster really gone, though? Or just sleeping?

CHAPTER THIRTY-ONE

Regan

Since people learned Jack was alive, it's been a hell of an undertaking explaining to everyone how that's possible. I'm exhausted from distilling history and details into bite-size sentences to offer up multiple times a day when it's truly none of their business. Of course they want to know. It's shocking. All of it is too much to wrap their heads around, but it's the same for me, too, so I try to lie low as much as I can.

When I walk into the pub for Tia's memorial gathering, I pull my woolly hat down over my ears, keeping my eyes downcast while I make a beeline for the booth I see Andi and Roxie sitting in.

"Hey!" I hear a few guys at the bar yell. One starts to sing "for she's a jolly good fella," but the man next to him gives him an elbow in the ribs, reminding him of the occasion. I give them a nod of recognition. Someone shoves a drink in my hand and pats me on the back. Before too much fuss can be made, I slip into the booth and Andi pulls me in for a hug.

I have to hold back tears as we hug each other for a long moment. We've talked about it so many times now—I didn't save her life; the medics did. She didn't single-handedly bring down evil—it was a strange series of events and all of us played a part we never wanted to be cast in. But our lives are forever entwined now in the baffling, unsettling turns they've taken.

It's really Roxie and Drew who should be taking the credit, but Andi reminds me of all the illegal things they did to get the information they got, and she doesn't want their lives even more disrupted, so Sasha and I both agreed to leave their names out of it.

"How's Drew liking Tucson?" I ask Roxie.

"He likes it, I guess. He's taking a photography class and his Instagram is full of cactus photos. Looks boring to me."

"But we'll drive down so she can visit this spring," Andi says, and Roxie nods.

"And you?" I ask Andi, who is zoned out watching Ray across the room sobbing into his handkerchief while some older woman I don't know hugs him.

"Huh?" she says, missing the question, but I don't repeat it. It was a stupid question.

"I just stopped in to pay my respects, but I'm gonna just say hello to Ray and then head out. Jack has a doctor's appointment." And then I hug them both and slide my drink to Andi. On my way out, I dodge a few people who want to ask me questions about the whole tragic night that I have no intention of answering, and I just make sure Ray sees me wave to him before getting out of the crowded bar and heading back home.

It's a strange feeling, not knowing which place I want to be in less—surrounded by friends and loved ones at O'Malley's, or home spending time with Jack. Before, either option would have been top on my list of favorite things to do. Now I'm looked at differently by people, bombarded, praised or judged or pitied. Everyone has an opinion about my life. And going home . . . it's changed.

When I walk in the door with burgers from Kellers, Hallie has Jack's feet up on a pillow on the coffee table and they're watching *Curious George* while she makes tiny ponytails in his hair with rubber bands. She's careful not to jump on him or get close to his wounds. She understands on some level what's happened, but I don't know how much.

"Hi, Mom!" She beams and then giggles when she sees me notice the glitter nail polish Jack has let her paint his nails with.

"You should open your own shop," I say, handing her the bag of takeout. She opens it and starts plucking out the food, looking for her waffle fries. I sit down next to Jack and hand him a burger.

"Thanks." He kisses me on the cheek, and we eat while we watch George learn how to paint with watercolors on the television for a few minutes. All I've ever wanted. This. I would have given up just about anything in life to have one more day like this with Jack—just his presence and the minutiae of the day-to-day, the simple things that aren't in themselves exciting but having him close makes them perfect. Why can't I feel that anymore?

I know why he did what he did. I know that it destroyed him and that he thought it was the right thing to do—the only thing. I can't really hate him for that, because it was incredibly selfless. Not only was he looking over his shoulder every day, running constantly, trying to survive, but he gave up the only family he had and went through mourning all of that alone. He should get a medal, if anything.

But there is a part of me that deeply resents being abandoned. It feels like a betrayal no matter how many ways I look at it—no matter how understanding I try to be.

"We should get ready for your appointment," I say after everyone finishes eating. I pull his walker from the hallway and set it next to the couch. Then I give him his afternoon meds before I go to warm the car up and pull it around. Hal likes to help him put his coat on and run ahead to open the car door.

"It's a long road to recovery," Hallie says, not for the first time today, repeating something she's heard us discussing. She wants to take care of him, and it's heartwarming. As we pile into the car and pull away for another doctor's appointment, I look over at Jack and smile. I want to feel something different. He's a hero, really. I want to see the sacrifice and love when I look at him now, but . . .

He's a stranger to me.

EPILOGUE

Sasha

Six weeks later

It's finally sunny. I sit in the courtyard of Raffy's rehab center at a stone-carved table, eating a cheese sandwich in the bright sunshine. Tucson had the best dual-diagnosis facility, and so we came here. I've always wanted this warm, happy climate but would never have believed the road I'd take to get here.

Chloe adores her school, and of course it's difficult, but she's adjusting to this new life. Drew has taken up photography and seems a little lighter—sometimes I even see a glimmer of something resembling a regular teenager who's excited about stuff, playing pickup basketball and talking about colleges. We don't turn on the news or follow the updates on Al Blanc's trial or all the coverage on Tom's heinous crimes over the years. We go to the state park and botanical gardens, we watch British baking shows, we grow lemon trees in pots on the patio, and we watch fireflies blink in the backyard of our tiny rented house. And I visit Raff every afternoon when the kids are at school.

I'll likely have to testify, but I don't let myself think about that now. I won't be a good witness anyway because I never suspected a thing—not one of the horrors going on right under my nose. I just want to put it all behind me.

It wasn't hard to walk away from the very comfortable life I was used to. It was the easiest thing I ever did, because it never felt quite right no matter how much I convinced myself it did. I suppose I wouldn't have lied and spent so much time at Raffy's if I'd felt . . . safe.

Everything was in Tom's name, so it will be seized by the state, and even that can't possibly be enough to pay his lawyers and debts to the families he's destroyed—victims that seem to surface one by one with each passing day.

The state can have it. I don't want it anyway. I never really did. The little house on the cliff that Raffy and I bought was modest and had wooden shutters and flower boxes and a vegetable garden in back, and that was home. I wonder if I should have fought harder to keep that all together—if I helped him enough or gave up too easily.

I won't give up on him this time. We're selling the cliff house and the money will get us by while I look for a job. We've been left with next to nothing, but I couldn't be happier. The man who ruined Raff's life and held him emotionally captive all these years is gone, and he finally can be free now. Maybe letting go of that will finally allow him the space to recover.

I sit across from him, the sun on his face, light in his eyes for the first time in many, many years. I push a bottle of lemonade Chloe made for him across the table. He smiles. We eat our sandwiches and watch a goldfinch hop from branch to branch of the desert willows above the courtyard, and I pray to myself, silently . . . a quiet plea that Raff stays with me. That I don't lose him again. That he doesn't lose himself.

I stay until dusk, hanging out in the rec room and pushing pieces of a jigsaw puzzle together and talking with him about his plans—the business he could rebuild, the fruit trees we could grow, the years we still have. Then, when it's time for him to go, I walk inside with him. I hold his face between my hands and kiss him goodbye before he walks down the long hall leading to the group therapy room, and I turn to go back out to the lobby and leave. It's dark outside and I'm excited to pick Chloe up from her ballet class and bring dinner home for Drew. I feel something I haven't felt in a very long time—something like happiness, I think.

When I pass through the lobby to the front door, I stop when I hear my name. It's the news playing on the TV above the waiting area chairs near the front desk. They are talking about the events that happened—the tragedy, and the arrest of two seasoned killers. I moved far away from Connecticut, but I know the story has made some national news outlets. But this time what I hear is different, urgent, horrifying.

I look up at the screen and see the face of a young reporter with a microphone saying words I cannot believe I'm hearing.

"*Breaking news: Thomas Blanc has been reported missing from Mercy General.*" I instantly become so dizzy the rest of the report blurs before my eyes and only some of the words reach me—a buzz in the air like electricity. *Escaped, manhunt, armed and dangerous.*

I have to rest my hands on my knees as I lose my breath. A desk clerk rushes out to steady me and tries to help me to sit down, but the world is spinning all around me as sparks of light detonate across my vision.

I have tried to avoid hearing that name. I have gone out of my way *not* to loop all the horror in my mind and let it erode my psyche and sink into my bones. But now it's in front of me. They say he escaped yesterday. He could be anywhere. My phone rings; it's Regan. A text buzzes. Andi. Everyone is trying to warn me, but it's too late.

"He's free," I whisper to myself as the desk clerk fans me and a woman who was sitting in the waiting room gets me a paper cup of water.

"Are you okay, ma'am? Should I call a medic?" the woman asks.

Suddenly, there is a pop, the hiss of electronics shutting down, the shock of the power halting suddenly, and then the building is dark. There are gasps and murmurs around her. Footsteps, shouts, a couple staff trying to find a flashlight. Shouts of "What happened?" and "Oh, my God" whirl around me, and I know. I fall to my knees, I try to breathe, but I know what's happening.

He's here.

There's no panic right away because nobody else knows what is really happening. They still live in a safe world where a benign power outage can happen anytime. It's true that brownouts aren't uncommon, but I know what's coming. First, I start to run for the front door, because I don't want to be trapped inside. But then I immediately think, *Raffy*. Tom's not here to kill me. He wants Raff. I push through the double doors and start to run down the corridor leading to the staircase up to Raff's room.

I hear mumbles about the generator not kicking in. Of course it hasn't. Tom's a master criminal. He would have thought about disabling the generator. It's not the first time he's skillfully planned a murder in a short amount of time. How could he have even found out which hospital Raff was at? He's so seasoned at this, I imagine there are ways—as complex as hacking a system or as easy as calling and asking to talk to Rafael Carro and having some college student working the front desk give out too much info. Somehow, he's done it. All these thoughts spin in my head as I run—my mind's attempt at making sense of how this could be.

I imagine him flying here under one of his fake names, researching the hospital, looking at the layout on Google Earth, accessing the blueprints, which are public record—all the things he could have done to get his ultimate revenge, he would do. He would sink to any level and he has the expertise.

Then something stops me cold. I hear a pop. A gunshot. A scream. That's when the chaos starts. Residents who were hovering in their door frames, looking to see what was happening with the power, are now panicked, rushing for the stairs, falling over each other with fear. Active shooter. Common, everyday words in this country. I'm sure they can imagine themselves on the news tonight. Another mass shooting we will forget about in a couple weeks. No power, no generator. Gunshots.

The shouting is deafening. When I reach the second floor, I'm almost trampled by the crowd of residents rushing me.

Nurses are screaming evacuation instructions, but nobody is listening. It's sheer desperation to get out, to run. There is one security guard who seems to have been swallowed up in the confusion. Could it have been him? Did he shoot an intruder?

No. Thomas Blanc is a man with nothing to lose. He knows he's going to prison for the rest of his life no matter what, and he will take as many people down with him as he can.

It happens so fast that I can't be sure what occurred in which order, but a staff member was shouting for people to stay in their rooms and lock their doors and get on the floor, and when I finally reached the top of the staircase, I see Tom, right there—just his profile—and I can see he's pointing a gun and standing perfectly still. Raff is just outside the open door to his room. He has his hands up and fear in his eyes, but there is something stopping Tom from killing him. The security guard is there—on the opposite side of the hall in front of a nurse's office. He's a scrawny, sandy-haired man—a kid, really, scared to death. His hands visibly shaking, but he holds his gun with both hands and shouts orders at Tom.

There's a woman on the ground. The one I heard shouting orders. She must have gotten in Tom's way. Was that the shot I heard? Is she the only victim so far? She's groaning in pain, but she's alive. The three men stand in a triangle—a standoff. But the second I saw Tom is the exact moment he registered me, and it all somehow feels like slow motion and like a flash all at the same time. In one swift movement, he grabs me by the hair—before I can even absorb what I've just encountered and turn to run. He pulls me into him, and before I can scream, he has me in a chokehold with the gun pointed at my head.

"I never wanted to hurt you, Sasha," he says, and all of it

hits at once—the hopelessness of what is happening. My legs go weak and the adrenaline surges through me, making my whole body tremble. I could never get out of his grip twice. I beg him. Reason with him.

"You can run. You're free. Why are you doing this when you could still escape? You could be in Mexico by now!" I say, because those are the first questions that come to mind. Truly, why wouldn't he disappear now that he's somehow gotten himself free? How could revenge and hatred burn this hot in someone?

"Don't worry, sweetheart. I can do both," he says, and a chill runs through me. I look at Raff and see he's gone white as a ghost. His eyes flit from the guard to me, filled with panic, and I can tell he's desperate to do something, to save me. But there is nothing he can do.

"We're moving. We're going this way," Tom says, using me as a shield as he inches us both closer to the stairs. "Don't try to be a hero and do something stupid," he tells the guard. "You want everyone out alive, just stay right the fuck there," he says, and I suddenly feel a new panic surfacing. Maybe he didn't come for Raffy. Maybe he came to take me with him. Oh, Jesus. No.

"Please, Tom. You can run right now. Just let me go and nobody will . . ." Before I can finish, I hear sirens howling in the distance. Helicopters overhead.

"Fuck," Tom says.

I would be relieved, but if there was a chance, moments ago, that he thought he could get out of here with me or kill Raff and run, or likely both, now he really has nothing to lose. If he'll be caught anyway, we're all fucked.

"Fuck!" he screams again with a guttural sound, spit flying from the sides of his mouth and his face reddening. Then in a sudden and shocking move, he points the gun at the security guard and shoots. The guard is hit in the thigh and falls to the ground in an agonizing cry. I use the brief second of chaos and bite down as hard as I can on Tom's wrist; his grip around my neck loosens, just barely, as he lets down his guard. I bite so hard I feel like I break a tendon. I taste blood. He screams and drops the gun involuntarily, his hand seizing up.

I drop to my knees and scramble to pick it up before he even registers what's happened. He's paralyzed in pain for a moment, and I use that fraction of a second to move, to grab the gun and run. Raff runs, too. He follows me, and we fly down the concrete stairs two at a time. I know Tom will grab the guard's gun and be only steps behind us. Tears are streaming down my face as I pray we can make it to the front doors. The police are coming. I don't know if we will be shot in the back before we get that far. The fear and panic has me shaking so violently, and my knees feel so weak that I miss the last step and fall hard on the polished concrete floor. The gun skids down the empty hall. Everyone has fled. I hear it echo as it ricochets off the wall and I hear Tom's footfalls on the steps above us.

Raff pulls me up, and I feel blood seeping from where I must have cracked my chin open. I think about it again—trying to get outside means running down this long hallway to the doors, and I can almost feel the bullet to my back if we try that. I know Raff knows it, too.

"This way," he says, and he pushes open the door to the kitchen and locks it behind us. It's just a flimsy doorknob twist lock, but it feels like a moment of safety. The kitchen is a big, industrial room with stainless-steel countertops and walk-in coolers, pots and pans hanging from racks on the ceiling.

"There's a delivery door," he says. "We can get out!" He takes my hand, but before we can run the length of the kitchen to the side delivery entrance, Tom kicks in the kitchen door and the plywood easily cracks and flings open, the lock broken. We both instinctively hide. I duck, but Raff doesn't. He tries to slip inside the door of the pantry, but he never had a chance. Tom sees him.

"Well, well. Shit. It's my lucky day," Tom says. "It's almost like you've gift-wrapped yourself." I watch him glance behind him, looking for me or maybe making sure there are no other armed guards around. He closes the broken kitchen door and pushes a crate of potatoes in front of it with his foot, clearing the space visually. He might think I made it to the delivery door and out to safety, but he has to find me. He won't leave here without me; we all know that by now. I'm lying on the floor behind the washing station, blocked by metal and racks of dishes. I hold perfectly still.

"You can come out or I can enjoy blowing you to bits through the door," he says, but he won't do that. He has no idea if I'm in there, too. Does Raff know that? Does Raff know he should stay inside? Pile shit in front of the door? Wait for police rescue? At least that's possible. It's something. But no. Raff walks out with his hands up.

"Please just leave Sasha alone. Please. You have me now. You win."

"What a martyr. Where is she?" Tom asks. He doesn't shoot him right away. He needs him to find out if I'm long gone or still reachable.

"What do you care? You're surrounded. You're going to

prison. What does it matter where she is?" Raff says. And this is when I start to move. I have precious little time.

"Prison, I can beat. I think I've already demonstrated that. But taking care of you? This may be my only chance," I hear Tom say as I crawl on my hands and knees across the floor as soundlessly as I can. I hold a pair of kitchen scissors that were lying on the bottom of a plastic dish tub on the floor tightly in my fist.

"Please," Raffy pleads. "Let her go."

"Shut up! Shut the fuck up. She's not yours! She's mine," Tom screams, and then he cocks the gun and the expression on Raff's face falls. A recognition that it's his last moment on this earth—a look that's indescribable and heartbreaking. And then there is a glint in his eye when he looks up, something catching in the corner of his vision. Movement. He sees me standing up, moving silently behind Tom's back and holding the handle of the scissors so hard my knuckles feel like they're bleeding. Tom must register the change in Raff's face, because he hesitates and then starts to turn, to look behind him, but it's too late.

With a scream so hard and loud my lungs ache, I thrust the blade into the side of Tom's neck. He doesn't cry out or scream. Eerily, he doesn't make a sound. The gun softly drops from his hand. His eyes bulge and blood starts to pour from the side of his neck. More blood than I've ever seen. And then he collapses, wordlessly, almost gracefully, to the floor and begins to convulse.

Raff runs to me, pulling me away from the body, taking the weapon. I fall to my knees and hold my head in my hands, shocked at what I've done even though I know I had to do it.

Tom's body goes still, and Raff just holds me in his arms on the floor, letting me sob.

"It's okay," he says, and he keeps repeating it until I can breathe again. The sirens are louder, the front doors open, and medics and police are shouting.

"You're okay. I'm here. You're okay, Sash. It's over."

★ ★ ★ ★ ★

ACKNOWLEDGMENTS

Thank you so much to all the people who make a book come together, especially my biggest supporter and husband, Mark Glass, and my amazing mother, Dianna Nova, and my family and friends.

I'm profoundly thankful to Leah Mol, Sara Rodgers and Erin McClary for their insight and eye for detail, and for reining me in when I get too weird.

Thank you to Sharon Bowers for her patience, humor and collaboration. I couldn't ask for a better agent.

I'm so grateful to Erika Imranyi, Leah Morse, Ambur Hostyn and the whole team at Park Row, and all the other forces behind the book that make it possible.

And a huge, heartfelt thank-you to all my wonderful readers.

QUESTIONS FOR DISCUSSION

1. Cloverhill Lakes and its surrounding woods serve as a backdrop to the story. How does the setting influence the atmosphere and mood of the story?

2. Andi, Regan and Sasha all find themselves in situations out of their control. Do you think they dealt with their problems well? How would you handle these problems differently?

3. How do social status and wealth shape character interactions and conflict in the novel?

4. Explore the role of deception in the novel. Which characters embody this theme the most?

5. How does the narrative benefit from multiple character perspectives?

6. What does the title, *Too Close to Home*, signify in relation to the core themes?

7. How do friendships among the main characters evolve? What role does friendship play in supporting or hindering Andi, Regan and Sasha?

8. Motherhood is an important theme in *Too Close to Home*—how does the author use the challenges of motherhood to enhance the plot?

9. What techniques does the author use to weave suspense and foreshadowing through the story?

10. In what ways is the theme of mental health addressed?